"Trevor is a master."

—*Denver Post*

"Skillful as ever at stretching suspense to the screaming point."

—*Publishers Weekly*

"Trevor's simple and direct style creates such wrenching suspense that the story remains haunting long after the last page is turned. MAGNIFICENT."

—*Library Journal*

"Elleston Trevor has long been one of the world's best novelists. THE SISTER, with its dark look at the emotional carnage of failed families, is perhaps his best book yet. A HORRIFIC NOVEL OF SUSPENSE WITH A STARTLING CLIMAX!"

—Ed Gorman, author of NIGHT KILLS

"A master. One never doubts the reality of every page he writes."

—*The New York Times*

THE SISTER

ELLESTON TREVOR

A TOM DOHERTY ASSOCIATES BOOK
NEW YORK

This is a work of fiction. All the characters and events portrayed in this book are fictitious, and any resemblance to real people or events is purely coincidental.

THE SISTER

Cover art by Jim Thiesen

A Tor Book
Published by Tom Doherty Associates, Inc.
175 Fifth Avenue
New York, N.Y. 10010

Tor® is a registered trademark of Tom Doherty Associates, Inc.

ISBN: 0-812-53337-2
Library of Congress Catalog Card Number: 93-35852

First edition: February 1994
First mass market edition: December 1994

Printed in the United States of America

0 9 8 7 6 5 4 3 2 1

To

DOLLY

PROLOGUE

Father Giovanni was standing below the archway at the end of the passage, his face strained and his eyes hollow in the lamplight as he stared at Nicola and asked the guardian to leave them.

Nicola watched him, waiting.

"I'm sorry I had to wake you," he said.

"No problem." She thought she smelled lamp oil on his coat.

"There's just been an accident, Nicky," he said, "involving the two young sisters. I need—"

"They okay? Just tell me."

"Yeah. No one was hurt." He moved close to her, the raw smell of the lamp oil strong now. His voice was low, hard, as he said, "But they could have been. Debra could have been burned alive. So—"

"Oh Jesus Christ—"

"So listen, you've got to give it to me straight now, Nicky. You understand?"

He waited, not letting her eyes go free. Somewhere the guardian was talking to somebody in the shadowed passage near the staircase; the rest was silence, the whole building, the whole night resting on silence as Nicola stared into the dark face of the priest. Then she took a deep breath and spoke, because now she knew she must.

"All right, Johnny. Debra thinks her sister's trying to kill her. And I think she's right."

He closed his eyes, then, just long enough to let a prayer fly upward.

"That's all I need to know."

1

Glass crashed somewhere downstairs in the house, waking Madlen. There was silence for a minute, then the voices began again, muffled by all the walls and the doors, so that Madlen couldn't make out the actual words; she only knew that they were cruel, and brutal, and full of spite and hate, because there had been a time when she and Debra had left their room and crept along to the top of the stairs to listen. Then they had stopped doing that, not wanting to hear any more.

A door slammed now, and in another minute there was the scream of tires on the concrete driveway, and the fading roar of Dad's car down the street. Hearing the rustle of bedclothes, Madlen looked across the room and saw that the noise had wakened her sister too; she could see that Debra had her head and shoulders raised from the pillow as she stared at the bedroom door. Moonlight was in the room, slanting through the shutters.

"It's okay," Madlen said quietly, and saw her sister

turn her head to look at her, then back to watch the door.
Debra didn't answer—or her silence was the answer: It
wasn't okay, it was never okay in this house.

They both waited, not able to go to sleep again yet,
and after a while they heard Mom coming up the stairs,
and when she was passing their door Madlen called out
to her—"You okay, Mom?"

They could hear she was crying—she was always crying after one of these fights—but she managed to call
back, "Yes . . . I'm okay. . . . Go to sleep."

They heard her going along to her room, the one she
shared with Dad, and in a moment they heard the door
close.

Madlen settled herself again under the bedclothes.
"Go to sleep," she told her sister, "like Mom says.
Okay?"

A deep sigh came across the space between their
beds. "Yeah, okay."

But Debra was awake for longer than Madlen, and
that always happened. Maybe it was because she was
a year younger and felt things more, though a year
shouldn't make all that difference. Maybe it was because
Madlen was kind of more than just a year older, in spite
of the calendar, older and stronger, able to take things
more in her stride. When they'd been thirteen and fourteen and these terrible fights had started between Mom
and Dad, she and Madlen had had their own separate
rooms, because Mom had said they should have their
privacy now they were growing up; it would help them
become independent. Then, when they got to be fifteen
and sixteen, like they were now, Madlen had seen what
all of this was doing to her sister, and had told Debra that
if she wanted she could move in with her. And that was
what had happened, and even though it helped Debra to
have someone in the same room, she still felt terrible

every time another fight started downstairs after they'd
come up to bed.

She watched the moonlight shining on the picture
above the dressing-table, the picture of Mom and Dad at
the football game at Weldon High four years ago, hugging and laughing when the home team won by three
goals. They'd looked like they loved each other, then,
and everyone had had a lot of fun, but that was before
things started going wrong at Dad's office and he'd gotten worried and began drinking.

Debra felt her eyes stinging, because it was worst of all
for Mom, of course, having to listen to all those terrible
things Dad said to her when they were fighting, throwing
glass tumblers around and slamming doors and everything. But he'd never hit Mom, they knew that; it was one
of those things Debra and Madlen had come to know as
time went by and they sat huddled together on the stairs
listening and sometimes actually watching when the
doors down there had been open.

"If he ever hit Mom," Debra remembered her sister
saying once, "if he even *touched* her, I'd kill him."

And Debra knew—because she knew her sister very
well—that this was true.

Three days later there was a lot of commotion going on
in one of the hallways at Weldon High when Madlen and
Debra came back from their lunch break in the Hi-Value
Supermarket cafeteria. Kids were milling around everywhere, and there was the smell of gunpowder or something in the air.

"Oh, Jesus Christ," Madlen said, "what now?" There
was always some kind of drama going on in this place.
Mrs. Rosenberg was pushing everyone back from the
doorway of the boys' rest room and telling someone to
dial 911 and ask for the police and an ambulance.

"What happened?" Madlen asked Alice Thompson.

"One of the guys shot himself." Alice was looking pretty shaky, her eyes frightened behind their glasses. "Eric Holloway."

"Playing Russian roulette," somebody else told them, and Madlen rolled her eyes and took Debra's arm and said, "Come on, let's get out of here."

When they were in the playground sitting down at one of the scarred wooden tables with Coke stains on the top and used gum stuck under the edge, Madlen let out her breath explosively—"Well, *shit!*"—and slapped her hands on the table. "This fucking *place!*"

"It's awful," Debra said quietly. Her sister was better at expressing herself about things like this, about life in general, and all Deb could do was shake inside of herself with her mouth dry and her nails picking at her cuticles.

Madlen was staring across the worn crummy grass of the playground. "It's a madhouse, you know that? It's a goddamned funny farm for freaks."

"Poor Eric," Debra said.

"Poor *Eric?* So what was the idiot doing with a gun in the first place? And is that all these punks can think of doing to prove what they think is their manhood?"

"Maybe he's not dead," Debra said.

Madlen put her arm round her sister's shoulders as they heard a siren coming in from the distance. "Maybe he's not," she said, but she knew he must be, because with that stupid game you hold the stupid gun to your stupid head when you pull the trigger. Something inside of her was trying to bring out some tears for Eric Holloway, who was—who'd been no more and no less than a typical sweaty jock with a bright red Corvette and a raucous laugh, but she was too angry. This place was meant to be a school, not a bear garden. "You know this is the second time there's been an accident with a gun in the past six months," she told Debra, "if you want to call it an accident. Maybe I'll write a complaint to the school board."

"Yeah?" Debra said, impressed. That was like Madlen, to go stir things up when she was mad at something. Debra wasn't like that, and there was a reason for the difference between them. Soon after she'd had Madlen, Mom was told she couldn't ever have another child, or not without a lot of risk, so she and Dad went to an agency, because they wanted two kids who could keep each other company, and Dad didn't want a son, so the infant they brought home with them was Debra. She'd been told all this on her fifteenth birthday, a year ago, and she'd been pretty shocked, but Madlen helped her through it, like she always helped her through everything, and they'd grown up together real close—closer than Debra had ever felt toward Mom or Dad. Mom was busy running a realty office and Dad was a Cadillac salesman working all hours too, and they were always doing their own thing and staying out a lot or bringing friends home that didn't have any interest in a couple of kids. But it didn't matter too much, except for the terrible fights, because she had Madlen and Madlen had her.

"It's not just the guns," she heard Madlen saying, "it's the drugs too, with half the guys buying or selling or dealing in the hallways and behind the gym."

There were a lot of flashing lights outside the school now, and Debra felt really bad because she hated any kind of violence going on, and after this Eric Holloway thing she was beginning to wonder where she'd rather not be—at home or at school.

That night there was another fight downstairs.

Madlen and Debra had gone to bed at the usual time, but neither of them could get to sleep because of what had happened today to Eric Holloway, so they switched the light on again and sat up in bed against the pillows,

and Madlen began studying her part in the next Halloween play—*The Angel from Hell*—that the local amateur
theatrical company was putting on, and Debra found a
book to read.

Then around midnight they heard Dad's red Charger
turning into the driveway from the street, and they could
tell from the whimper of the tires that he was in one of
his moods: He and Mom had been out to the Marco Polo
Lounge with some friends, according to the note Mom
had left, and they'd obviously started to fight.

"Shit," Madlen said, looking up from her script.

Debra didn't say anything, but felt herself kind of
gathering tighter inside of her skin, trying to get smaller
and hide herself away from what was going to happen—
for the second time in just a week.

There were raised voices as soon as Mom and Dad
came into the house, and before they went into the sitting
room Madlen and Debra caught some of the words and
put them together to make sense.

"She can look at a guy, for Christ's sake, can't she,
without necessarily wanting to get into bed with him?"
That was Dad.

"The kind of look she gives you, she—"

"Oh, Jesus—last week it was Phyllis Kramer and this
week it's Bette Jordan, you'd think I was—"

A door slammed and then there were just voices, the
house slowly filling with spite and hate and anger, like
dark water creeping under the doors and across the hall
and up the stairs, higher and higher, until Debra felt she
was drowning in it.

Then suddenly Madlen flung her script across the
room and jumped out of bed and snatched her bathrobe
from the back of the door and shrugged herself into it
while Debra watched with her eyes wide and a little bit
frightened, because she knew that when her sister decided

to blow up, she blew up, and there was usually a whole lot of fallout.

"Madlen, where are you—"

"I'm going downstairs, sweetie," Madlen said through her teeth as she jerked the knot in her robe like she was strangling something, "to kiss Mummy and Daddy goodnight. O-*kay?*"

She pulled the door open and it banged back against the wall as she went down the stairs with her hand sliding on the banister rail and her hair flying out. The voices were still coming from the sitting room and she turned the handle and hit the door open with the sound of a bomb going off and stood there looking at her parents while they swung round and stopped yelling at each other and just stared, as Madlen's voice came tearing into the silence.

"I've had enough of this shit!"

Debra sat listening from the top of the stairs, bundled in her bathrobe, shivering.

Madlen looked at her father standing there with his mouth open, then looked at her mother, backed up against the fireplace like she expected an attack. And in their daughter's voice they heard all the rage and hate and contempt she'd been bottling up for months, for years.

"Now *listen*—if you two guys don't get your fucking act together we're going to leave this house and we're not coming back—now do you *get* that?"

In the silence they heard the grandfather clock ticking out there in the hall through the open doorway. Then Madlen's father started walking toward her, his hands clenched and his knuckles white.

"Go back to bed *at once!*" He was standing over her now, his right fist raised, but she didn't take a step back, didn't even flinch.

"Madlen—" her mother began, her face strained.

"Shuddup. Shuddup, *both* of you, okay? Because I'm doing the talking." Her eyes narrowed as she stared up at her father's face, and her voice was suddenly lower, coming from between her clenched teeth. "And by the way, Daddy dear, if you're thinking of hitting me, *don't.* Or I swear to Christ I'll claw your eyes out and leave you looking like a fucking beefsteak—okay? We don't take self-defense class for nothing, and I'm pretty good." It sounded like somebody else talking, because she'd never come right out and told her parents what she thought of them. She sometimes felt like this, like she was two different people, especially when she got really mad. Wasn't that what the Bard meant when he talked of people in a rage being "beside themselves"? But it didn't bother her; she wasn't mad too often.

She turned away, digging her hands into the pockets of her robe, turning back, noting that her father had lowered his fist and was just standing there like he was trying to work out what could be happening here. "We had a bad day today," Madlen said. "One of the guys at school shot himself dead." She was aware of the drama, like she was saying her lines on the stage. "He was playing Russian roulette, and blew his brains out. Big deal—something's always happening in that goddamn place. But it gets to us—you know?"

"That's terrible," she heard Mom saying.

"Yeah, Mom. But that's also life—life and death at Weldon High—good title? But the thing is, you guys have got to pull your own lives together, because we need you, Debra and I." Her voice was calmer now as she spoke to both of them. "So try talking it over, or go for counseling. Or you could just try love. Try and get back the love you once had for each other, way back when. Try understanding. Try anything, for God's sake, but don't just go on this way." With a shrug—"So, like I say, we had a bad day at school today, and it would've been

nice if we could've come home and gone to bed and tried
to forget it, or deal with it somehow in our heads. But
then you two came home, and it was too late to tell you
what happened at school and how we felt about it, and—
you know—look for a bit of comfort, and anyway you
wouldn't have listened because you were too busy yelling
at each other—*and suddenly I couldn't take it any more.*"
She gave another shrug, tucking her robe tighter inside
the belt, turning away from them toward the door. "So
do something, is all we ask. We have lives to live too, and
believe me, right now it's not a whole lot of fun." Turning in the doorway she said quietly, "There'll be parents
going to the school tomorrow, protesting—again—at the
conditions there. Not that it's ever done much good. But
they'll try." She looked at them both in turn. "I hope
you'll be there with them. At least do that."

The banisters creaked as she went back up the stairs,
the anguish drained out of her and the first tears creeping
onto her face.

2

"Hey, Madlen? Deb?"

"Yeah?"

They both stopped as Alice Thompson came across the grass, bulky in an extra sweater, her eyes excited. It was almost the end of the semester, and the evenings were starting to close in.

"Have you heard about Dolores?"

"What happened?" Madlen asked with her stomach tightening, because there was always some kind of drama going on here. But this was news of a different kind.

Dolores Garcia, Alice told them, had made up her mind to quit school and become a nun—"to take holy vows," was the way she put it. And what made it more interesting still was that Dolores was the most popular senior there'd been at Weldon High for years, tall and graceful and kind of dusky skinned with huge olive-black eyes and a smile that lit up your soul.

"She'll make," Madlen said, "a really *fantastic* nun."

"All in black?" Debra couldn't see it.

"She has it all in the eyes," Madlen said, "and that hood and everything's going to make a frame for them. You can see her walking down the aisle of the cathedral with the sunlight coming through the stained-glass windows and throwing colors all over her . . . the word is *beatific!*"

Debra had always thought the word was "beautific," but she never questioned what Madlen said because she knew it must be right; she'd proved that a lot of times, looking up words in the tattered blue Webster's in secret. And she knew how Madlen could imagine things like that, Dolores in a cathedral with the colors and everything: Madlen had been in every school play since Deb could remember, and loved parts in stuff like *Dracula* and *The Phantom of the Opera,* any kind of play where she could put on a vampire's mask or stab someone with a stiletto and burst the little plastic bag of ketchup underneath the costume. She'd learned to do what she called "fiendish laughter," and was so good at it that when she did it at Halloween with dripping fangs from the joke store sticking out of her mouth it made Debra's flesh creep.

"We don't know everything," Marianne Pauley said, "of course." She'd come across from the gym and had stopped to listen.

"About Dolores?" Alice asked her.

"Well, you know, there's rumors running around that behind that fantastic smile she's hiding a lot of pain and guilt about an abortion she had during her last vacation, and other people are saying she's so scared of guys that the only place she can go where there aren't any is a convent."

"Look," Madlen said, "it's just that people can't see someone like that just giving up on the world, so the guys say she's scared of getting laid and the girls say she must have had an abortion and things like that. But—"

"Right on!" said Alice.

"But the way she's always seemed to me," Madlen nodded, "is like I say, beatific, and I think she's kind of spiritually turned on by the whole idea. And you know something? I don't think it's impossible that she finds the world she's giving up on so completely shitty that she's decided to try a different one, where at least she's not going to get hustled all the time by drug dealers or shot at or what the hell. Have you thought of that?"

And then less than a week later the young Cuban doctor at the clinic was saying to Debra, "Okay, will heal very soon now. You like to go, or feel like more rest?"

They all waited, looking down at Debra lying on the treatment table—the doctor, Mrs. Templeton from the school, and Madlen. Then Debra said, "No, I'm fine." And the doctor gently helped her to get up.

"Just sit," he said, "for a minute," and took her blood pressure again. "Yeah. You fine now." He turned to Mrs. Templeton. "A little high for her age—130 over 80—but still some shock, you see?" He looked searchingly at Madlen. "You in shock too, yes?"

"You bet," Madlen said with a tight mouth. "You bet I'm in shock, Doctor."

"Just take it easy. All over now."

"No," Madlen said, "it isn't all over now." But he didn't seem to know what she meant, and they filed out of the treatment room in silence.

In Mrs. Templeton's car, as she drove them to their home, Debra said to her sister, "It's scary, the way you said Dolores had decided to go someplace where she wouldn't get shot at, only last week. Almost like you knew."

Madlen was sitting right up close to Debra, holding

her tight but taking care not to touch the bandage on her upper arm. She was looking at the scenery going past the windows but not seeing it, just keeping very quiet all the time, with the color not back in her face yet.

"Of course I knew," she said in a moment. "It was just waiting to happen." Then she said under her breath, like she'd done a few times before, *"Shit,* you could've been killed. . . ."

An hour ago they'd been sitting in class and Mrs. Templeton had been asking them if anyone could name six well-known women novelists who'd published their books under a man's name.

Debra didn't know even one of them, and was waiting for someone to put their hand up when she noticed T-Tommy Friedeck in the row in front of her, sitting at his desk kind of hunched up and looking around him like he didn't want anybody to look back. Debra knew he wouldn't be putting his hand up, because even if he knew the answer to Mrs. Templeton's question he wouldn't want to say anything, because he had a real bad stutter. That was why everybody called him T-Tommy, after someone had first started it—Frank Bullen, she thought it was, just the kind of thing he'd do. T-Tommy hated it, but even people who didn't mind him called him that, because everyone else did; it had gotten to be a habit.

"George Eliot," Mrs. Templeton was nodding, *"every-one* knows that one. Who else? Only five left."

Debra was watching T-Tommy Friedeck all the time now and couldn't look away, because he was acting so weird, still hunched over—hunched over *something,* she thought now, and breathing in a funny way like he couldn't get his breath—and then he was suddenly on his feet and so fast that Amy Green in the next desk gave a little squeal of fright, and T-Tommy was scrambling between the desks and swinging around to face them all and the gun in his hand went off with a bang that filled the room like a thunderclap and he was shouting something at them, like *"I hay-hay-hay—"* but that was all he could say, and people began screaming and he fired again, waving the gun around just anywhere with the smoke blue in the light coming from the windows and the screaming worse now with everyone ducking down and trying to get under the desks as the gun fired again and then Mrs. Templeton managed to get close to T-Tommy from behind and was knocking the gun downward very hard, hitting and hitting at his wrist while Jeff Soderberg went darting away from his desk to help her keep T-Tommy from moving, and the gun was on the floor and one of the kids kicked it away into the corner as the door came open and one of the other teachers stood there with her eyes staring, and it was then that Debra felt a hot tingling in her arm and looked down and saw blood creeping down from under her sleeve and heard Madlen saying, *"Oh Jesus Christ—are you all right, are you all right?"*

Now they were going home in Mrs. Templeton's car, with the smell of the disinfectant making Debra feel a bit nauseous and Madlen holding her sister very close and looking out the window and saying again under her breath, "You could have been killed . . . oh, Jesus, you could have been killed. . . ."

"But she wasn't," their father said.

Madlen stared at him. "And that's all that matters?"

"Sure. She wasn't killed, so let's forget the amateur theatricals and get on with life."

They were in the toolshed at the back of the house, where he was varnishing a fishing pole, and the smell of the varnish reminded Madlen of the smell of the clinic. Debra was upstairs in bed, and Madlen had told her to stay there, no matter what anybody else said. Mom wasn't home from the realty office yet; she'd come straight here when Mrs. Templeton had called her, and then gone back to work when she saw Debra was okay.

"Are you going to the school meeting?" Madlen asked her father.

It was very quiet in here, with some twigs outside tapping the tin roof in the breeze, making it quieter still.

"Sure." He didn't meet her eyes very often; he listened to the things she was saying like she was on the other side of a screen or something, not really in his world. Maybe nobody was, except for himself. "Sure I'm going to the meeting. We both are."

"You and Mom?"

"Sure. We'll get something done. We'll ask that the principal—what's his name?—resigns from his job there." He drew the brush slowly down the length of the fishing pole, concentrating, a little frown on his face that meant she was interrupting him; the frown was always there whenever Madlen came to ask him something important.

"You've never known the principal's name, have you, Dad? The principal of our school?"

He half-looked at her, his glance dipping away, the frown deepening. "You wouldn't believe how many names I have to remember, in my job."

"In your job. I can believe that," Madlen said. "Do you know my name?"

"Now listen here—" he slapped the brush down onto the newspaper "—it was a bad experience for you today and it shook you up a little, but let's not get into anything, okay?" He was meeting her eyes now, angry, and that was all she saw in them, anger, with nothing to soften it. "When you go back tomorrow," he said, "you'll find things have—"

"Go back where, Dad?"

The twigs tapped at the roof.

"To school." He was looking puzzled now, because of something in Madlen's voice.

"We're not going back."

Then that awful smile came on his face, the one he used for telling her she was being stupid, was just a silly school kid. "Aw, c'mon, now, for God's sake. All the kids'll be going back there in the morning—"

"Some of them won't. Three of our best friends won't—they told me. One's the daughter of a judge."

"I don't care who they are—"

"That's okay, Dad, you wouldn't know their names."

He didn't pick up on that, maybe didn't hear. "You'll be going back to your school in the morning like always, do you understand?"

"Yeah, I understand what you're saying, Dad, but that's got nothing to do with anything." She looked into the hard, glittering eyes and found herself wishing her father were dead, but it was just a passing thought. "We're not going back. That's what I came to tell you."

He took a deep breath. "You'd better speak to your mother about this."

Passing the buck like he often did—let Mom sort things out, he didn't have time. "I was going to," Madlen said. "But she was kind of busy—you know? Had to get back to the office as soon as she found things were okay." She took a step toward him, daring him to look away from her. "But they're not okay, Dad. My sister and I have had enough of the shit we get here at home and we've had enough of the shit we get there at school. Like the man said in that movie, remember? We're not going to take it any more."

But he couldn't hold her eyes, and looked away, and saw the varnish had started to run on his fishing pole, and half-turned from her and picked up the brush and tried to fix the run while Madlen watched him, disbelieving, disbelieving this even of him.

"So just what are you going to do?" he asked her, still busy with his brush, like he was talking to a kid of six, with that terrible faint smile on his face that she could see even at this angle.

"You mean it would interest you?"

He swung round on her and the brush went skittering across the workbench and hit the can of varnish. "Now listen here, you sassy little bitch, while I tell you something!"

But she'd had enough now and wanted to get away from him, feel free of him, so she turned and went through the doorway into the breeze and looked back once and said, "Go fuck yourself, Dad," and walked on past the woodpile into the house.

That night, when Madlen came out of the bathroom after brushing her teeth, she sat on the edge of her sister's bed and stroked her soft fair hair, her hand as soothing as a mother's.

"How are you feeling, sweetie?"

"I'm fine." Debra's arm was still a bit numb, but it didn't hurt. What worried her was that she kept seeing T-Tommy Friedeck staring at them all with his eyes wild and the gun waving around in the air while he yelled at them—*"I hay-hay-hay—"* What had he been trying to say?

"Get it out of your mind," Madlen said quietly; she often knew what Debra was thinking. "Just forget it. We're not going back there again."

"Back to school?" Debra sat up higher against the pillows, smelling the fresh, somehow comforting smell of her sister's toothpaste.

"Right. I told Dad. Tomorrow I'll tell Mom. But the thing is, sweetie, they'll make an awful fuss about it and start fighting again, and we can't go on staying here with all that stuff going on forever. So we'll get out, before it drives us crazy. Okay?"

"Get out?"

"Leave home. Leave school. Leave the whole stinking mess behind. It's no big deal. They won't even care. And that's perfectly okay with us, right?"

In a moment Debra nodded. "Sure. Whatever you say."

"You're a champ. We'll find someplace where we can't get raped or shot at, or treated like we don't even exist."

Debra looked at her in the soft light of the lamp. "You mean like Dolores?"

"Yeah," Madlen said. "Like Dolores."

3

"My name is Sister Marie Teresa. How can I help you?"

The nun folded her hands on the table, offering a gentle smile.

Madlen and Debra were in two creaky upright chairs, facing her. Everything was a bit bleak-looking in this place, Madlen thought, except for a big colored poster on the wall with Jesus in a pale blue robe with light shining out of him and the words in gold along the top: SISTERS OF NOTRE DAME DE MONTPELLIER. But it looked kind of old-fashioned.

The only things on the bare scrubbed wooden table were a Bible and a yellow legal-size writing pad and a black ballpoint. The early autumn wind fretted at the single window—this was a small office next to the church.

"I'm Madlen," the darker girl said, "and this is my sister Deb. Debra. We want to become nuns." Then Madlen remembered how Dolores Garcia had put it. "I mean, we want to take holy vows."

Sister Marie Teresa took off her glasses to polish them, giving herself a moment to think. Her first thought was that these two kids were here to waste her time, and Mother Superior was coming here straight from the airport this morning and would have to be met.

The two girls looked quite nice, and they'd put on clean white sweaters and jeans and weren't chewing gum or anything; it was just their approach, that was all. They couldn't have talked to anyone about this before they'd come here.

"Just like that?" Sister Marie said.

"Excuse me?" Madlen leaned forward slightly.

She was the elder sibling, the nun decided—more assertive, the spokeswoman for the two, less pretty than her sister but still attractive, with clear eyes and a strong straight nose and a firm mouth. She wasn't wriggling her ankle, like Debra.

"You want to become nuns," Sister Marie said, "just like that?"

Madlen didn't seem to understand the question. "I guess. Sure."

"Why?"

"Home sucks, and school sucks."

Sister Marie's delicate eyebrows lifted slightly. "I see. And in what way do your home and your school—er—suck?"

So Madlen told her the whole story, not making it too hard on Mom and Dad because it wasn't their fault, they were just screwed up. But she was pretty hard on Mr. Crawford, the principal of Weldon High, because she thought he was bad for the whole community, letting things like that happen to the kids there. In fact she thought Mr. Crawford was a shitty old bleeding-heart wimp, though she didn't use those exact words because the nun hadn't gone for "suck" too much.

"I see," Sister Marie said, and turned her head slightly

to look at the other sister. "Do you think that gives a good picture of things, Debra?"

"Yes, ma'am. That's exactly it." She realized she was turning her ankle round and round, and stopped.

Sister Marie laid a pale, long-fingered hand on the legal-size notepad, lifted it once and laid it down again. "Well, now. We'd very much like to offer hospitality and shelter, here at our convent, to all who are suffering and feel they have nowhere to go." She gave each of them a very direct look, and spoke more slowly for a moment. "And please be assured that I fully understand that feeling. I've experienced it myself, and that is why I am here now. But I was older than you when I took my vows, and I understood at the time that the only choice for me was to serve God and to devote and dedicate the rest of my life to Him. Now that's a rather big thing to do, you see."

"Sure," Madlen said. She wanted to get all this over with and sign up.

"If you had come to me today," Sister Marie said, a little quicker now because Monsignor Jeaumont's plane would be landing in less than an hour, "to tell me that your privations and sufferings have led you to understand that your only choice is to devote the rest of your lives to the service of God, I would be pleased to help you follow Him. But you're too young to commit yourselves to the vows of poverty, silence, and chastity, good gracious me! You'll know from talking with your friends at school that your case is sadly not uncommon. Parents are tending to lose touch with their children in the increasing stress and pace of their lives, while school administrators are engaged in a constant battle with the moral concepts of the movies and television, where wholesale sex and violence are portrayed as the norm, even to be encouraged. You might consider that when you think of your principal at school—he can use your understanding, believe me." She lifted her hand again and slowly laid it down. "So you're not alone, you see. But nothing in life is forever. I'm sure you both have some very nice boy-friends, don't you?"

It was a curve ball and Madlen wasn't ready for it. "Boyfriends? No. I mean, yeah, sure, but I mean—you know—nothing serious."

"Well it won't be long," Sister Marie said, "before you fall for two fine young men, and soon after that your thoughts are going to be turning to marriage and raising a—"

"Marriage sucks," Madlen said. "Excuse me. It—er—doesn't work."

"Just because your parents have their problems, Madlen, it doesn't mean that you and your sister can't launch out one day into a wonderfully happy and re-warding marriage for each of you. In family lives, the past doesn't always dictate the future." She managed to look at the clock on the wall by the chance turning of her head. "So what I'd like to do for you is to give you the name of a counselor." She wrote on her yellow pad. "She's a sister like myself, so of course her services are free. And she can help you, I know. You're both going through a very miserable time, I quite realize that." The gentle smile came again as she handed Madlen the note and rose from behind the desk. "You're not in the least obliged to see her, of course. But I hope you will."

Madlen looked at the yellow sheet of paper like it was something in the mail she hadn't ordered.

"You've been real kind," Debra murmured.

"Less than I would have liked," Sister Marie said with a sigh, "but at least I can wish you luck and give you the Lord's blessing." She followed them to the door and watched them go down the steps, the autumn wind catch-ing at their long brown hair. They looked so very young, she thought, and so very lost.

*   *   *

"So what brings you here?"

This nun was different, Madlen thought—still quite old, maybe thirty or even forty, but more smiling than the first one, with little gaps in her teeth that made her kind of more human. But she was thin as a rake—did they get enough to eat in this place?

"We feel called by God," Madlen said quietly.

In a moment the nun gave a nod. "I see." They'd all said who they were—she was Sister Denise. "But I asked what brought you *here.*"

"Oh. We like the name of your order. Sisters of the Sacred Light. That's terrific."

Sister Denise was wiping her thin red nose a lot; it looked like she had a cold. Or maybe she'd been crying about something—her eyes were a little red.

Debra liked Sister Denise already. She looked like someone you could confide in, no matter what it was about. And that could make a whole lot of difference if she and Madlen joined these people. It would help with the fear—because it was still with her, the feeling that the world she'd known was slipping away and leaving her alone with Madlen in a huge kind of nowhere.

The fear wasn't anything to do with becoming a nun, or setting out to embrace the Redeemer—which was how Dolores Garcia had put it. The fear was about Madlen, and Debra had been able to handle it okay at home with Mom and Dad and their friends around, and even at school, because there were a lot of people she could go to. She'd never really been alone with her sister in that world, but if they cut themselves off from everyone they'd ever known, then she would be, and for the first time. Alone with Madlen.

Debra shut it out of her mind, like she'd had to do so many times as they'd grown up together. They loved each other, that was all that mattered, and things would work out okay. But she was glad there'd be Sister Denise in their new world, if they could ever get into it.

The nun was asking more questions, and Madlen was doing real well. She'd always been pretty good when she'd been on the stage, and Debra had sat there in the front row feeling proud of her, and in awe.

"You've both been baptized?"

"Sure," Madlen said. It was true, though she didn't remember anything about it—Mom had told them, that was all.

"Do you know the Order of Mass?"

Sister Denise looked this time at Debra, who panicked and looked down as Madlen said quickly—"Oh, sure. The priest begins by saying, 'In the name of the Father and of the Son and of the Holy Spirit,' and we all say 'Amen.' Then he says, 'The grace of Our Lord—' "

"You're quite conversant," Sister Denise said with one of her gentle smiles.

"Thank you," Madlen said, but Debra still couldn't look up, in case the nun turned to her again. She and Madlen had spent an hour in a Catholic bookstore called The Lantern yesterday and come away with a whole lot of little booklets and pamphlets and stuff, and they'd sat up in bed till midnight "rehearsing." "It's no good just saying it over and over," Madlen had said. "The trick is to see what the words actually mean, then they're easier to remember." But Deborah hadn't ever studied school plays like her sister, and not much of it had gone in. And besides, she hadn't really wanted to learn this stuff, because secretly in her heart she was hoping they'd never find a convent to take them, and they could stay in the world where they lived now.

"And your parents approve of your wanting to take holy vows, and live away from home?"

"Oh, sure." These were the easy questions, because Madlen had known they were coming—they were the obvious ones, and she'd rehearsed the answers. Anyway it was true about Mom and Dad. When Madlen had told them what they wanted to do, Dad had frowned like a thunderstorm and said, "What in God's *name*—" and Madlen had cut in very fast and said, "That's exactly it, Dad," which Debra had thought was really cute, she told her afterward. Mom had just raised her eyes to heaven— which Madlen thought was laughably appropriate—and said they'd all have to talk this over when they found the time. But wouldn't you know, the only time they could find had been five minutes one evening when their friends were late arriving for dinner, and Mom had just said, "Whatever makes you happy, but you'd just better talk it over with Mr. Crawford and take his advice before you burn your boats like this."

The impression Madlen got, the very distinct impression, was that Mom and Dad were actually quite happy with the idea, because it would save the expense of college and they wouldn't be interrupted any more in their careers and their dinner parties and their endless fights. Well, shit, Madlen had thought, that was okay with her and Deb too, they wouldn't have to listen to glass smashing all over the place and tires screaming and everything when they were trying to go to sleep. And yet . . . it had felt like a knife going into her, when she woke at night and thought about it, the way Mom and Dad didn't give a damn what she and Debra did or where they went, and it was a while before she got over the feeling.

"You should know," Sister Denise was saying, "that we're rather a poor convent. This is a very old building, as you can see."

They were in the parlor, and everything seemed to be made of wood—the floor and the table and all the chairs, though not the walls, of course: They were made of huge stone blocks. It looked kind of cold, because everything was polished up really bright, you could smell the stuff.

They must have a pretty good staff here to keep the place like this, Deborah thought, even though Sister Denise said they were rather poor.

"But poverty's a virtue, right?" Madlen said. "That's one of the vows we're going to take."

Sister Denise wiped her nose again and put on a new smile. "I like the way you said that, Madlen, but there are practical considerations too, and you should think about them. There's no electricity here right now, because the generator's broken down and we can't afford to have it repaired." She added bravely—"Though we're busy fund-raising. But the point is that it can be rather cold in Connecticut in the wintertime, and this whole building is of stone."

"Real ancient," Madlen nodded. "It's great."

Sister Denise didn't give up. "We think it's beautiful, too, but with no real heating except for one fireplace in the Great Hall, the winters can be quite sharp. There are quite a few other convents where I think you'd be more comfortable." She watched them steadily.

Debra was still trying to think of a suitable answer when Madlen came right in—"How much more comfortable could we be, as long as we're serving God?"

Sister Denise lowered her lids slowly and raised them again. "I like the way you said that too, Madlen." But she still didn't give up. "But life in a convent for two young people can be rather restricting, you must understand. Rather . . . cloistered. Are you sure you wouldn't miss the great big world out there?"

"The great big world out there," Madlen said, "is going crazy. Haven't you heard? Excuse me—sure, I guess you've heard. Shootings, drugs, girls getting raped and all that good stuff. And people who don't care about you, who don't even *care.*" She heard her voice echoing in the bare little room, and finished more quietly, "I think—we think there's a bigger world in here, and it's filled with the love of God."

In the silence Sister Denise looked at them both in turn again for a long moment, then got up from her chair, her smile shimmering. "I'll go and see if Father Giovanni is in his office. I think he'd like to meet you."

She went out through the arched doorway, and the long wrought iron hinges gave a little squeal.

Madlen swung her head to Debra and said quietly, "Looks like we could be in."

"Yeah," Debra said, and shivered suddenly.

"You okay?"

"Sure," Debbie said.

Madlen was watching her steadily. "Are you cold?"

"No. It's—well, yeah, I guess." She rubbed her arms a little.

Madlen glanced across at the arched doorway and looked back at Debbie and put a hand on her wrist, bringing her voice down low, almost to a whisper. "Look, Deb, it's got to be okay for you too, this whole thing we're doing. You want to go back to all that stuff, we'll go back."

"No," Debbie said, but couldn't make the scared feeling go. She wanted to get up and run, get out of this place before it was too late, run all the way to . . . where? There wasn't anywhere she could run, except back to "all that stuff."

"There's nowhere else," Madlen said, her eyes deep now as she watched her sister.

"I know."

"I mean sure, there are other convents. But—" she glanced at the doorway again "—but if we're going to get any peace for ourselves and leave all that shit behind, this is the only way to go. We agreed on that, didn't we?"

"Sure." She felt the strength in her sister's hand, gripping her wrist, and felt scared.

"I don't want you to be scared of anything," Madlen said softly. "Not ever."

She always knew what was in Debbie's mind. That was scary too.

"I'm okay," Debbie said, turning her head and meeting her sister's eyes, seeing how deep they were, how concerned.

"I never want you to be scared," Madlen whispered urgently. "Not of anything." Her grip on Debbie's wrist was harder now, almost hurting. "There's nothing you have to be scared of, ever. Okay?"

"Sure," Debbie said. But she shivered again, because she knew there was.

4

It was like dying.

"Okay," Dad had told them. "You can do it so long as you don't come running back home here after a couple of months, you'll have to understand that. You leave home, it's for good. Now get that."

"I just think he feels kind of bitter," Debbie told her sister. "It's like we're saying home isn't good enough."

"God," Madlen said as she packed the blue plastic trunk she'd bought from Hi-Value, "you're always so charitable, Deb. You bet your sweet ass home isn't good enough, and he knows it. He's glad to get us out of the house so he can fight with Mom without us listening, so he won't have to feel guilty anymore." She threw her hair dryer into the trunk and then took it out again; they'd been told what was going to happen when they entered the convent, and one of the things was they were going to have their heads shaved. She dropped the hair dryer into the big cardboard box in the corner where they were putting things to give away to their friends.

That was why it was like dying—they were kind of going through their unwritten wills and leaving stuff to people.

"You think Mom's going to be okay," Debbie asked, "alone in the house with him?"

"Look," Madlen said, "she doesn't have to take it anymore if she doesn't want to. She can pick up a bread-knife, can't she, or get the gun he keeps in the bedroom drawer—she doesn't *have* to take it. But you know what? I think she likes it, the same as he does. It's *passion,* right? I know it sounds screwy but I think that's all that keeps those two people together. So sure, she'll be okay without us. If not, she knows where the bread-knife is. Don't worry about it."

Debra held up the strawberry-red sweater she'd bought from Hi-Value only a couple of months ago on sale, the one Alice Thompson admired so much at school.

"Should I give this to Alice?"

Madlen glanced across. "I guess she'd have to go on a diet." Deb had always been wonderfully slim, which was a real pain because it was a high standard to have to live up to, weight-wise, French-fries-wise. "But she's crazy about it, sure," she told Deb, "so why not? What've we got to lose, when we're losing everything we've got?" She threw her red-and-white Nike Cross Trainers into the big cardboard box and tried to stop herself thinking about not ever running through the park again. Nuns didn't run. *What did they do for exercise, for God's sake?* She and Deb hadn't asked questions like that in the convent parlor when they'd been talking to Father Giovanni. What did *he* do for exercise? He looked awfully fit—and awfully good-looking for a man his age. It was going to be real nice having him around. She dropped the silver belt that Mom had given her last Christmas onto the bed, so Mom could wear it instead; people bought things they liked themselves for other people, right?

Deb had gone quiet, and Madlen glanced across at her again. She was just standing there with a lost look on her face and the little turquoise sequin purse dangling from her hand, the one Madlen had given her on her sixteenth birthday.

"Deb. You okay?"

It broke the spell. "Yeah."

Madlen went over to her and put her arms round her and squeezed gently. "We don't have to do it," she said, "unless you're sure. Always remember that."

"I know. But I'm okay." Her small body was trembling, and Madlen waited till it stopped. "We're in this together, pal, and it's going to be really great, remember? We're going to walk away from all this shit we're getting from everybody, just walk away and shut the door on the whole goddamn world."

"You bet," Debra said at last.

"Attagirl."

It had happened a couple of times before—Madlen had seen her sister getting cold feet, and had had to give her a quick fix to pull her out of it. She'd be okay when they'd settled in to their new life together at the convent.

That evening when Debra got out of the shower she looked at herself for the last time in the mirror—because that was one of the things on the list of personal possessions they were *not* to bring with them to the convent—a mirror. As she rubbed herself with the towel the two scars came up a bit red as they always did, the one on her left arm—that was when the car had run down the driveway into the street when she was four years old and she'd been dragged out screaming—and the longer one on her right leg, which had happened when she was twelve and her horse had bolted and she'd woken up in the hospital two

days _ater with Madlen sitting by her bed looking like she
hadn't slept for two nights, which was true, because she'd
thought it had been all her fault.

Then the mirror slowly steamed up, and Debra
watched herself gradually become lost in it, just a blur of
pink, till she looked away and vanished from all the
mirrors she'd ever seen herself in, because this one was
the last.

Mom and Dad didn't come.

There were six other girls here, looking cold but rather
ethereal, Debra thought, in their white dresses as they
stood on the grassy slope outside the huge doors of the
Convent of the Sacred Light as the big bell tolled in the
tower and the nuns gathered around the eight postulants
like they were herding sheep.

The parents of all the other girls were here, looking
awkward in their best clothes, two of the mothers sniffing
a lot into their handkerchiefs.

"We didn't want them here," Madlen told Debra, saying it between her teeth. "I was hoping all the time they
wouldn't come, you know?"

"Sure," Debra said.

But Alice Thompson was here, squeezed into the
strawberry-red sweater and holding a bunch of flowers
with a silver ribbon curling in the breeze as she looked
from Madlen to Debra and back like she wasn't sure
whether she should be happy or sad for them. And Jeff
Soderberg had come, giving Alice a ride in his beat-up
Volkswagen, and he was looking all the time at Debra,
because their whole class knew she'd started blowing his
entire mind since the first time she'd sat down at the desk
next to his two semesters ago. He'd only drummed up the
courage once to try dating her, and when she'd said she
hadn't started dating anybody yet he took it to mean he
was going to be the first of them all when she finally got

around to it, and had bounced along in her shadow ever since, in the special gold-ribbed high-deck inflatable Superking shoes he'd bought the day after he'd first seen her. He too was clutching a bunch of flowers tied with string, their stalks still dripping because he'd kept them in a jar of water in the VW till they got here.

He wasn't saying anything; he spent most of the time swallowing. The breeze fretted at the lock of straw-colored hair he'd been trying to keep stuck down with water.

"It's going to be great for you," Alice said to her friends.

"You bet." Madlen had told Alice about their life at home, the noise and the fights and the atmosphere of hate all the time, and of course Alice knew what things were like at school. "Will you come see us sometimes?"

"Absolutely!" Alice tugged her sweater down, sucking her stomach in.

"We can receive visitors," Madlen said, using the correct term for it, "once every two months."

Alice swallowed. "That's great!" But oh, God, she'd seen Madlen and Deb every *day* at school and a lot of times between semesters. "That's really great!"

Madlen was watching Deb, stealing glances from time to time, but she seemed okay, she was holding up pretty good, even though this was the clincher right now as they stood only a few yards away from those enormous wooden doors over there that were going to slam shut after them when they went through, any time now.

It had been like dying, she thought, up there in their bedroom in the house yesterday, throwing stuff into the cardboard box for the Salvation Army and kind of bequeathing their special things to Mom and their friends, and now it was like the funeral, with people standing around holding flowers and the big bell tolling solemnly in the tower and some of the moms crying and everything. But there'd be a new life in there for them, and everyone would only be thinking about love instead of hate, and they wouldn't have to think about getting raped by some guy every time they were alone anywhere, especially Deb, because of her fair hair and her deep blue eyes and her pretty mouth—she'd been a target for hassling all the time at Weldon High, and Tom Stokes had come close to getting his hand in her blouse one time until Madlen had pulled off her shoe and smashed it into his face and there'd been a trail of blood all the way to the boys' room.

Goodbye to all that, hallelujah. . . .

Then the nuns began bearing down on the postulants and the visitors and there was a lot of hugging suddenly and a dog started yelping, shut up in somebody's car and wanting to get into the act.

"Gonna miss ya," Alice said, and gave Madlen the bunch of flowers. "That's for you both, okay?"

"Well, gee, they're so pretty!"

Jeff Soderberg pushed his own flowers at Debra, staring into her face like he was scared of not being able to remember how it looked, once she was gone. "I'm coming to see you," he said, and swallowed again. "Okay?"

"Sure," Debra said. One of the flowers had gotten away from the string, and dropped onto the grass. They didn't notice.

"I'll come every time," Jeff said. "Every time it's allowed." He went on gazing into Debra's eyes, full of courage now because there was only a minute or two left and he could handle that. "Till—you know—till you get out."

"Now we'll say our goodbyes," one of the nuns told them—it was Sister Denise—and waited, bestowing her gracious smile.

Madlen whispered quickly—"Tell him he's the only guy you'll want to see, Deb."

"What? Oh. Sure. You're—"

Another nun began clapping her hands—"Come along, now, it's time to go in!"

"You're the only guy—" Debra began, turning to Jeff, but Sister Denise put an arm gently around her shoulders and led her away, and Jeff Soderberg stood rooted, staring after them, the benediction filling his head with the sound of a heavenly choir. . . . *You're the only guy . . . the only guy.* . . .

"C'mon, Jeff," Alice said, "I guess we gotta go."

She turned and walked a little way down the grassy slope, then looked back and saw Jeff hadn't moved. The other visitors were going back to their cars, most of them carrying stuff they'd brought with them to leave for the postulants to take into the convent with them—boxes of candy and cookies and a six-pack of Coke and things like that. But Alice had heard one of the nuns saying that flowers were the only "acceptable offerings."

"Jeff!" Alice called. Now that she couldn't be with Madlen and Debra anymore she wanted to go, and fast, before she started sniffling like some of the moms were doing. God, this whole thing had seemed like a funeral service. "Jeff!" she called again, and he turned and came bouncing down the slope in his totally outrageous multi-colored rubber shoes.

"There *is* a God," Jeff said, his face radiant.

"There's a *what?*" Alice asked him, because it had sounded kind of weird for Jeff Soderberg to say a thing like that.

"There is a *God,*" he told her, and went bouncing on down the slope to the beat-up Volkswagen. "I just found out," he called over his shoulder.

A throng of nuns was gathering now at the entrance to the convent, climbing the worn stone steps and shepherding the postulants in their white dresses, all of them carrying their little beribboned posies. The bell was still booming in the tower, floating its solemn notes on the light autumn air across the knoll of beeches below the hill.

"Come along, now. Don't look back."

But some of the girls were turning their heads, wanting to give a last wave, or to see one of the people down there by the cars.

"Don't look back!" another nun called sharply. "You're leaving that world behind you now." She was taking their flowers from them as they filed past her, saying they would be placed below the high altar as an offering to Christ.

Madlen glanced quickly at her sister, but Deb seemed okay; she was keeping pace with the rest of them, her head down as she looked at her clasped hands, where the flowers had been. They were the last of the postulants to go through the huge wooden doors, and could feel the chill of this place as they left the sunshine and walked through shadow, their shoes tripping sometimes on the edges of the rough gray stones.

The only sound now was their footsteps, and Debra felt the urge to turn and run back into the warmth of the sunshine out there while she had the chance, but the great doors slammed shut suddenly, sending echoes thudding along the walls, and the bell in the tower stopped ringing at last, and a deep silence fell.

5

"The Sisters of the Sacred Light is a small Order, and ours is a small convent."

Madlen and Debra and the six other girls were sitting in a row along a wooden bench, in a small room with only a desk and a few chairs in it. The nun was standing in front of them below the painted wooden crucifix on the wall. She'd said her name was Sister Carlissa, and that she was the Mistress of Novices. She didn't look that old, Madlen thought, maybe in her thirties, but life had been a bit rough on her or something, because she had deep shadows under her eyes and her mouth was kind of tight all the time as if she was having to keep things back and not tell anybody. Her pale skin looked thick, like a lizard's.

"We therefore have only a few teachers, and for this reason you will enter the Order straight away as novices, and take your studies as postulants with the novices already here." She was looking at each girl in turn, leaving her almost-black eyes on her for a minute before passing on. "In one way this is a privilege for you—an immediate promotion, if you will—but on the other hand it will mean you must study harder in order to catch up."

Debra wanted badly to scratch her head; she supposed they all did, because earlier today they'd filed into a room near the Great Hall and taken their turn on the upright chair in the middle, while a nun had wielded a huge pair of scissors and another one had scooped up their hair from the floor with a dustpan and shook it into a bucket, blond and chestnut and black and ginger, and all this in complete silence except for the snip of those awful scissors. Then a razor had been brought out and their heads were shaved right down to the skin, and now as they sat listening to the dry monotonous voice of Sister Carlissa they wanted to scratch their heads like crazy under their veils.

"You may have heard of the so-called Vatican II Conference of 1965, where sweeping changes were proposed and some adopted within our Church. But you should know that each Order has the right to conduct its protocol of worship according to the original edicts and dogma established centuries ago, and here in this convent, as is the case in many others across America, we adhere to the rules and regimen of earlier times." Her eyes moved on to study Debra, who held them for a moment and then looked down. "I shall now give you some of the basic instructions that will govern your daily lives."

The girl next to Madlen was sitting with her black-stockinged ankles crossed, swinging one foot all the time, and Sister Carlissa stared at her in silence for a moment. The novices began leaning forward to stare too. The foot didn't stop swinging.

"What did you say your name was?" Sister Carlissa asked the girl. Her voice had become quieter, and it didn't sound nice at all.

"Who, me? Nicola."

"Sister Nicola, I am waiting for you to compose yourself and sit perfectly still."

The foot went on swinging, and Debra looked across her neighbor at Sister Nicola, recognizing her as the girl who'd come to the convent yesterday on her own, without anyone to give her flowers or say goodbye.

"I am waiting . . ." Sister Carlissa said. Her voice was very soft now, and a glitter had come into those very dark eyes.

The silence in the little room was so intense now that Debra heard the girl next to her swallowing. And then there was the rustle of Sister Nicola's robes as she uncrossed her ankles and put her brand-new polished black shoes together on the floor.

In a moment Sister Carlissa said, "Now sit up straight." She waited. "Straighter than that." She waited again. "Thank you." Her voice was still ominously quiet. "You see, Sister Nicola, even with your slack and undisciplined body you can manage to sit up straight. That's very good. Because otherwise I would have to give it the discipline required. I would avoid the necessity for that, if I were you." She looked away at last and began pacing slowly, her thin white hands clasped together and her head down, eyes on the floor. "To continue with our basic rules and customs here at the convent of the Sisters of the Sacred Light, this is how we walk the halls and passages, just as I am doing now, not looking around us or at anyone else; our thoughts, being constantly with God, must not be distracted. If you feel the need to communicate at all, such as when you are passing Father Giovanni or Mother Superior or myself, you may say 'Praise be to Jesus,' or 'May the Lord be praised,' to which you may expect the reply, 'Praise be,' or 'Let us praise Him.' "

Sister Carlissa stopped pacing and faced the row of novices again. "As to your daily schedule, you will rise at

5:30 in the morning when you hear the bell and your cell guardian calling out the 'Benedictus Dominus.' Your first action on leaving your bed will be to kiss the floor. To forget to do this is considered a sin, and remember that sins are punishable. Remember too that Profound Silence, which will have begun after Recreation the evening before, will continue until after your first meal of the day."

Debra's mind wandered as the Mistress of Novices went on with her instructions. This wasn't the fun part, any more than the head-shaving business had been, but she and Madlen weren't here to have fun; they were here so they could go to bed at night and listen to the peace instead of those terrible angry sounds downstairs, which had often left Debra shaking with nerves as she tried to ignore them and get to sleep. And they were here to be able to spend their whole day, every day, knowing they were safe from trouble, instead of having to struggle through every hour at Weldon High in an atmosphere where the shouts of the guys and their hooligan laughter and the slamming of locker doors had been a kind of orchestration of wild, primitive, machismo force. Compared to that, Profound Silence was going to be something out of this world. Debra was happy, for the first time since she could remember, and she had Madlen to thank for it, because it had been her idea to bring this wonderful change into their lives.

"... And if the period bell sounds in the middle of your chores, whatever you may be doing, you will stop at once, cross yourselves and kneel. Remember that the bell is the voice of God."

Madlen, sitting as upright as she could on the bench without touching the wall behind, wondered if all the nuns were going to be bitches like this one, and if sooner or later she and Deb would get fed up with kissing the floor and crossing themselves and doing chores, and decide to quit. But maybe it wasn't going to be as bad as it looked right now, and in any case if they left this place they couldn't go back home and they certainly wouldn't go back to Weldon High. They'd become runaways, like the kids you read about in the paper, selling their bodies to creeps in cruising limos on Broadway so as to have enough food to eat, or waitresses or checkout clerks working ten hours a day with their feet killing them. So it was this place or nothing, and she hoped Deb could be happy here in spite of people like Sister Carlissa. As long as Deb was happy, nothing could spoil it for them.

". . . And you are strictly forbidden to talk about yourselves to your fellow novices, or to anyone else, or about the world you knew before you came here. The only One we talk about here is God." Sister Carlissa swept her gaze along the bench, resting for a moment to study Sister Deirdre and then passing on. "You will be allowed to receive visitors once every month in the parlor, but never more than two at one time, and in the presence of a superior sister. Again, you will not talk about yourselves to your visitors, even if they are your parents, or discuss your life here or anything that happens between these walls. Do you understand?"

Only a few of them had the courage to answer, and their voices were barely audible.

"Yeah—"

"Sure—"

"Yeah. . . ."

There was silence for a moment, and then, "My name, as I believe you know, is Sister Carlissa. The correct answer, then, must surely be 'Yes, Sister Carlissa.' I trust you agree?"

"Yes, Sister Carlissa!" It was a chorus this time, and she nodded briefly in satisfaction.

They didn't know how long it was before the period bell sounded—their wristwatches had been bequeathed to relatives or friends—but it seemed an awful long time, and when they heard it, a young novice who'd come here yesterday, Madlen remembered, in the company of a priest, slipped quickly to the floor and crossed herself, kneeling. The rest followed suit as a team, and the long wooden bench was left rocking on its legs.

"What is the sound of the bell?" asked Sister Carlissa, and got another chorus.

"The voice of God!"

"Think it's going to be okay?" Madlen whispered.

"Sure," Debra whispered back. "It's going to be great!"

They were in the double cell that had been allotted to them as close relatives, unpacking the rest of their things; there hadn't been time last evening because instead of Recreation, Sister Denise had "given them the tour" as she'd called it, taking them through the halls and the passages and the chapels and the kitchens, her habit flying out behind her as she led the way.

"But what about that Carlissa creep?" Madlen whispered. Profound Silence had begun immediately after Recreation tonight, and to break it was a sin—as they'd been warned—and sins were punishable.

"She's okay," Debra said. "She just gets her jollies that way." She laid her white woolen nightdress across her bed, and the binder beside it. Their instructions were that the normal bra was not to be worn under their habit, but only a wide cotton binder, stretched tightly across their chests.

The cell was half the size of their bedroom at home, which made things a bit cramped, but then there wasn't much in it besides the two narrow beds, a rickety table— no bigger than a stool, really—and two rickety straight-backed chairs. An ancient wardrobe with great splits in its woodwork and one end jacked up on a brick, a small

metal sink, a crucifix on the wall, an oil lamp, and that
was it.

"Look what I brought," Madlen said, and held up her
Dracula mask.

"Oh, God . . . don't let anyone see it!"

Madlen put it away. "You look cute," she said, "with
no hair. Like Sigourney Weaver in that space-alien
movie." It was true: It made Deb's eyes look even bigger.
She'd always been pretty as anything, and it figured that
Jeff Soderberg had come all that way to say goodbye.
Madlen had been asked for a few dates, sure, at Weldon
High, but she hadn't turned heads like her sister. She felt
a twinge of envy, but let it pass. She'd felt it before, a
hundred times, while they'd been growing up; it was
nothing new.

"We could have brought wigs," Debra said, "if we'd
known." She looked around her. "Where do we put our
trunks now they're empty?" There was so little room for
anything in here, with their beds almost against the wall
and only a narrow gap between them.

"On top of the wardrobe."

"Are we meant to study these prayer books by the light
of an *oil* lamp?" Debra asked.

"Keep your voice down . . ." Madlen hissed. "You
know what we get for breaking Profound Silence?"

"No . . ." in a whisper.

"They make us eat our next meal kneeling."

"Kneeling?"

There was a knock on the door and they froze. Someone must have heard them. . . .

Madlen slipped quickly to the door and opened it, and
saw a face in the shadowed passage outside. It was
Nicola.

"I brought you some soap."

"Soap? Come on in."

"And keep your voice down," Debra said. She thought

having to take an entire meal on their knees would be the pits.

"We have some soap already," Madlen said, and closed the door carefully.

"This is scented. Ivory. I brought a supply with me." Nicola held out a small white box. "The stuff we're expected to use is the same as we use for scrubbing the floor." She glanced around the cell. "You get moved in okay?"

"Sure. You want to sit down?" She put the box of Ivory onto the shelf above the sink.

"Don't put it there," Nicola said. "Hide it somewhere. They check out our cells when we're not here." She perched on the bed, and her black woolen ski hat with the bobble on top made a weird shadow against the wall. "Aren't your heads *freezing?*"

"Now that you mention it," Madlen laughed softly. It was already November, and the nights were cold. "You really get things organized, don't you?"

She felt slightly in awe of this girl Nicola, though not just because of her looks—she had the tan, dark-eyed features of a southern European, maybe Spanish or Italian, and her hair had been thick and raven-black when she'd arrived at the convent yesterday, a red carnation setting it off flamboyantly. Her teeth were very white and her smile was quick; her eyes had gold flecks in them as she squatted on the bed near the oil lamp. But it was the scene in the classroom this afternoon that had got Madlen's attention—and everybody else's.

Sister Carlissa, as Mistress of Novices, had been taking them through the whole curriculum at the convent, including things like protocol, dogma, and the confessional, and near the end of the period she'd asked for questions. Sister Patrice—the quiet one who was always the first to kneel whenever the bell rang—had wanted to know if she could sing in the choir because she knew the whole of the *Messiah* by heart, and somebody else had asked if they could have a lesson in fixing their veils because there were so many pins, and Nicola had waited her turn and then asked:

"Why do we get our heads shaved?"

"It's symbolic of humility," Sister Carlissa told her.

"Don't you mean humiliation?"

In the silence Madlen heard someone suck in their breath.

Sister Carlissa watched Nicola with her black obsidian eyes. "I don't believe I could have heard you correctly."

"Humiliation—you know? It's what they do to prisoners in China and places like that, to humiliate them. So I think it's symbolic of humiliation, don't you?"

Sister Carlissa turned to her desk and wrote something on her scratch pad. "Have you any other questions for me, Sister Nicola?" Her voice had gone very quiet—something they'd all come to recognize by now.

"Yes. Why doesn't Father Giovanni have his hair cut off? Is it because only women have to do it and he's a man, like the Pope's a man too and he calls the shots? Isn't that really the way it goes, because women are thought of as inferior in the Vatican like everywhere else?"

Debra was holding her breath; she imagined they all were. Nicola was asking her questions in a perfectly normal voice, like she really wanted to know the answers, but underneath the tone of innocence you could tell there was a lot of rage boiling up.

"Sister Nicola," the Mistress of Novices said, "you will take this note to Mother Superior, so that you can ask her the same questions you have just asked me." She tore the slip off the scratch pad, folded it, and gave it to Nicola. "I'm confident she'll satisfy your curiosity."

"You want me to go right now?"

"Of course."

And here was Nicola sitting on Madlen's bed in her

black woolen skiing hat, and Madlen felt slightly awed.

"That was a class act," Debra said, "you know? This afternoon?" She admired courage in people, maybe above all other things, because she didn't have any herself, could only ever try and put on a show.

"Oh," Nicola said, "the Carlissa thing? She kind of goads me."

"What happened when you went to see Mother Superior?" Madlen asked.

Nicola shrugged, and they noticed that even under the black robes she had eloquent shoulders, maybe had been a model once—she sure had the looks. "July Fourth firework show," she said, "you should have been there. You think Sister Carlissa's the chainsaw massacre queen? You should try Mother Superior. First she said she was going to throw me out of the convent because she didn't need anybody here who wanted to challenge the Pope. So I tried my best to look like a saint—a tough shot for someone with my track record—and I convinced her I was really only trying to learn about the ways of the Vatican, and she finally said I could stay. But of course she threw me a whole lot of shitty-type chores like cleaning the johns and emptying the trash and scrubbing the kitchen floor. You two kids orphans?"

The question threw them both.

"Kind of," Madlen said.

Nicola watched them for a moment in silence. She'd seen them coming into the convent yesterday and noticed there'd only been a couple of friends their own age who'd come to say goodbye to them, so she figured they didn't have any parents. Today they'd always kept close to each other in class and during prayers and stuff, and she thought that was nice to see, because sisterly love wasn't always the norm in families these days; some of them spent their whole time scratching each other's eyes out, you ask Nicola Maria Montini and she'd tell you.

She didn't ask Madlen what she'd meant by "kind of" when Nicola had asked if they were orphans a minute ago. She just said, "I happened to notice there wasn't anyone from the older and wiser generation around when you got here yesterday, which would make you the same as me. But I'm a bit older than you myself, I'm twenty-five, and I checked out the background to this whole thing while I was waiting to be accepted, so I thought maybe—you know—I could help you guys a little, show you the ropes. Have you got a hang of these habits yet, how to make them stay on so you don't moon Father Giovanni by accident when you're walking in front of him?"

Madlen began laughing, and Nicola hushed her quickly. "Watch it, for God's sake," she whispered urgently. "Talking during Profound Silence is bad enough, but the one thing you don't want to do in Sin City is to laugh, because it means you're happy, and that's the one thing they can't stand."

Debra got her veil from the wardrobe and held it up. "Sure, I can use some help with this." She'd felt it trying to come apart all afternoon.

"Where's the headpiece and everything?" Nicola got off the bed and stood behind her. "Keep still, okay, and hand me the pins when I'm ready. There are fourteen of them, starting with the robe and the bib." Some of them were in the wrong way, so she began taking them out and putting them back in. "So what about that Father Giovanni," she said, "isn't he just gorgeous?"

"Yes," Debra said, surprising herself. She'd never thought much about boys so far in her life, let alone men. She suppressed an *ouch!* as Nicola stuck a pin in her neck.

"Whoops! Sorry—did you feel that?"

"No."

"I think I'm going to start working on that man," Nicola said contemplatively, "give him some fun, love him to death. Isn't that the name of the game in this

place—love? Now you hold this bib down at the back
with a pin through the loop—you want to look and see
what I'm doing, Madlen?"

"I'm watching."

"Because you have to dress each other, see, it's the
only way to go, unless you're a contortionist."

"They haven't heard of zippers?" Debra asked.

"Honey chile, they ain't even heard of *sex.*"

"How d'you mean," Madlen wanted to know, "you're
going to 'work on' Father Giovanni?" She didn't know
Nicola well enough yet to tell when she was joking.

Nicola turned her head to look at her, and Madlen
could certainly tell now that she wasn't joking. Her dark
eyes were intense, and there were those gold lights in
them again. "I knew a priest once," she said softly, and
Madlen almost flinched at the tension suddenly in the air
between them. "And I've been waiting to meet one
again." Then Nicola went back to her pins, and Debra
could feel the tension too, in the sudden sharp move-
ments of her hands. There was a strained silence for a
moment, except for sounds of whispering from one of the
other cells across the passage, until Nicola said in her
normal tone, "See, Madlen, you pull the underbonnet of
the headpiece together with this string, using the pin at
the back of the head. Then you put the stiff black bonnet
on top, and then the veil, and you fix the veil with three
more pins—you watching?"

"You bet," Madlen told her, but she couldn't forget
what Nicola had said about the priest, and the way she'd
said it.

"Then finally," Nicola took up again "—and you have
to do this real careful—you go under the black bonnet
and fix it to the white one with the last three pins. And
watch your scalp, because you're playing with fire here."
She stood back. "Have a look in the—oh, that's right, no

mirrors. How's it feel, Deb? Or do you prefer to be called Debra?"

"Deb's fine. It feels great—thanks a lot. I got a headache this afternoon, trying to keep this thing on by tilting my head all the time. I still can't see sideways from under the bonnet, but—"

"We're not meant to, honey—we're here to learn tunnel vision." Nicola's eye fell on the long width of cloth on the bed. "Oh, Jesus, you're not wearing *binders,* are you? Didn't you bring any bras?"

"They were on the forbidden list," Madlen said.

"Right, we're not meant to have breasts, because breasts are sexy." Nicola put her hands on her hips, unconsciously striking a pose. "But what if—"

"Were you a model?" Madlen cut in.

"Huh? Yeah, I kicked my heels up and down a few runways for the rag trade one time. But with these damn things—" she took the binder and held it up like a dead fish"—what if we want to quit the brides of Christ business one day and marry a live male of the species and have kids—how can we feed them the real Half-and-Half if we've had our boobs flattened out in this place? If we—"

"Shhh . . . " Debra whispered, "someone'll hear you!"

"Shit, I was forgetting." Nicola lowered her voice. "No tongues and no titties, right. But listen, tomorrow I'll get you a pair of bras I smuggled in. I've got a deal going with my dentist, see. When I go for a clean-up every six months he's going to give me a package from a girl friend of mine—new bras, soap, tampons, stuff like that. So there'll be things to spare for you guys if you need them. I knew a nun in New York, where I come from, and she gave me the whole picture. She—"

"You knew a nun," Madlen said, "and a priest? Is that why you decided to enter a convent?"

Nicola's eyes darkened and she looked away. "The nun happened to be my sister-in-law." Then a steely undertone came into her voice. "The priest I met when I was seven years old. But they're nothing to do with why I decided to enter a convent."

"I guess I shouldn't have asked," Madlen said quickly, wishing she hadn't. You had to watch what you said to Nicola; it was so easy to run slap into trouble.

"Oh," Nicola said, throwing out a graceful hand, "it's okay. I don't like these people too much, the way they look at life. But I'll tell you one thing—" and her eyes were fixed on Madlen's again, with the gold flecks smoldering like sparks "—I like them a whole lot better than the people I knew outside." Then she flashed her dazzling smile and broke the tension and Debra let out the breath she'd been holding without knowing it. "It's a long story," Nicola said, "and maybe one day I'll—" she left it as the bell for lights out began ringing from the end of the corridor.

Later, Debra lay on her hard narrow bed with thoughts of Nicola circling around in her mind. She couldn't stop wondering what could have happened to the girl from New York, to drive her into a place where she didn't even like the people who were going to control her life for as long as she was here.

The only window in the cell was a small oblong of bottle-green glass set high in the wall above the beds, and pale light was washing through it as the moon topped the hill to the east. Over the door was an open fanlight, with a notice beneath it in red capital letters conveying the strict instructions that it must never be closed under any circumstances—for the obvious reason that anyone breaking Profound Silence could not then be heard by a guardian passing outside.

Someone was there now, moving along the passage in slippered feet, the shadows of her robes flying like bats across the fanlight from the lamp she carried, and Debra gave a sudden shiver, turning on her side and pulling the blanket across her head.

But her thoughts of Nicola wouldn't stop, and she found herself wondering why she'd talked so strangely about Father Giovanni—*I think I'm going to start working on that man . . . give him some fun, love him to death. . . .*

Why did she say *to death?* How could you love someone *to death?*

Then sleep came at last, and Debra's thoughts slipped into a dream, and she was walking along a corridor with the priest some way ahead of her, his feet in slippers and his lantern sending the shadows of his robes flying like bats along the walls.

"Father Giovanni!" Debra called out, *"Father Giovanni!"* She walked faster to catch up to him, but he walked faster too, and in a moment she was having to run. *"Be careful, Father Giovanni! She's going to love you to death!"* Then he was running too, the three gold crucifixes on his robes glinting in the light from his lantern. *"To death!"* she called desperately, frantic to warn him. *"To death!"* Then someone else's footsteps began sounding from behind her, and she turned and saw Madlen coming, her black robes swirling around her like smoke and the red-fanged Dracula mask on her face grinning in the dark—and Debra screamed, running faster and faster so her sister couldn't reach her, faster and faster to catch up with Father Giovanni so he could save her, but she could hear Madlen's footsteps close behind her now, closer and closer, and she went on screaming because Father Giovanni couldn't save her now, no one could save her now as her sister's hands reached out at last and caught her with their sharp vampire's claws and there was nothing left but one last scream, a shred of terror torn from her in the night. . . .

6

"Divine Mercy, gushing forth from the bosom of the Father. . . ."

"I trust in you."

"Divine Mercy, greatest attribute of God. . . ."

"I trust in you."

"Divine Mercy, fount gushing forth from the mystery of the Most Blessed Trinity. . . ."

"I trust in you."

The sweetness of incense lay on the air, and Madlen consciously breathed it in. It wasn't as good as "Scarlet Sin"—a half-full splash-on bottle of which she'd bequeathed to Mary Beckwith from next door—but it was better than the smell of furniture polish and boiled cabbage and the general odor of antiquity that no amount of scrubbing would ever get rid of.

"Divine Mercy, which flowed out from the open wound of the Heart of Jesus. . . ."

"I trust in you."

Mary Beckwith from next door . . . Madlen could hardly remember what she looked like, after only three weeks here. Being so closed in and never going outside—except across to the vegetable gardens or the woods to cut lettuces or gather mushrooms—had done something funny to their sense of time: It seemed like they'd been here forever.

"Divine Mercy, shielding us from the fire of hell. . . ."

"I trust in you."

Madlen loved the ritual in this place, the drama. She'd told Debra, "It's so wonderfully theatrical, as good as *Grand Guignol!"* She'd had to explain it was the traditional French theatre of the grotesque. "All this talk of open wounds and blood, and pretending to drink it, and eating the flesh of the Savior—that's cannibalism, right?" Deb had said it probably had a deeper meaning than that, but Madlen wasn't to be put off. All the other sadomasochistic stuff was good theatre too—shaving the head and kissing the floor and begging for mercy all the time; it was really great, and far better than any of the plays she'd acted in, except maybe for *Dracula* at Halloween.

And she'd been exploring this place over the weeks, admiring the beautiful stained-glass windows and the archways and the beamed ceiling of the Great Hall where they took their meals—what a set!—and finding nooks and crannies and hidden staircases and the Big Secret itself, which she was dying to tell Debra about—but nobody else.

"Divine Mercy, delight and ecstasy of holy souls. . . ."

"I trust in you."

Then Sister Faustina's Praises were over at last, and for the next hour there'd be free time, today being Sunday, with no lessons.

"There's something I want to show you . . ." Madlen

told her sister as soon as they were out of the chapel.
"You'll absolutely flip!"

Debra looked quickly around them. She was always
excited by Madlen's obsession with what she called the
"psychodrama" going on here, and willingly shared in
her various escapades; there was no harm in them and
they kept the boredom of convent routine at bay.

"What have you found this time?" Debra asked her.

"It's in the North Chapel," Madlen whispered, and
took her arm. "Come on, we've only got an hour!"

"It's going to take a whole hour?"

"It's going to take *days,* to do it thoroughly. . . ." They
slowed their walk as Sister Carlissa passed them in the
corridor.

"Praise be to Jesus," Madlen murmured devoutly.

"Let us praise Him," Sister Carlissa answered, and
went on her way.

It was late afternoon, and soft winter sunlight played
in the colored windows as the sun neared the hills. As
Sister Denise had told them when she'd given them the
"tour," the North Chapel was seldom used for services,
since the roof tiles had been damaged by a winter storm
two years before, and as yet there were no funds for
repairs.

The chapel was deserted as they went down the aisle,
but Madlen stopped at the altar and turned round to
make sure no one else had come in before she led Debra
onto the worn red-carpeted dais and around the altar to
the wall behind it.

"Madlen . . ." Debra whispered, "this is strictly off-
limits!" The area behind any of the three altars in the
convent could be entered only by sisters of high rank,
from the Mistress of Novices on up.

"Shh!" Madlen whispered, and took an oil lamp from
behind a stack of boxes, where she'd obviously hidden it
earlier. Lighting the wick, she took Debra's hand, lead-

ing her along the wall to where an ancient door leaned on its side against the granite stone. Heaving it upright, she told her sister to hold it steady as she ducked behind it, and in a moment Debra heard the squeal of rusted hinges. "Come on," Madlen said, and Debra let the door fall back against the wall as she followed her sister through the opening.

"A secret passage?"

"Our very own . . ." Madlen lowered the lamp to the floor. "It's ages since anyone else came through here, look . . . those are the footprints I left the first time I discovered it, and the dust's pretty thick all around them. It's been years . . . maybe centuries." She held the lamp high again. "Phantasmagorical?"

"What on earth's that?"

"Means fabulous." She drew the door shut on its rusty hinges and Debra shivered, the sound shrilling along her nerves.

"Is there another way out?" she asked uneasily.

"There could be. I haven't explored it all yet."

"Then what happens," asked Debra slowly, "if we don't find one before we have to leave here the way we came in, and there just happens to be somebody in the chapel . . . like, for instance, Sister Carlissa?"

Madlen's face was close to hers in the lamplight, her eyes wide with excitement. "You chicken?"

"I'm never chicken," Debra said, "you know that." It was true: She had to try so hard to prove to herself she was brave that it had begun to look like the real thing.

"I shouldn't have said it," Madlen told her, and gave her hand a quick squeeze. "That's absolutely right— you're never chicken."

"But it's still a good question. . . . What if we get caught going back into the chapel?"

"Call it Russian roulette." Madlen was grinning in the lamplight, and something flashed into Debra's mind—

the terrifying dream she'd had three weeks ago on their
second night at the convent, the one where Madlen had
been running behind her along a passage, the Dracula
mask on her face and her clawed hands reaching out for
her. Debra had forgotten it within a day or two, and
there hadn't been another one since then. But now she
remembered it, and it disturbed her.

"You okay?" Madlen asked, watching her closely.

"Sure." A dream was a dream, and this was the real
world, where a severe disciplining from Sister Carlissa
was the worst that could happen.

"Look," Madlen said, "I take most of the fallout if we
get caught, okay? I'm the eldest, and I'll tell them I got
you into this—which I did. Now come on, we're wasting
time."

She turned away and started along the passage, her
shadow flitting across the walls like Father Giovanni's
had done, Debra remembered, in the dream. But she
braced herself and followed, because she was brave, as
brave as they came, wasn't that right?

The passage seemed endless, and she thought it must
run the whole length of the convent, but it opened at last
into a chamber, and their shadows flew higher suddenly
against the ceiling, like a cloud of bats.

"This is as far as I've been," Madlen said, staring
around her. "See the fireplace?" It was set in the wall
opposite the passageway, a crude pile of granite, with the
cold embers of the last fire still lying among the ashes.
Nearby was a huge stack of firewood. "It looks like they
were here for a long stay, but then something happened."

"What like?" Debra shivered again, wondering if they
were trespassing on hallowed ground, disturbing the spir-
its of the dead.

"I don't know. Maybe somebody found them hiding
out here, and they had to abandon the place, or they got
taken away and killed or something. I—"

"But who were they?"

Madlen gave a short laugh. "Look, I just found this place, that's all. Sister Denise said the convent used to be a monastery way back in the seventeenth century, so maybe these people were a secret cult, hiding from the monks, or they were the monks themselves, hiding from some kind of enemy; it's anybody's guess." She gazed around the huge shadowed chamber. "But isn't it great?" It reminded her of the set for the robbers' cave in that Swedish opera, though she couldn't remember the title.

There were two other passages leading away from the chamber, and she told Debra to wait there a minute while she checked things out. Debra watched her vanish into the nearest passage, until there was only a fading glow of light against the walls, and the shadow of Madlen's robes.

Don't let her leave you.

The voice sounded quite clearly in Debra's head, like someone had actually whispered to her in the darkness.

Go after her—you could get lost in this place.

I know, she thought, and the idea scared her, but she didn't move. Madlen always knew how to figure things out, so she'd learned to trust her. She could still see the glow of light, and the moving shadow.

It was cold in here, colder than in the main part of the building, where everyone gave off body heat and there was the fire burning in the Great Hall. Here it was cold and it was dark, and Debra stood with her arms folded across her chest for warmth, hugging herself for comfort. *Madlen?* she wanted to call out. *You still there?* But she kept silent. This was a test, maybe, of her courage, and she mustn't be found wanting.

Then the light brightened and Madlen was there suddenly in the mouth of the passageway—"It's a dead end, there's just a lot of rubble and stuff where maybe the wall caved in." She came close to her sister and held the lamp higher. "You okay?"

"Of course I'm okay." She tried to sound surprised at the question but didn't quite manage it, because she was too relieved. "It's cold in here, that's all."

"Then jump up and down," Madlen said, "while I check the other one out—it might not go anywhere either."

And she was off again, and light bloomed suddenly in the mouth of the next passageway, then gradually began fading. Debra did as she was told, jumping on the spot in her heavy black regulation shoes until she was out of breath. The light in the passage was very faint now.

"Madlen?" She called out without thinking about it first: There wasn't time now to wonder about tests of courage. "Madlen?"

"I'm here! Come on—this one's okay!"

Ashamed of herself, Debra moved across to the mouth of the passage and saw the light brightening, and her sister standing there waiting for her. "There's another kind of room," she told Debra, "just up ahead," and she swung the lamp and got going, with Debra on her heels.

It was a smaller chamber than the last one, with the ceiling hewn out of solid rock. There was no fireplace this time, but only a stone dais in one corner, covered with some kind of rubble. Above it there hung something that turned slowly in the light, and Madlen took the lamp over there to get a better look.

"What. . . ." She held the lamp higher, and the shadow of the thing flew against the wall like a great bird—because that was what it was, the remains of a rook, bigger than a crow, bigger than a raven, its ragged feathers half-concealing the white bones of the skeleton beneath, the shadowed eyesockets staring blindly into the light, the big hooked beak gaping as if its last screech had been one of rage.

Madlen brought the lamp down almost to the floor, and now they could make out what the rubble strewn across the stone dais actually was—a mass of scattered bones, small and fragile-looking, some still discernible as a ribcage, or part of an arm or a leg . . . a human arm or a human leg . . . with among them, here and there, the roundness of human skulls.

"Oh, my God . . ." Madlen said softly, and with her free hand crossed herself.

Debra stood holding her breath, staring down at the skulls as they stared back at her. Then she heard herself whispering, "But they're so small . . . why are they so. . . ."

In a moment Madlen said quietly, "Because they're children. . . . They were children . . . infants. . . ."

They stood together in silence, shocked, feeling themselves to be mourners, here too late to attend the obsequies, to hear the prayers. But then, they wouldn't have understood them anyway; there hadn't been the rites of God performed in this place, but of Satan.

"Human sacrifice?" breathed Debra.

"Yes." In a moment Madlen moved back from the dais, bringing the lamp with her. "So now we know, don't we? It was some kind of pagan cult."

Debra couldn't move, couldn't look away from the little round skulls, feeling she could hear faraway laughter, distant cries, sending their faint, frantic echoes for the last time around the cavernous chamber, never to be heard again.

"It's horrible," she said at last.

"Greek theatre," Madlen nodded. "Greek tragedy. It's incredible." She was moving the lamp around, exploring again.

"You know what you did?" Debra asked her.

"Huh? When?"

"When you saw what we were really looking at."

Madlen held the lamp closer, puzzled. "What did I do?"

"You crossed yourself."

"I did?" Madlen gave a short laugh. "Well, Jesus. I guess we've done it so many times in this place it was from sheer habit. You know what? This stuff's getting to us—we're turning into a couple of *nuns!*"

Her kidding didn't fool Debra. Madlen had a heart too, and the sensitivity of an actress, and she was trying to come out of her shock the quickest way, by turning the whole thing into a joke. She'd always done that in the past, as Debra knew, and maybe it was as good a way as any of getting rid of something you couldn't handle.

Quietly Debra said, "You did it so naturally."

"Well, sure. Ain't I a bride of Christ?"

She explored with the lamp and saw yet another passage leading off from the chamber. "This place is a labyrinth! Wait there, Deb, while I check this one out."

"I'd like to go back now," Debra said quietly. This whole place gave her the creeps, and she couldn't stop thinking about those tiny skeletons lying there in the corner.

But Madlen was barely paying attention. "Just give me a couple of minutes more, okay? This one's *narrower,* why's that?"

Debra watched her go through the mouth of the passage, only just able to walk straight forward with her shoulders brushing the walls, her robed figure blotting out the lamplight. Waiting in the pitch dark, Debra didn't know how long it was before she decided she could call her sister's name without seeming to panic. But it didn't matter how long it was . . . she was now beyond caring.

"Madlen?"

In a moment, "I'm coming!" Her voice was very faint. "But the darn lamp's gone out."

Oh, Jesus. . . . "Have you still got the matches?"

"Yes." Madlen added something else, but it was too faint to understand.

"What did you say?" Debra called.

"The lamp's out of oil."

Debra felt instant goosebumps. She had to catch up with her sister and she had to do it *now*. . . . But she'd need to go slow, because in the darkness she could miss the mouth of the passageway. She began walking with her hands in front of her, sliding her shoes over the rough earthen floor to prevent herself tripping on rubble.

In the corner behind her, on the dais, the tiny skulls watched, and listened. A trickle of nerves flowed down her spine.

"Madlen?"

She needed her sister's voice to guide her, but it came so faintly now that she could barely hear the words. Something about "another way out," it sounded like. She kept on moving cautiously through the dark, knowing the entrance to the passage must be almost straight in front of her, but when at last her hands touched the wall she knew she'd gone off course, and began moving to her right, taking a guess. The granite was cold against the palms of her hands, so she used just her fingertips, working her way along. In another minute she called out again, needing Madlen's voice to guide her, needing *Madlen*.

But there was only silence this time.

"Madlen!"

Silence.

Silence and the smell of lamp oil and the chill of the stone wall under her fingertips, and the echoes of those infant cries . . .

"Mad-len . . ." in a sing-song tone this time, the way they'd called out to each other once playing hide-and-seek—which was all this was, a game of hide-and-seek,

because Madlen had gone dashing off in the dark somewhere and Debra had to catch up and surprise her.
"Mad . . . len. . . ."

Silence.

Debra stopped moving. She wasn't getting anywhere
in this direction; it had to be the other way. But first she
stood back, trying to make out the blacker mouth of the
passage against the blackness of the wall. But that didn't
work, because now the lamp had gone out there was no
other source of light in this place at all, no windows, no
doors with cracks at the edges, no fireplace in here with
a flue that might have filtered the glow of the sunset
down to help her.

The darkness was *total,* and she remembered watching
Madlen rehearsing one night as the star of a play called
Butterflies Are Free, and the producer—the head of the
school drama department—saying, "Okay, Madlen, now
shut your eyes and cup your hands over them—switch
that light off over there, someone. . . . Thanks—cup your
hands over your eyes and sit like that for a minute at the
table with this one thought in your head: you are blind
. . . you are completely and totally *blind* . . . and that's all
you can ever see, complete and total darkness . . . blackness . . . because you are *blind.* . . ."

Debra stood trembling, having to get used to the idea
that she didn't have to shut her eyes and cup her hands
over them to see this complete and total darkness, blackness. . . . It was *there* for her.

"*Madlen!*" Close to a scream now, a cry for help.

Silence. Darkness and silence and the fear coming up
into her throat in a cold wave because she knew now that
the game of hide-and-seek was over, and this was for
real. Madlen had gone blundering on in the dark, looking for what she thought was another way out—if that
was actually what she'd called back the last time. Or
she'd bumped her head on a low archway or the mouth

of a passage and knocked herself out and couldn't hear now, couldn't answer.

Would never be able to hear, never be able to answer.

Debra felt the shock run through her, and then, strangely, found a kind of courage, because her sister might need help too, more than she did, could be lying there in a pool of blood or—*Whoa there, Deb, get a grip on yourself.* Okay, but Madlen might need help, so she'd just better *get* there and find out.

Move to the left, fingertips tracing the cold granite slabs, shoes shuffling sideways, kicking at something—*it doesn't matter what, don't worry about it*—moving on slowly, it has to be here, the end of the passage, somewhere close now, fingertips freezing, no feeling left in them—then her left hand pushed suddenly forward into space and she caught her breath.

The passageway.

"Madlen?"

Silence. But the fumes of the oil lamp were stronger now. It had gone out a while ago but the fumes had lingered, and Debra took a shred of comfort from this fragile link with her sister.

The passage was so *narrow*. She walked with her hands raised head-high in front of her, because if Madlen had hit a low archway she was liable to do the same, and now she was the rescue team and she had to take care for both their sakes.

"Madlen?"

She stopped, listening to the silence, then hearing, she thought, her sister's voice, ever so far away, calling her name. . . . *Debra . . . where . . . are . . . you?* Or she imagined it, trying to believe she heard it.

"You know, Debra," the school drama coach had told her once, "you've got just as much imagination as your sister if you wanted to use it. You'd do well on the stage, and you've certainly got the looks for the star parts. So why don't you show up at the next audition? I'll help you through."

Okay, Debra had said, but she never showed up. Her sister was the star of this show, and she was quite happy to let things stay that way.

"Madlen?"

Calling her name now just so Madlen would hear her if she was still near enough—or still conscious. The thing was to press on, and sooner or later she'd find her sister, and everything would be back to normal.

This wasn't normal. She was wandering blindly through the dark in a place where they'd made human sacrifices, *where they'd murdered babies* and left them to turn into tiny skeletons under the hanging bird of prey, under the effigy of their god or whatever it was. *Or had they sent living birds into the chamber to feast on every new sacrifice, tearing with their great hooked beaks at the tender flesh, so they wouldn't have time to rot slowly away and bring the rats?*

"Madlen?"

Seeking comfort in the sound of her own voice, that was all. Madlen wasn't here.

Or had the infants been still alive when they were thrown onto the dais and the birds were sent in? Was there a law in those pagan rites that—

"You know, Debra, you've got just as much imagination as your sister. . . ."

Too much. A whole lot too much.

"Madlen?"

She moved forward into the dark, her arms beginning to ache from having to hold them up, and after a time, after what was maybe a long time, she stopped.

Because Madlen wasn't here anymore. She wasn't anywhere. She'd found the other way out of this place and she'd be waiting for Debra to follow. But she didn't want to follow. This was the turning point. She didn't know what was ahead of her in these passages, in this blackness, but she knew what was behind, so that was the way she'd take, go back through the . . . through the place where the bird of prey was hanging in the dark above all those little bones . . . and through the bigger chamber where the fireplace was, and through the long passage to the end, to the secret door in the North Chapel, to the normal world, with the lamplight and the voices of people and the sound of their prayers and their singing.

Go back.

For the last time—"Madlen?"

Silence.

Go back.

Debra turned in the narrow confines, bumping her shoulder and feeling her veil catch against a jutting stone. Then she moved forward, her hands touching along the wall now because she knew there weren't any low arches to bump her head against. She could still smell the lamp oil, even though she was used to it; otherwise she might have thought this whole thing was a dream, a nightmare, that Madlen had never been here with her lamp at all.

Touching the wall as she moved, so her shoulder didn't bump into it, touching the wall and listening all the time for the faint far sound of her sister's voice, in case, just in case Madlen had decided to come back to find her. But if she heard her voice again she wouldn't be able to trust her ears; in this dark void and in her loneliness her imagination was going slowly wild. She understood the danger in this, and knew she must keep her thoughts under control.

Touching the wall on one side only now, finding it easier to walk sideways a little because the passage was so narrow and the stones kept tugging at her veil.

Touching the wall . . . but she should have reached the smaller chamber by now, where the bird hung in the dark—should have reached it *before* now, surely, because she hadn't come very far along this passage before she'd decided to stop and turn back.

She'd come too far. But how could she have come too far without reaching the sacrificial chamber?

Debra stopped, and stood still.

It couldn't have happened. She couldn't have come too far. And there was something else that was trying to get her attention as she stood there in the darkness, feeling the stillness, listening to the silence. It was a moment before she knew what it was.

She couldn't smell the fumes of the lamp anymore.

This wasn't the same passageway.

This wasn't the way she'd come.

Putting a hand to the wall to steady herself, she felt the slow chill of understanding lifting the hairs on her arms as terror came, blocking the breath in her throat.

She was lost in the labyrinth.

7

She screamed as wings brushed her face and claws plucked at her veil.

Lord, thou art my Savior, and my only hope.

Screamed again as the bat swooped, squeaking, its droppings flying across her cheek, acid and scalding.

Lead me from the darkness into Thine eternal light.

The words ran through her mind at random, learned from habit and now repeated instinctively as a silent cry for help.

The bat swooped again and she struck out at it and for an instant felt its fur and its leathery wings against her fingers, like thin gloves, with the small hooked claws catching at her skin and trying to cling on before she flung the thing hard into the darkness and heard it thud against the stones. Silence came back and the squeaking stopped.

Debra leaned against the wall, her head back against the cold granite and her eyes closed, the nerve light flashing in brilliant colors beneath her lids.

Divine Mercy, lifting us out of every misery, I trust in Thee.

When she moved at last it was to wipe the stuff from her cheek and get rid of it against her robes, disgust bringing saliva into her mouth.

Nothing had changed. Nothing had changed because of the bat. Nothing was different except that it lay dead somewhere near her with its blood creeping in the dark across the stones. There was still nothing in her world except for the darkness and the silence and the cold, and the knowledge that she was lost in the labyrinth and that if she couldn't find her way out in time she would gradually become a skeleton, like the children, like the bird, like the bat.

There must have been a fork in the passage. She'd been touching the wall on only one side, moving forward at an angle because the passage was so narrow, and she'd led herself into a new one, where she couldn't smell the lamp oil anymore.

So there was no problem, was there? She'd simply turn and go back, touching the wall on the *other* side this time until she came to the fork; then she'd turn again into the other passage, the familiar one where the lamp fumes lay on the air. Go back to the chamber where the . . . where the dead bird hung above the little white bones, the little white skulls . . . and make her way back to the North Chapel from there. There was no problem.

Except that it would be impossible for her to do that now. It was beyond her.

She had tried to do something, and she had failed. She had tried to keep her imagination under control, and hadn't managed it. Things weren't normal anymore; she couldn't think normally. *You've got just as much imagination as your sister. . . .*

More, maybe, much more. And that was the problem. She knew what would happen if she managed to find her

way back to the place where . . . the dead bird was
hanging, like a mobile made by the devil to decorate hell.

They would hear her coming.

They would hear her coming and scramble up from the
floor with their little bones rattling as they swarmed toward her, their cries filling the chamber as they begged her
to help them, to give them life again, clamoring against
her with their tiny skeletonic fingers reaching for her, the
weight of their numbers bringing her down, while—

Something was making a sound, and she listened to it,
her shoulders and the palms of her hands pressed to the
wall as the sound went on, softly, the sound of crawling,
of something crawling across the stones toward her—*and
she screamed.*

Pressed to the wall, screaming, sobbing, as the stress
broke and swamped her, tiding through her mind and her
body and leaving her limp and without strength, without
the power to stay on her feet as the soft sound of crawling
went on, close to her now.

Then her strength came back and she was running
blindly through the dark with her hands skinning themselves against the walls to guide her, running and running
until she was out of breath and had to slow down, had to
stop.

It had been the bat, that was all. She hadn't killed it.
It had started crawling across the floor, trying to fly
again.

Normal thought.

That had been a normal thought, thank God.

*Divine Mercy, shielding us from the fires of hell, I trust
in Thee.*

Her breath coming painfully as she leaned against the
wall, her heart hammering in her body, hammering in her
chest and her eyes and her head. The wall cold against
her shoulders, the air chill, moving across her face, bring-

ing relief, cooling the red-hot blaze of her imagination, her *goddamned* imagination.

Take it easy. . . . Take it easy, we're through it now. We're on the other side, where things are normal.

So let's think a minute. Let's check things out. There's no light anywhere, but I can feel the air moving . . . *moving across my face.*

This was what Madlen had felt, then—she'd shouted something about another way out; she'd felt the air freshening. *She must have been here somewhere,* and then gone onward and found the way out, expecting Debra to follow.

She was getting her breath now, could think straight at last, could realize now that there was something else: If bats could get into these passages, she could get out. In fact Madlen *had* got out. Hadn't she?

So let's go. Keep on going in this direction. If she—
What was that?

Stood holding her breath, stood listening.

It came again, a scuffling, a kind of scuffling, though not close, not anywhere close. Now it was silent. Now it was—

Scuffling again. Farther away, this time.

Had Madlen got out?

Silence again.

"Madlen!"

Listening. Very far away now, the scuffling sound, if she could still really hear it, if she had ever really heard it, if it hadn't been just her imagination.

"Mad . . . len . . ."

Echoes. Just the echoes of her voice.

It must have been another bat. Maybe they weren't so smart with that radar stuff of theirs after all, sometimes hit the walls. Though it hadn't been that kind of sound; it had been heavier, not just wings brushing the stones.

But it couldn't have been Madlen, either. She would have answered.

Then what had it been?

She didn't want to think about it, because if it couldn't have been Madlen and it couldn't have been a bat, there were only two possible answers. Either it was something heavier than a bat or she'd simply imagined it . . . and had started losing her reason, hearing things that weren't really there.

Before the panic could start again she moved, quickly and decisively, feeling her way in the darkness with the fingers of one hand tapping their way along the wall like a blind man's, because they were so sore now that she was certain they must be bleeding. She kept her other hand raised in front of her head, to stop herself walking into an archway and knocking herself out, because if *that* happened, she'd never—but it *wouldn't* happen, because she was making sure it didn't, okay? So don't even think about it.

This was the way. This was the right direction. This was the only way Madlen could have come when she'd realized there was an exit somewhere, with fresh air coming in. This was the way . . . saying it again and again in her mind, like a litany. This was the way. . . .

Now that she was certain of it, now that she knew she'd soon be out of this hellish place, she felt cool waves of relief flooding through her like a blessing, an almost physical reassurance that her prayers had been answered. And as if doors had been suddenly opened in her mind she was able to think of other things now, allowing images to flow behind her eyes, bringing back the world of reality . . . the crowded tables in the Great Hall, where in a little while she'd be taking her evening meal with Madlen and all the others . . . the lush and carefully-tended vegetable garden behind the West Chapel, where yesterday she'd helped start the first bonfires of the au-

tumn, raking the dead leaves into piles well clear of the
trees and putting a match to them, watching the first
tendrils of blue-gray smoke climb through the morning
air . . . the real world, and she'd soon be part of it again.

She kept moving, sliding her feet along in case there was
anything to trip over or suddenly kick against. She didn't
want any more problems; her problems were over now.

Kept moving, the sweet smell of the bonfires in her
mind, in her senses, as the passage turned now and she
felt small rocks against the toes of her shoes, and then
bigger ones. She didn't stop; she just kicked them aside.
There wasn't anything to stop for, the thing was to keep
going, keep moving, because it wouldn't be long now
before she was free.

A really *big* rock now, a small boulder, and this time
she had to go around it, one hand still waving in the air
to protect her head from any archway there might be.
And then another boulder, and another one—and suddenly her hand met stonework, and she explored its surface with her fingers, going higher and then lower and
then to one side and then the other . . . until she realized
it was a wall, a wall blocking the passage, blocking it
completely.

A dead end.

She stood perfectly still, listening to her own breathing, its sound magnified by the confinement. If there had
been light here, she would have seen herself standing with
her face up against the wall, staring at it like a dumb
idiot.

Okay, then, we have to go back. There's no need for
panic.

But it's a dead end.

Well, sure, yeah, it's a dead end, but that just means we
have to turn around and go back and—

Go back to what? To where?

Go back the other way, that's all.

Keeping her breathing slow and steady, keeping control of things.

But you've just been back there. You said this was the way out.

Yeah, well I—I just thought—

Question. *Why had she been thinking about the bonfires?*

That was easy. Because she could smell the smoke.

What smoke?

It was getting stronger all the time, starting to sting her eyes. It was creeping along the passage behind her.

The smoke from what? Not from the bonfires: They'd burned themselves out by this morning, and tomorrow they'd be raking more leaves for them.

The smoke from in here, then, from somewhere in these passages.

Fire in the labyrinth.

She felt her heart bumping suddenly, running wild.

Oh Jesus Christ, sweet Jesus.

She spun round and got past the boulders, grazing her legs and bruising a knee, clambering past them and going on down the passage, one hand to her face now as the smoke thickened, sharp in her lungs and pricking at her eyes, lurching on and not stopping, her shoulders hitting the walls as she half-ran, tripping over debris and small rocks but not stopping, not stopping for anything now because she had to get out of this place before the smoke got so bad she wouldn't be able to breathe anymore.

No, the good-looking young guy had said, *they don't die of their burns.* He'd been the fire captain from No. 2 Brigade a mile from Weldon High, and he'd been asked to give them a fire drill and tell them a few things about his work. One of the girls in her class had told him the thing that terrified her was the thought of being burned alive, and he'd been reassuring her, kind of. *They don't*

*die of their burns—they're no longer alive when the flames
reach them. They die of smoke-inhalation.*

She was running, stumbling, running on again as fast
as she could, as hard as she could through the blinding
dark with her eyes streaming and the smoke tearing at
her lungs and her hands flying out as she tripped and
went down and scrambled up again and ran on through
the thick gathering smoke.

Jesus, be with me now, be with me now.

As fast as she could, as hard as she could, blindly
through the dark with her breath sobbing and her tears
flying from her face as she ran and ran and ran.

They die of smoke inhalation.

Lying on the ground, she was lying on the ground, face
down.

The world came and went, came and went away in
waves of reality and limbo and reality again, came back
as she dragged the air into her lungs with the sound of the
wind moaning in the dark, the world coming and going
and coming back as she felt the floor of the passage under
her hands, sticky with something, sticky and smelling of
acid, and that was strange.

The air was clear, except for the acid smell.

And there was light.

*Lord, you didn't abandon me. Let there be light, you
said, and there was light.*

It was so long since she'd seen it that she'd thought at
first it was just in her mind, a square shape in front of her
eyes with bright white sparks in it.

The world came back and didn't go away again. She
knew it was called consciousness, and that she was conscious now.

It was in front of her and above her head, the square
of light, no more than a faint glow in the darkness all
around. She thought it must be the sky, the night sky,

and those bright white sparks must be the stars. But she
didn't move yet, because she needed to get this business
of breathing done with: She didn't know how far she'd
run through the passages but it had been a long way and
it had taken a long time, and she wanted just to lie here
for a while and get her breath back and put things together in her mind.

Breathing . . . breathing the clear air, and trying not to
cough anymore; she'd been coughing an awful lot, she
remembered now, because of the smoke. Breathing was
all that mattered for the moment. But she was puzzled by
the sticky stuff under her hands, and it was a little while
before she realized it must be bat droppings, a whole lot
of the stuff, because this was where they came in to sleep
during the day, hanging upside-down from the ceiling
above the square entranceway in the stones.

Cold air moved against her face, coming from the
opening in the granite walls. Clear and pure, the air drew
her upward from where she lay, and she stood leaning
against the wall, pulling the clear pure air into her lungs
as she watched the stars out there. And at last, feeling
strength coming back into her, she moved to the opening
and looked out. It was big enough for her to go through,
easily big enough, twice as wide as her shoulders. The air
was cold against her face, and for a while she closed her
eyes and let the coldness wash over her like cleansing
water, and felt the magic of being alive again, after dying
so many times in there, in the dark passages.

A coward dies many deaths, a brave man only one.

Yeah, sure, that's very true, but how do I get to be
brave? You think I don't want to be, or something?

She opened her eyes at last and looked at the stars, and
then lower, at the tops of the elder trees, and then lower,
way down below her, at the ground, where shrubs had
been planted and kept trimmed to make walkways,
something like a maze, where the nuns could go with

their rosaries and their prayer books, to read and pray and meditate on the miracle of Jesus Christ.

Way down below, way down.

A sheer drop.

She looked to one side, then to the other. There was no parapet, or any kind of plinth along the wall. She looked upward, way up, and saw a break in the wall and then a roof, and even from this angle she could recognize the bell tower. There'd been steps, maybe, at one time, running down from the platform around the bell, from the low stone wall she knew was there. She'd been in the tower, but hadn't ever looked down over the low stone wall. But she could see now there must have been steps, long ago, because there were wooden beams jutting out from the wall at intervals, slanting at an angle from the opening here to the platform in the tower. The rest of the steps had broken away after all those years, or maybe they'd *been* broken away to stop people going down into the passages anymore.

The bits jutting out weren't very long, only six inches or so, and their ends were splintered.

A night wind was rising, blowing softly against her face, and the moon was coming out from behind the clouds in the east, sending the shadows of the cypresses slanting across the maze, way down below there. She would go there tomorrow, with her Immaculate Conception Novena, which she was studying for class. That would be nice; she found the story of Eve and Ave Maria pretty neat.

She was trembling a little now, looking upward from the maze of shrubbery below to the broken ends of the beams sticking out from the wall above, trembling because she knew that the way to the maze, and the morning, was up those jutting bits of wood to the tower.

She couldn't go back through the passages and she couldn't stay here, because she'd freeze to death by morning or die from lack of water—all that smoke had dried her mouth and throat and she was already thirsty.

You're always dying of something or other. Why don't you just climb up there to the tower? You'll have to do it some time, so what's wrong with right now?

Trembling.

The low wind tugged at her robes.

It would be a good idea to call out, and hope someone would hear her before morning, but with her throat so sore she wouldn't be able to manage much more than a croak.

The only really good idea is to go up there to the tower. You know that.

Absolutely. That's absolutely right.

Then let's go.

The wind tugged at her, asking her to follow.

So she took a breath and clambered through the opening and reached up and got a grip on the beam above it and found the sill of the opening with her shoe and pulled herself upward, clinging to the wall, and then had to stay like that for a while to think about things, because there was something she'd only just realized. She couldn't go back into the opening now, even if she wanted to. It wasn't physically possible. It would mean having to reach below her for a handgrip, and she couldn't do that because there wasn't any room to turn around—she had to keep close to the wall, cling to it, or she'd just fall away into thin air and—

Don't think about it.

No.

And don't look down.

No.

But the trembling wouldn't stop, because she knew now that she was cut off from any possibility of going back, even if she wanted to. It had been a kind of option

she'd had, before she realized that—well—she didn't
have it.

She looked upward; it was okay to look upward, because the tower was quite close compared with the
ground. She could count ten or maybe twelve bits of
wood sticking out between here and the low stone wall of
the platform. That wasn't so many; it wouldn't take long.

She pulled herself up again and got a grip on the next
beam, feeling its surface crumbling a little under her
fingers. That wasn't a very good sign. There could be
some really rotten ones up there, too rotten to bear her
weight. She hadn't thought of *that* before, either.

The wind tugged at her robes, flapping them against
the wall, and she began coughing as the cold air touched
her red-raw throat. She stopped the paroxysm at once,
forcing herself, because it had been shaking her whole
body and she couldn't allow that to happen.

Clinging to the wall, resting a minute, one hand on the
beam above her, one shoe on the beam below. What did
she look like? she wondered. Like a ragged black crow,
spread-eagled against the wall in the moonlight with the
wind ruffling its feathers. I wish . . . I wish . . . she
thought, because crows, after all, could fly.

She reached up again, way up, and found the next
beam and pulled, feeling the beam below her crumbling
under her shoe, sliding her shoe right up against the
wall—*quick*—right up against it where the wood felt
more solid. The shock was tingling in her nerves, and she
had to wait for a bit until she felt ready again. Then she
reached up, and found the next beam. By her count, it
was number seven, seven from the tower platform.

Six . . .

Five . . .

Four . . .

It was number three that was the problem.

She felt how short it was the moment her hand found

it *and slipped off again,* sending her heart into her mouth as she clawed for a hold again on the rotten wood.

It was too short, this one, and too rotten.

She kept still, shutting her eyes again and letting the freezing fire of the shock go on flickering through her nerves. When it was over she took a deep breath and then another, opening her eyes at last and staring upward at the short stump sticking out from the wall.

Three or four inches, that was all, and with the end badly splintered. Within her reach, if she wanted to try it again. The third one from the bell tower, from home, from continued life.

So get moving, we're nearly there.

Not really, no. Suddenly we're miles away. It's too short. . . . I'll never get a grip.

You've got to. You've no choice.

But she waited, had to wait, till she was ready, and it gave time for her imagination to take fire, and she could hear the short stump crumbling, breaking away in her hand, could see herself from above, falling, falling away, floating down through the moonlight with her robes fluttering in the wind as her body turned with its arms flung out in the shape of a cross as she became smaller and smaller, a shred of black rag above the trees . . . below the trees . . . above the ground . . . then on the ground, on the ground now among the shrubbery of the maze as the silence and the dark drew down. . . .

Then the wind tugged at her and she opened her eyes and shook the images out of her mind and reached up for the short stub of wood and tested it and pulled and gave it all her weight as she brought her legs up and with one foot found a purchase, but the stub was too short and too rotten and she felt it giving *and then her hand slipped toward the splintered end and she gripped harder but it went on slipping* so she straightened her leg and pushed upward, pushed hard upward and reached higher and got hold of the next beam and clung to it and hung there until she could gather the strength she needed to pull herself upward again and find a new purchase for her foot, and when she'd managed it she had to rest for a while because the moonlight on the wall was kind of pulsing, light and dark, light and dark, and the same pulse was going on in her head, a slow heavy throbbing, and she knew she'd been pushing things too hard and it was going to be a matter of time now before she passed out.

Better move on, Deb.

I can't. I can't.

Hung there in the coming-and-going moonlight with the wind on her face and her arm-muscles burning and the throbbing in her head counting the seconds for her, telling her the time.

There's no time left—get moving.

I can't. I—

Get moving!

So she dragged her weight upward again and reached higher and found the next beam and dragged her weight upward again and reached higher and found the top of the low stone wall of the platform in the tower as the throbbing in her head became a hammering that roared in her ears and the moonlight flashed on and off and her breath sawed in and out of her throat as she pushed herself higher, dragged herself higher and hung jack-knifed across the top of the wall and couldn't move anymore, just hung there with her legs in space and her arms dangling inside the tower, couldn't—

Move.

Just the roaring in her ears and the—

Move!

So she swung her legs up and tilted forward, tilted back like a seesaw, swung her legs up again and tilted

forward and slid off the wall and dropped onto the platform and rolled and lay there with her face to the stars
and the roaring in her ears dying away, the moonlight
dying away, the night dying away . . . dying away. . . .

8

"Sister Anne Marie?"

"Here."

"Sister Barbara Teresa?"

"Here."

"Sister Debra Lorraine?"

The Mistress of Novices waited.

"Sister Debra?"

In the silence Sister Carlissa looked along the rows of novices, stopping at Madlen. "Where is your sister?"

"I don't know, Sister Carlissa."

The black eyes watched her for a moment. "You do not *know?*"

"I haven't seen her since the end of Recreation."

"But you are always together."

Nicola was eyeing Madlen from the row behind, thinking she sounded worried.

"I know," Madlen said. "I was going to report her missing."

The Mistress of Novices looked back to her roster. "Sister Evelyn Julia?"

"Here—"

"I think we ought to start a search for her," Madlen cut in, and Sister Carlissa swung her head.

"If you'll allow me to complete roll-call, Sister Madlen, we shall go into the matter. Sister Laura Jane?"

"Here."

Sister Denise, the professed nun who had interviewed Madlen and Debra when they'd first come to the convent, moved from behind the Mistress of Novices and walked quietly down to the row of benches, beckoning to Madlen. She thought the Mistress of Novices would probably reprimand her later for interrupting roll-call, but it couldn't be helped—this poor child was looking really concerned.

"Come with me, Madlen," Sister Denise said quietly, and drew her aside. She used the title "Sister" only on formal occasions, and the Mistress of Novices didn't approve of that either: It smacked of familiarity, not to say intimacy. "Where was Debra when you saw her last?"

"She said she was going to polish one of the silver candlesticks again in the West Chapel," Madlen said, "because she wasn't satisfied with it. I had to go to the bathroom, and when I went to find her she wasn't there."

"She wasn't in the West Chapel?"

"No."

Sister Denise's quiet blue eyes watched her with sympathy. "And you've been worrying, Madlen?"

"Yes."

"You should have come to me before." Then Sister Denise lifted her head and began sniffing the air. "Is that smoke I can smell?"

"I was thinking the same thing," Madlen said.

"Go into the Great Hall and see if there's a fallen ember in the fireplace. Then come straight back here."

The Great Hall was only just along the passage, and Madlen was back inside of a minute, looking alarmed. "The smoke's not coming from the fireplace—it's pouring down the staircase!"

The Mistress of Novices was still calling the roll, but the nun interrupted.

"Sister Carlissa, there seems to be a fire on the upper floor—we should sound the alarm!"

It was an hour before the smoke started clearing. Mother Superior had given orders for every door and window in the building to be thrown wide open to let the wind blow through the building, and some of the nuns had gone for their woolen shawls, the night was so cold.

It was the bed in a novice's cell upstairs that had caught fire, and Father Giovanni had organized a bucket line from the nearest bathroom to put out the flames. A white china candlestick, blackened with soot and cracked by the heat, had been found among the ashes of the bed, and Sister Patrice—whose cell it was—had been questioned. She had no idea how such a thing could have happened: She'd left the cell at the end of Recreation, which she'd spent tidying her things, and there'd certainly been no candle burning; it was still daylight at that hour.

Sister Patrice, a young, quiet, and devoted novice whose obedience and fervor had already caught the attention of her superiors, had of course been believed without question. Nor did there seem any possible reason why anyone else should have gone to her cell and lighted a candle, let alone set fire to the bed.

It was a total mystery, and Father Giovanni was still pondering it in the Great Hall, soot still on his hands and face, when Sister Denise came to speak to him.

"One of the novices has been missing, Father, since Recreation. Sister Debra Lorraine."

"She missed Vespers and roll-call?"

"Yes. Her sister Madlen is quite worried. I would have come to you before, but the fire took priority."

The priest's dark Italian eyes shared the concern in hers. "You think we should make a search?"

"As soon as possible."

The night had started strangely in the convent of the Sisters of the Sacred Light, as the wind moaned through the open doors and windows and the nuns hurried from room to room and from cell to cell, calling Sister Debra's name as they went, the light from their oil lamps casting their restless shadows against the walls.

Mother Superior was in the vestry behind the main chapel, beating at the hanging robes in case for some extraordinary reason Sister Debra had decided to hide herself away.

Father Giovanni was searching the closets under the great staircase, swinging his lamp and calling Debra's name, by now thoroughly concerned and beginning to wonder what a missing novice might have to do with a bed being set on fire.

But it was Sister Denise—guided by divine intuition, as the priest said afterward—who climbed the narrow stone steps to the bell tower and went out onto the platform and found Debra lying there in the moonlight, her young face deathly pale and her hands dark with blood and her robes torn and covered with filth.

A moment later every soul in the building was startled by the sudden booming of the bell in the tower, and Father Giovanni was the first to reach there.

9

Madlen's face was like a rainbow, running with colors.

The huge bell kept on booming . . . booming . . . in Debra's head.

Why was her sister's face like a rainbow? She wasn't wearing a mask; she didn't look like Dracula. She looked beautiful with all those colors on her face. Was it really Madlen? Maybe it was somebody else.

"You okay?"

The bell stopped booming.

Madlen reached out and put a hand on hers. Was it Madlen?

"Are you okay, sweetie?"

Nobody else ever called her that, and Madlen only called her that when she was very concerned about her for some reason.

"Are you concerned about me?" Debra asked, and saw her sister starting to laugh, very quietly, and the rainbow flowed across her as she moved her head. It was the light

coming through the narrow stained-glass window above
her bed, Debra saw now. Madlen was sitting in the light
from the window. "What's funny?" she asked.

When her sister finished laughing she said, "Nothing
. . . nothing at all. You just sounded so—so formal when
you said that, and also it's the first time I've heard you
say *anything* since we brought you in here last night, but
that isn't funny either, it's—terrific."

"Is it today?" Debra asked. She wasn't quite sure what
she meant.

Madlen leaned over and hugged her gently and said,
"It's always today, sweetie, every day, but it's the next
morning now, I would think around eleven o'clock."
Then her body was shaking and Debra felt the hot tears
dripping onto her face.

"Why are you crying? You were laughing just now."

In a moment Madlen said with her eyes red and glistening, "Sometimes it's almost the same thing."

"Oh. Why are my hands bandaged?"

"You kind of skinned them, I guess, in that place."
Madlen glanced behind her to make sure the door of the
cell was closed, and lowered her voice. "Father Giovanni
told me you said you couldn't remember anything. You
couldn't remember how you got there, to the bell tower."
Her eyes were serious now.

"That's right," Debra said. She remembered telling
him that. He'd come to see her sometimes in the night;
there'd been a candle burning all the time and Sister
Denise had been here all the time too. "Sister Denise was
sleeping in your bed," she told Madlen. "What was she
doing that for?"

"She was looking after you all night. She's a registered
nurse."

"Where did you sleep, then?"

"In a spare cell." She wiped her eyes with the back of
her hand and then snuffled a bit into her handkerchief.

"But have you really forgotten everything, like you told Father Giovanni?" She was watching Debra steadily now.

Debra shut her eyes, and the tiny skeletons rose up from the huge littered stone and came crowding toward her and the bat squealed, clawing at her veil, and she ran and ran and ran with the smoke stinging her eyes and getting into her throat.

"No," she said in a moment, and opened her eyes and looked at her sister. "I haven't forgotten anything."

Madlen took a deep breath. Her eyes were very deep as she cupped Debra's cheek with one hand and said softly, "So why did you tell Father Giovanni you had?"

Debra didn't look away. Her sister knew, of course, why she'd told the priest she couldn't remember anything; it was just that Madlen wanted to make sure they both knew what was going on here.

"It would have got us into trouble," she said, "wouldn't it?"

"You bet," Madlen nodded. "A whole lot of trouble. Especially me, because I told you I'd take all the blame, or as much as I could." Her eyes began glistening again and she said, "So that was—pretty nice of you."

"No big deal," Debra said. She was waiting for her sister to tell her how she could have gotten herself lost in those passages, how she could have left her there without even trying to find her. But she wasn't going to ask.

"Sister Denise said you must have had what she called 'retrogressive amnesia,' " Madlen said.

"What's that?"

"It means when people have some kind of a shock, like a car crash or something, they can't always remember what happened to them for quite a while before." She got off the bed and went to the door and opened it carefully, looking into the passage and coming back, shutting the door again. The fanlight above it was open, and they weren't ever allowed to close it, because the guardians needed to listen at night to make sure no one was breaking Profound Silence. She sat on the edge of the bed again and said softly, "Don't you want to know how I lost touch with you in there?"

"Yes," Debra said, and felt a kind of weight lifting off her chest; she'd been thinking maybe her sister wasn't ever going to tell her, because it was just something she couldn't explain. "Yes," she heard herself saying again.

"I felt a breeze," Madlen said, "blowing along the passage. That was just after the lamp went out. Didn't you hear me calling to you?"

"Sure. You said the lamp had run out of oil."

"Right. Then I said I thought there was another way out of that place—you heard that too?"

"Yeah. Or some of it. You sounded pretty faint by then."

"I guess I must have, because I was trying to find the way out, to save going back all that way to the North Chapel. I could smell fresh air, so I thought I must be close. And then, gee, I just got lost. That place is a *labyrinth*."

"I know." Debra wanted to hear about all the smoke in there, but again, she wasn't going to ask. There were things she'd never been able to ask her sister, all through their life together. She just knew she mustn't, because the answers would be terrible.

"You okay?" Madlen asked her.

"Sure."

"You want me to get Sister Denise here?"

"No. I'm okay." Madlen always knew when there was something on her mind, even just a passing thought, but there were things she couldn't ever tell her, like there were things she couldn't ever ask.

"Well," Madlen went on, "it was so *dark* in there, and that's how we lost each other. You know what happened? When I finally felt my way back to that big room where the fireplace was, you weren't there. You weren't anywhere. Did you hear me calling to you?"

In a moment Debra said, "No."

Madlen rolled her eyes. "Well, gee, you must have been too far away, because I was calling you all the time—panicking by then, as you can imagine! But I wasn't going to leave till I knew for certain you'd found your way out *somewhere,* so I got a bit of the brushwood by the fireplace and used the matches and got it going, made a kind of torch, and went all the way back along the passage to where I'd started from, but you weren't anywhere, and it was right then I felt sure you must have found a way out, the one I'd been looking for." She closed her eyes for a moment. "And I was so *relieved.* . . ."

Debra didn't say anything.

"You can imagine—" Madlen said, but Debra stopped her, because the bell had started booming out from the tower.

"What's that?"

"That'll be Mass. But don't worry—I've been excused, so I can look after you. Sister Denise says you're through the worst."

"Oh."

There was silence for a bit, and Debra hoped her sister hadn't finished. There was such an awful lot to explain. She waited.

"Then I saw smoke coming along the passage," Madlen said, "and heard a crackling noise, so I ran back to the big room where the fireplace was, and oh, Jesus, you know what? The whole pile of brushwood was on fire. . . ." She rolled her eyes again. "I must have set it going when I'd been there with the matches, making the torch. There wasn't a hope in hell of putting the fire out, with no water or anything, so I just got out of there as fast as I could, back to the North Chapel."

The bell in the tower stopped tolling, and Debra was relieved. It didn't sound all that loud down here, but when Sister Denise had found her up there last night and pulled on the rope it had brought Debra out of her coma with a real bang, and the first thing she remembered doing was to cover her ears. Since then, she'd jumped every time she heard the bell start ringing.

That was what she'd been in, according to Sister Denise—"a coma induced by prolonged shock." Maybe that was true. They didn't know what had been happening to her—nobody knew except Madlen—and she hadn't told them, but by the mess her hands and her robes and everything were in they could see she'd been through a pretty rough time somewhere.

"Then the worst thing of *all*," she heard Madlen saying, "was when I got back into the convent and couldn't find you anywhere. I looked in our cell and Nicola's—in case you might be in there with her—and everywhere else I could think of. But I was still certain you'd found your way out of that place, or you would have answered me when I called out. But I didn't wait any longer than roll-call to tell Sister Carlissa we had to make a search for you. She tried to bitch me about but Sister Denise came to the rescue. By that time I was *scared,* and if they hadn't found you up there in the tower I would have told Father Giovanni about the secret passage and started a search in there." She gave a big sigh suddenly. "Thank God I didn't have to."

It had been awful for her, Debra could tell. With her white face and her red eyes Madlen looked like she hadn't slept a wink all night, and when Nicola had come to spend a little time with Debra this morning she told her that Madlen had been crying so bad in the spare cell where she was meant to be sleeping that Nicola had heard her through the fanlights and gone in there to keep her company.

It helped Debra to know how much her sister had suffered through this whole thing, because it kept away the thoughts she'd found herself thinking in the night when she'd woken up and couldn't get to sleep again for a while.

She was trying to kill you.

Thoughts like that.

She's tried before.

Thoughts like that too.

She'd started shivering in the night when the thoughts had got real bad, and Sister Denise had noticed and gone for another hot water bottle.

"You've got rainbows all over your face," Debra said now. It was nice to think about, instead of the other things.

Madlen was staring at her. "Rainbows?" Then she got it, and glanced up at the stained-glass windows. "I must look weird!"

"No," Debra said, "you look pretty."

Then Madlen's rainbow face crumpled suddenly and she threw her arms around Debra and started crying and crying with her whole body shaking the bed while Debra sat there bewildered, watching a goose feather come loose from one of her pillows and go floating through the colored light, turning red and blue and yellow as Madlen went on crying and crying, and finally stopped.

"Only you could have said that," she managed to get out at last, snuffling a lot into her handkerchief. They weren't allowed Kleenex in this place—they were an expense, Sister Carlissa had told them, and worse, encouraged self-indulgence.

"Said what?" Debra asked her.

"That I look pretty—after all I did to you, taking you into that hellhole and then losing sight of you. Jesus, I

could have got you *killed,* with that smoke and everything. . . ."

There was silence for a moment, then Debra said, "I
know."

"I don't even want to think about it," Madlen said.

"Neither do I."

The small colored feather settled onto the blanket, soft
as a blessing. Debra had caught herself looking for meaning in small things since she'd been a Sister of the Sacred
Light—finding sermons in stones, you could call it—and
it was surprising how often it happened, like with the
feather just now, seeing it as a blessing.

Madlen got off the bed and pushed her handkerchief
into the soiled-linen bag and got a clean one from the big
wardrobe, the heavy door squeaking like it always did
because the brass hinges were dry and corroded. Watching her, Debra felt a rush of compassion; she really
looked frazzled out with all that crying. Those thoughts
Debra had had in the night were crazy—of course
Madlen hadn't been trying to kill her; it was that weird
imagination of hers, that was all, and anyway she was
still trying to recover from everything and didn't feel
herself again yet.

"So you must have found the other way out," Madlen
said, and sat on the bed again, her robes rustling in the
silence. "The one I was trying to find."

"Yeah. Eventually."

"Where was it?"

Debra told her, shifting over in the bed to give her
sister more room. "But I'm glad you didn't find it first."
She told Madlen about the rotten stumps of wood and
the sheer drop and everything.

"Oh, Jesus," Madlen said when she'd finished, "I don't
know how you can still speak to me."

Her eyes were waiting, Debra saw, and said quickly,
"It wasn't your fault."

"Of *course* it was my fault! It's time I grew up, you know that? Only kids want to explore everything they come across. I—"

"You're into drama, that's all. Dramatic things. I understand."

Madlen managed a watery smile. "No one else would. Only you." She glanced up at the open fanlight, then back at her sister, playing with her handkerchief while she got up the courage to say what she had to say next. "So . . . you're never going to 'remember' what happened, is that right?" She waited.

"Of course not. It's our secret."

"Forever?"

"Forever."

Madlen let out a long sigh. "Okay." She kept her voice low. "When they asked me where I'd seen you last—you know, when you were 'missing'—I said you were going to polish some candlesticks again in the West Chapel, because you weren't satisfied with them. Remember, we were doing them the day before?"

Debra had to think. Such a lot had happened since the day before yesterday. "Yeah," she said at last. "I guess."

"Okay. Then I said I had to go to the bathroom, and when I came back you weren't there in the West Chapel after all. That make sense?"

"Sure," Debra said. She thought it was pretty clever, as a matter of fact, but then Madlen could always work things out like that.

"Okay," Madlen said, "it's a deal." She laid her hands gently on Debra's bandages, her dark eyes going deep as she gazed into her sister's. "I'm going to take better care of you from now on, sweetie, *much* better care. That's a promise—to both of us."

In a moment Debra said, "It all came out okay."

Madlen pressed her lips together. "But it mightn't have." She glanced up at the fanlight again. "Sister Denise is coming to check on you as soon as Mass is over, and then I'll have to go." She lifted the lid of the earthenware water jug on the bedside table. "Half full. You want me to get you some fresh?"

"It's fine."

"Remember the days when we could put ice in our drinks?"

"It's self-indulgent," Debra smiled, quoting Sister Carlissa, "and bad for the stomach lining."

"This is an *American* convent, all the same."

"But it's run by those goddamned Italians in Rome," Debra said, this time quoting Nicola. What made it funny was that Nicola was Italian herself.

"I'm going to tell her you're *much* better," Madlen said, making the connection. "And give her your love?" She said it in a whisper, defiantly, and Debra understood. It was strictly against the edicts to feel love for anybody in this place except God, or even to make friends.

"Sure," Debra smiled, and felt, just for an instant, a soupçon of the excitement that Madlen must feel when she deliberately defied the rules. "Give her my love."

As they heard footsteps along the passage outside, Madlen said in a dramatic whisper, "Remember, we are the Keepers of the Secret! That's our special credo."

"Our what?"

"Something we believe in. Can you remember it?"

"Sure. We are the Keepers of the Secret."

Madlen gave her a last hug. "You're such a terrific sport, Deb. I don't know what I'd do without you."

Debra said in a moment, "I hope you never have to."

10

Listening at the keyhole.

Madlen stirred in her sleep.

Listening to the voices, Mommy's and Daddy's.

She knew the dream, was familiar with it, though it wasn't quite a dream, it was something that had happened in the past, coming around again every so often like a carousel horse, something terrible and bewildering she would never forget, something she'd been living with all this time, since she was just a little kid of four-and-a-half.

She'd always listened at keyholes. You could learn secrets that way.

Mommy was saying, "But suppose it just slips out. What would she think?"

Madlen stirred again, wishing she could sleep. She didn't want this thing coming back to haunt her again, a carousel horse with its mouth screaming and its eyes ablaze and its mane flying like flames in the windy dark . . . but she couldn't ever stop it . . . she couldn't ever stop the carousel horse. . . .

"Of course it won't slip out," Daddy said. "Don't worry about it."

She felt the warm air coming through the keyhole against her ear; they had a nice big fire burning in the hearth in there, and she and Debbie had been allowed to sit by it for a little while like always, before they went to bed. "I want you toasty warm," Mommy always said, "so you'll stay toasty warm all night."

But now Mommy was saying something different. "A kid this age, if she finds out Debbie's not her real sister, it could—you know—be a shock for her. And what would Debbie think? There's that too."

Suddenly she felt coldness creeping all over her, like she was standing here in cold water, like it was pouring over her, and there was something funny happening with her breath, she couldn't breathe properly.

Debbie wasn't her real sister? What did that mean?

Pressing her ear to the keyhole, harder and harder, with the big brass handle of the door right up against her eye.

"Look," Daddy was saying, "when we brought Debbie into the house, Madlen was too young to know any different—they don't know what's going on at that age. You're just worrying. We'll tell them when they're old enough to understand. That's what we agreed, wasn't it, when Debbie was adopted?"

Cold, cold cold . . . pouring all over her so her teeth chattered and she had to pull the air into her body so she could breathe properly, but it wasn't air, it was water, cold cold water.

What did "adopted" mean? Found somewhere?

If Debbie wasn't her real sister, then who was?

Where was her real sister?

Shivering, shivering at the door.

"It's just that Maddie's so sensitive," Mommy was saying now, "so imaginative."

What did those words mean? Something bad?

And then Mommy said the most horrible, horrible thing of all, and Madlen put her fist in her mouth to stop herself screaming as she spun away from the door and scampered up the stairs and was in her bed by the time Mommy came up.

"You're so cold, Maddie!" she said. "How did you get so cold?"

Maddie didn't say anything, and Mommy got her an extra blanket and rubbed her hands while all Maddie could think about was where her sister could be, her real sister, and how she could find her.

Later in the night, much later, because the moonlight had gone from the window, Madlen stirred again, floating upward from the depths of sleep to the twilight zone, and the horse came swinging around again in the shadows of her mind, the screaming carousel horse.

"Why did you go off like that?" her Mommy was asking, tugging at her arm until it hurt. Mommy was very worried. "I've told you to always stay close!" Still shaking her. "Where did you go?"

They'd been in the supermarket, and somewhere along one of the aisles she'd glimpsed a little girl in a blue jacket just like her own, passing across the end of the aisle and vanishing again, and Madlen had gone running up the aisle after her, sure she'd found her sister now, the real one, not the hateful thing that lived with them in their house. But the little girl wasn't anywhere, and Madlen had cried and cried inside herself because it was like having something torn out of her, losing her sister the minute she'd found her, and she ran all the way past the other aisles, looking along every one of them, but her sister wasn't there, so she ran into the street to look for her but she couldn't see her anymore, and it was like losing a whole different world she knew was there somewhere, the world where her sister was, and she cried inside herself again until she was cold and shaking all over.

"Why did you run off like that?" Mommy was asking, her face very white.

"I thought I saw my sister."

"Your sister? But Debbie's at home, in bed with a cold! Don't you remember?"

And Madlen had said no, she'd forgotten, so Mommy would stop asking her about it, because she couldn't tell her the truth and say it wasn't Debbie she was looking for, it was her other sister, the real one. That was a secret she had to keep to herself, because people would get mad at her. They wouldn't ever tell her where her real sister was, so she better just keep quiet until she could find her.

The horse plunged past again to the mad brass music of the carousel, its eyes ablaze and the flames of its flying mane torching the windy dark.

And then, a long time after, there was Cathy.

"You don't need to come with me," Mom said, "I'll only be a minute, and you've got your book to read."

"Okay."

Madlen stayed in the car with her book, which was called VAMPIRE, The Complete World of the Undead, *by somebody named Mascetti. She thought that was a great subtitle, about the Undead, who were so very different from the living because they'd died and come back; it made you think of people clawing their way out of the sea with white faces and locks of black hair like seaweed and their eyes staring in the moonlight, or climbing out of a grave with the dirt dropping off them and worms everywhere. She loved books like that, and especially plays—she'd started acting in one or two plays at Weldon High, and that was a real* thrill, because one of them had been THE PHANTOM OF LAMAMOUR.

Mom had parked the car in the alley behind her real estate office because she only wanted to drop a load of flyers off, and it was now that Madlen noticed the blue and white pickup truck unloading.

A guy with red hair was taking stuff into the big clothing store a couple of doors away, heaving boxes and mannequins and clothes racks off the truck and bumping the door of the store open with his behind—it looked like he'd got nobody to help him.

And there was Cathy. . . .

The guy had left a mannequin standing against the back of the truck, a teenager dressed in a black ski suit, fair-haired and smiling, with a bright red scarf and woolen gloves, and Madlen just sat staring because the mannequin looked so like herself, and without even thinking first she put down her book and got out of the car and opened the trunk, watching the door to the clothing store and the one to Mom's realty office, but the mannequin was easy to lift, much lighter than she'd thought, and went into the trunk of the car easily too because the arms and legs swiveled around if you wanted them to, and the trunk lid was shut and she was back in the car with her book a good minute before Mom came along from her office and got in, and Madlen sat there aching to tell her to start the motor and floor the gas pedal before that guy came out of the store and missed the mannequin, but Mom got moving fast enough anyway because when Madlen turned round casually to drop her book on the backseat and glanced through the window she couldn't see the redheaded guy there by the truck or anywhere, he wasn't yelling and running after them like she'd imagined him doing.

"I guess I was a little bit longer than I thought I'd be," Mom said, and when Madlen didn't answer she glanced down at her. "You okay?"

"Huh? Sure, no problem, I was reading. It's a great book, a really great book." There was a sourness in her stomach that she knew was leftover adrenaline, but that would go, and it was nothing to the huge glow in her chest when she thought of what was in the trunk—a lifesize stand-in for her long-lost sister, the real one. And already she knew that she'd call her by her favorite name, the one she'd always wished had been her own.

Cathy.

11

"Come in!"

Father Giovanni Falconi was at his desk, phrasing a difficult letter to the relatives of the Sisters of the Sacred Light in the hope of raising funds for the restoration of the massive bronze Christ on the wall of the South Chapel, which was in danger of coming down. He glanced up as Sister Debra came through the door.

"My child," he said, and got up immediately to help her to a chair: She was still pale, and walked uncertainly. "I would have come to see you," he told her, "but of course I'm not permitted to visit the cells on my own."

"That's okay, Father. I've been walking around quite a bit this afternoon." Debra sat with her hands on the arms of the ancient carved chair, sitting up as straight as she could. To sit slumped was the seventh minor sin on Sister Carlissa's list.

"Lean back, my child," the priest said with a conspiratorial smile. "Lean back in your chair and relax. I won't tell anyone." Studying her for a moment, Father Giovanni wondered if it could be conceived a sin to look upon the innocent beauty of this young woman with a feeling of revelation, as he felt when watching, for instance, moonlight upon water.

The priest's office was small, dark, and cluttered with books and papers and a rickety-looking photocopier and a stained and dented coffee-making machine and a pair of old plaid slippers he'd forgotten to hide under the desk and a small dusty Christ figure on the wall whose left leg had been broken and then clumsily repaired with some rusty wire. But sitting in the old carved chair Debra felt herself to be several stations nearer to God. She also thought that Father Giovanni, with his lean, muscled face and his dark Italian eyes was "gorgeous," as Nicola had called him. And his voice was quiet and low, so low that you could almost hear every vibration, like on a cello. But she felt worried, as she sat so close to him for the first time in his actual room, about what Nicola had also said—that she was "going to work on" him, and "love him to death." Debra wondered whether she should say anything, but that would be telling on a friend, and she could only hope Nicola had been making some kind of a joke.

"So," Father Giovanni said, "you still can't remember anything about what happened to you last night?"

"No, Father."

We are the Keepers of the Secret. . . .

"Would it help you if I asked your sister to join us? Would she—"

"No." The word hung in the air, seeming to echo. She'd said it too quickly, and Father Giovanni looked a little bit surprised. She'd have to watch it. "I—I mean she wouldn't know anything, because she wasn't there."

In a moment the priest asked quietly, "Wasn't where?"

"Wherever I was, last night."

Father Giovanni watched her face in the fading light of the day as it gave way to evening in the window. This child wouldn't ever lie, he thought, to save herself. But she might lie to save somebody else.

In this case, whom?

"You don't remember going into Sister Patrice's cell last night," he asked her gently, "with a lighted candle?"

"No, Father. We're not—I mean I don't know her very well."

It was in Sister Patrice's cell that the bed had caught fire, and Debra believed she knew who had gone in there with a lighted candle; she believed it had been her own sister.

We are the Keepers of the Secret. . . .

Of all the secrets.

All of them.

Debra felt herself shivering a little, and tried to stop it by tensing her muscles. She'd never lied easily, and she was afraid Father Giovanni would trip her with one of his questions and get the whole story out of her. She mustn't let him do that. She mustn't ever betray Madlen. She wanted to say to him, "Look, Father, if I make a slip and tell you things, will you treat it like I was at confession?"

"Have you any idea," he was asking her, "who might have set fire to the bed in Sister Patrice's cell, by accident or . . . otherwise?"

"No, Father."

"You're aware, of course, that anything you tell me here is in the strictest confidence, as if you were at confession?" It was like he'd been reading her mind, Debra thought, and the idea gave her goosebumps. "If it wasn't an accident, you see," the priest went on, "it means that someone needs our help. They must be feeling pretty bad about themselves, right now." All day he'd been hoping someone would ask him to take confession, but no one had, except for Sister Nicola, but that was about something entirely different.

"I guess they are," Debra said. But Madlen hadn't even talked about Patrice's bed being set on fire when they'd been together this morning, and Debra hadn't mentioned it either; she hadn't wanted her sister to have to lie.

"You've been told," Father Giovanni said in a moment, "that when Sister Denise found you in the bell tower, your robes were torn and covered with some kind of animal excrement?"

"Yes." Debra swallowed.

"I'd say it came from bats. But there's none of it around in the tower, or on the bell. Can you think where you might have been, to get that stuff on your robes?"

"No, Father."

He let it go. This morning he'd been up to the tower and looked over the low stone wall on the east side, where there was a square opening in the granite below. Bats had a roost there, as he knew—he'd seen them homing sometimes at first light, when he'd been walking in the grounds before Mass. But this morning he'd observed particularly the broken struts of timber that must once have supported steps down from the tower; he'd been looking for a shred of cloth torn from a nun's habit, or any sign that someone had climbed from the opening to the tower. It had been a crazy enough notion, he realized, that anyone could have done that without getting themselves killed, but he'd wanted to set his mind at rest.

"How does your throat feel?" he asked Sister Debra gently.

"It feels okay."

"When Sister Denise checked you over that night after she found you, she said it looked quite raw, as if you'd been coughing a lot. Can you think why?"

The young novice shifted in her chair. "I—guess it was a cold night."

"That's true. But your habit smelled strongly of smoke. Do you think you'd been breathing maybe a great deal of smoke, during the time you were missing?" He wasn't going to mention the firing of the bed in Sister Patrice's cell again: He'd asked this child once about that, and didn't want her to think he refused to believe her answer—that she'd no idea who could have done such a thing. But it worried him, because she was so obviously holding something back.

"I don't remember, Father."

Again, he let it go. All their habits had smelled of smoke that night, of course—the whole building had been full of it—but nobody else had complained of a sore throat.

"Never mind," he said. "I'm glad you feel better now."

He kept her with him for another five or ten minutes, probing as gently as he could. He was determined to find all the answers, because it might even be that her life had been in danger last night. He also wanted to know if someone else was involved, and if they had in fact led her into that danger. Now that he'd questioned her, he wasn't any longer afraid he might stir her memory and release the whole content of last night's experience, bringing back the shock and overwhelming her. He believed the experience was perfectly fresh in her memory, but that she was concealing it, and not to protect herself but someone else. This child wasn't the sort to go off on some wild escapade on her own.

"Well, my child," he said at last, "I don't want to tire you." He got up from behind his desk and went with her to the door, his arm round her slight shoulders. "But if you start remembering anything, I want you to come to me about it, and nobody else. I understand things, you see, where others might not. If, for instance, you're keeping anything back, I'm certain it's for the best of reasons, but I'm also certain that you must tell someone about it as soon as you can, before it all goes bad on you. And when you're ready, I'm ready to listen." He turned her shoulders gently, so that he could look into her eyes. "And nobody else would ever know. Remember that. Nobody."

Sitting behind his cluttered desk again after she'd gone, Father Giovanni wondered for a moment if he were doing the right thing in taking personal and sole charge of this affair. Was it in part because it gave him so much pleasure to be close to this pretty young woman, physically and spiritually, while he was trying to help her? No question. But the vastly more important reason was that the idea of her having been in danger—and perhaps of her being in danger again—gave him infinitely greater pain. He wanted to protect her, just as she was protecting, he believed, someone else.

And besides, he thought, as the last of the daylight faded in the window and he switched on the parchment-shaded lamp, he must do everything he could to keep Mother Superior out of it. Even though she resented the presence not only of a mere man in her cloistered congregation of women, but of a man who outranked her in the diocese, Mother Superior was a good woman at heart. But when he'd talked to her about Sister Debra this morning after Mass, she'd run true to her characteristic bull-at-a-gate form and proposed assembling all seventy-five souls of the sisterhood in the Great Hall and exposing the whole affair in the hope of gleaning information, and he didn't intend letting her push the shy young novice under a spotlight. All that most people knew right now was that she'd been missing for a while last night and had then been found, and that was all he wanted them to know.

His fight with Mother Superior for control of the case

had been short and decisive, and he'd saved her face by choosing to win on points instead of going for a knock-out. As Father "Johnny" Giovanni he'd learned his foot-work on the streets of the Bronx, where for three years he'd fought to save as many as he could of a group of young, vulnerable and sometimes vicious crack addicts who had no other friend, and no other hope. But it was when he received the decidedly unsterile blade of a flick-knife through one of his kidneys and ironically lost it to the decidedly more sterile knife of a surgeon in Bellevue Hospital that the bishop of the diocese had called him in.

"You've done three years, Johnny, and that's enough."

"There's more to do, Bishop."

"Certainly there's more to do, but do you think you can do it all on your own? Besides, you take too many risks—you won't even wear the collar when you go down those streets."

"You have to be one of them, to be accepted."

"Let me put it this way," his bishop had told him finally. "First, you only have one kidney left, and you lose that, you go through the golden gates, and way ahead of your time. Second thing is, if that happens and it gets around that one of those crazy kids has put a priest in the morgue it could start a trend. You know how these things go in that region of hell—it could suddenly start to look chic. And there's a whole lot of my troops work-ing those streets the same as you, and I don't want them losing their kidneys too, or their lives. So I know you won't fight me on this, Johnny. I'm pulling you in."

And Father Giovanni Falconi had come out of New York with his one kidney and a bunch of minor scars and reported to Bishop O'Brien in Westbury, Connecticut, as per the instructions. Bishop O'Brien had talked to this young wounded soldier and had also listened a lot, and then he'd said, "Okay. You need a rest, Johnny, and I know just the place where you can get it."

Giovanni had fought this one, of course. He'd been saving lives back there in the Big Apple, and inside a convent full of nuns in picturesque Westbury, Connecticut, there couldn't be too much crack going around or too many lives to save.

"But if you're still interested in serving the Lord," Bishop O'Brien said, "even without the macho death-or-glory kick, I'll tell you how you can do it. I've been trying for a long time to get the Mother Superior to take in a priest to help her run things there, but she's very tough. The thing is, she's got a good heart, or I wouldn't let her get away with it. She's what a good Mother Superior is meant to be—a good mother. But a lot of those women there are still young, and they still feel the need of a father too. The need of patriarchal love, and patriarchal authority. Without it, the Mother Superior's just a single parent, and that doesn't make for happy families. Now, the reason I haven't sent in a priest before now is that, as I say, she's very tough, and so far I haven't found a man who could stay off the ropes for more than a couple of rounds with her." He looked at Giovanni with his pink bald head on one side for a moment. "But with a guy like you . . . I think I can go into battle. And win."

Giovanni still wasn't convinced. He didn't want to fight with a woman; he had too much respect for them. Men had been fighting them all through history, and now they needed a break. Also, it didn't sound like he'd be getting much of a rest.

Bishop O'Brien tilted his head again, smiling gently. "Look, Johnny, it won't really mean going into battle—that was just a figure of speech. I've been listening to you, and it sounds like you've got a good feeling for women, a respect for them. You're also young, Italian, and charming. So you can go in there without too much of a fight—you'll have it made."

Giovanni had decided to let the bishop win. If he could

do some good in this convent, then okay. He'd seen what the lack of a father had done to some of the kids he'd worked with in the Bronx.

Bishop O'Brien had given him an unexpected bear hug, smelling comfortably of Irish malt. Then he'd said finally, "There's one more thing, Johnny. You're going to be living your life among sixty or seventy women for a while, and they're not all dried-up septuagenarians and not all of them left their hormones behind them when they quit the outside world. And since they will also note that you're young, Italian, and charming, you may have problems. If you do, I don't want you coming to me with your confessions. I want you to put a stop to things before you've anything to confess."

But there hadn't been any problems in the two years Father Giovanni had taken up his duties with the Sisters of the Sacred Light—none, anyway, that he hadn't been able to handle. The bishop had been right: Just because a young woman decided for whatever reason to take the vow of chastity it didn't mean her glands were going to stop producing the kind of hormones that begged for release. Sister Nicola, one of the novices who'd come to the convent a few weeks ago, was a case in point: Her confessions were of a kind to tax any man's resolves. But he was confident he could handle things if she really came on too strong.

When night lowered and Vespers were concluded in the main chapel and Giovanni had managed to get through the stodgy beef dumplings that were Sister Gertrude's speciality in the kitchen—what was wrong with some good pasta, for God's sake?—he made his rounds before turning in. The wind had died away toward nightfall, and here and there it was possible to leave a window open to clear the last of the smoke that still clung to the carpeting and the drapes and the robes of the nuns throughout the building.

Passing through the North Chapel, where a lamp had been left burning by mistake, Giovanni thought the smell of smoke was stronger in here than elsewhere, particularly near the altar. He stood sniffing the air for a while, and then began moving around, still sniffing, until he reached the end of the chapel behind the altar, and heaved the old oaken door away from the wall.

The smell of smoke was strong now, and he unbolted the other door, the one set in the wall, and pulled it open a little, letting a blue-gray cloud of smoke come swirling from the passage beyond. He closed it again at once, and stood thinking.

Giovanni knew all about the secret door. He'd discovered it almost a year after he'd been installed at the convent, and had done a little exploring on his own. Following the passages that led from the door, and coming upon the tiny bones heaped in what had obviously been a sacrificial chamber, he had gone back to fetch a pitcher of water, blessing it before Christ at the altar and taking it along the passage and into the chamber, there to perform the Holy Sacrament over the relics of the departed, tears coursing down his face as he thought of what it must have been like in this chamber at the hour of each bloody sacrifice.

He'd told no one of his discovery. Bolting the secret entrance and dragging the heavy oak door across it, he had come away, and for the next month or so had examined records and archives in the nearby church, seeking evidence, however made threadbare by time, of the Satanic cult that had practiced its rites behind the inner walls of the convent long ago.

Tonight, after thinking awhile, Giovanni soaked an altar cloth in the little iron sink in the vestry, took an oil lamp and went into the secret passage, closing the door behind him. The smoke stung his eyes, as he expected, but with the cloth pressed to his mouth he was able to reach the first chamber, where the embers of what had once been a pile of kindling still glowed faintly in the shadows. Most of the smoke was drifting the other way, along the passages beyond, but his tears were streaming now and he had to turn back, regaining the North Chapel and blocking the secret door behind him.

Splashing his eyes with fresh water in the vestry, he wiped his face and hung the altar cloth to dry on the piece of string above the sink and then returned to the chapel, and without thinking went onto his knees before the altar, gazing up at the Christ figure above it, half lost in the shadows.

And here it was, as the night drew its silence over the sleeping stones and the souls they sheltered, that Father Giovanni prayed for guidance and enlightenment, for something strange was happening in the convent that he would have to deal with, and he might need the spiritual help of those more qualified.

12

Screaming, screaming, screaming as the big car rolled and the bushes and the trees started sliding past the windows faster and faster, screaming and screaming but it wouldn't stop and no one was there to help and the wheels went rocking and bumping across the bottom of the driveway and the sidewalk, faster and faster as horns began blaring suddenly and there was a terrible squealing noise and another car hit this one with a roar and the world outside swung upside-down and all she could hear was herself now, screaming and screaming as the tears sprang scalding on her face and her panties got wet through with pee.

"Are you okay?"

Screaming and screaming.

"Deb, wake up! It's okay, Deb, wake up!"

Shaking her, someone shaking her till the screaming stopped.

"It's okay, Deb. Everything's okay."

Madlen's voice. Madlen's hands, shaking her.

"Yeah," Debra said, getting her breath. "I guess I was dreaming."

"Sure." Madlen hovered over her, dark against the dark. "You were dreaming, that's all."

"Did I wake you?"

"It doesn't matter. Just so long as you're okay. You want some water?"

"Yeah." Debra struggled upright against the pillow, sipping the water slowly because it was cold and her throat was still sore.

There was a tapping on the door, and then a voice— "Are you guys all right in there?"

Nicola. She was in the cell next to theirs. Madlen went across and opened the door a crack. "Sure," she whispered. "It was just a bad dream. But thanks for coming."

"Any time you need me, you know my address."

Madlen closed the door quietly. "What was it about?" she asked her sister.

"What?"

"Your dream."

"Oh. Monsters." She always said that when Madlen asked what her dreams were about, because she couldn't tell the truth.

"I'll zap them good for you," Madlen said, "if they come again." She climbed back into her bed.

Debra couldn't tell the truth because it was more terrible than even monsters. She'd only got a few bruises that time when Dad's car turned over, but it had been ten years ago, when she was only five, and the dreams still came, bringing it all back to her. She'd been sitting in the car with Madlen, just sitting and stroking all the shiny chrome knobs and smelling the new-car smell and opening and shutting the glove compartment, and then Madlen had got out of the car and said she'd be back in a minute, and that Debra wasn't to touch anything while she was gone. But then after a minute the car had started rolling and rolling, and she'd begun screaming and screaming, and after the doctor had said there was no harm done and she was sitting up in bed with a brand new teddy, Dad had started asking her a lot of questions, and said she *must* have touched the brakes and the gearshift, though Mommy had said it wasn't possible for anyone to do that without turning on the motor, and there'd been a terrible fight because Dad hadn't gotten over the shock of running down the driveway to find his new Buick lying on its roof with the glass gone and everything and Debbie inside screaming, and the other man yelling at him because his car was damaged too.

In the end it was Madlen who got the blame, because she was older and should have known better than to take her sister to sit in the car with her and play, and it didn't matter how the brakes had come off and the gearshift had gotten moved, it had happened somehow, and little Debbie had been frightened out of her life and the car was all smashed up.

Debra had felt sorry for her sister, afterwârd, because Dad had finally yelled and yelled at Madlen behind the closed door of the dining room when Mommy was out of the house, and she'd come to bed as white as a sheet with her eyes puffy and red, and had tossed and turned all night long, till in the morning she looked worse than Debbie did after the accident.

"If it was my fault," she'd told Debbie with her mouth bruised-looking and her eyes like little pink bags, "I'm going to kill myself." Debbie knew that was pretty bad, because people who got killed went away and never came back and you had to go and put flowers on a stone in the ground. She didn't want that to happen to Madlen, so she'd given her the new teddy they'd bought for her, but Madlen wouldn't take it, because she said it *must* have been her fault if Daddy said so, and burst into tears again.

Debra lay watching the flicker of the nightlight in the passage through the fanlight over the door, thinking about Daddy's Buick. It had been a long time, years, before she'd come to know that yes, Daddy had been right, it had been Madlen's fault.

And it wasn't an accident.

No, that's wrong. Of course it was an accident. It's just this goddamned imagination of mine.

It was never an accident, any of those times.

That's wrong. They were all of them accidents.

Debra lay shivering in the sweat that had soaked her nightdress when the nightmare had come. If they hadn't been accidents it would mean that Madlen had been trying to kill her, and that couldn't be true.

You know it's true.

No, it can't be. It mustn't be.

Shivering, watching the glow of the candle outside in the passage, her only company, its light keeping the night away, keeping the truth away. If that little flame went out, the dark would come down and she'd know it was true—they hadn't been accidents, any of those times.

"She's a real quiet mare," the man at the horse rental place had told Debra afterward. "I've never known her to spook."

But suddenly the horse had gone wild under her, breaking into a gallop and thundering through the trees while she tried to cling on, cling on somehow because she didn't know enough about horses to make them stop when they went crazy. Thundering through the trees with its huge shoulders working and its mane shaking and its breath like bellows, flecks of foam flying back into her face and one sneaker coming out of the stirrup and then the other, and then she was pitching away from the horse and hitting the rain-sodden turf and rolling and sliding

with her shoulder on fire with pain and her leg hitting a
tree and then nothing, nothing, because she passed out.

But they'd found a patch of blood on the mare's rear
quarter, and the rental man had said it must have been
that—she'd caught a thorn from one of the bushes and
the pain had spooked her. He hadn't said it with much
conviction, and Debra privately thought he didn't want
to suggest she couldn't ride too well and had spooked the
mare herself, maybe by kicking its flanks too hard to
make it go.

Madlen had been shaken up by it all, because she'd
been riding close behind Debra and to one side, and
thought she might have bumped the mare by accident,
making her spook.

By accident. . . . It was always by accident. . . .

Accidents happen, don't they?

But she was always there with you, those times.

Of course she was. We did everything together. She
was there in the good times too.

*What did she use on your horse, where the blood was
found? A spike of some kind?*

I thought so once, but it was just my goddamned imagination.

The little flame burned out there, keeping the dark
away, keeping back the truth as she lay shivering, wanting to get out of bed and go along to the bathrooms and
take a shower, because of the sweat, but she'd wake
Madlen again and maybe other people too, and the
guardian would hear the water running and come to see
what was happening.

I was having a nightmare, Sister.

*Then pray to God for His forgiveness. Nightmares are
the progeny of guilt.*

Forget the shower. Try and go back to sleep.

But sleep wouldn't come. She started to think about
Mom now, and the time when she'd taken them both to

lunch at the rooftop restaurant in Dillard's department store on the day Debra turned fourteen, calling it a birthday party because both she and Dad had to go out that evening—she had a realtor's meeting and Dad was going some other place but she wasn't sure where. Deb found herself thinking it was a shame they didn't have any candles, though it was broad daylight so maybe they wouldn't have looked so good. Then, when they were just finishing their ripple fudge sundaes and Mom was putting her Visa card down on the check, she said—Debra thought a bit nervously—"Well, I guess you've heard all about some kids being adopted, haven't you?"

It threw them.

"Sure," Madlen said, sounding puzzled.

"Well," Mom started off, "when I had you, Madlen, it was a kind of close call, and the doctor told me I couldn't ever have any more children. It would be risky, is what he said. But we both wanted another one—" still looking at Madlen, though glancing down a lot "—to keep you company; so we decided to adopt one."

Debra started feeling weird. She'd heard a couple of the girls at Weldon High talking about this, saying they'd been adopted, and even though they were trying to make it sound like it was a perfectly normal thing, she could tell it bothered them. So she was wondering now whether she ought to be feeling bothered, and if Mom weren't her Mom, then who was, and if they'd wanted two kids so much why had they started to leave them to themselves all the time while they had their fights and their friends in and their dinner parties out and everything, all these questions spinning around in her mind while she watched Mom looking all over the place for the waitress, obviously hoping she'd come soon because she had a real busy afternoon, as she'd told them.

But most of all she felt sick to her stomach and didn't know why.

"Anyway," Mom—who wasn't Mom anymore—was saying, "you two guys have always got along pretty well and people say how close you are and how nice that is, so I—" she saw the waitress now "—I guess this whole thing doesn't amount to much more than a hill of beans, does it?" She was looking at Debra now.

Debra felt the ripple fudge sundae starting to act up on her, and tried to remember where the rest rooms were in this place. She wanted to look at Madlen, but they were sitting side by side in the booth and it would mean turning her head and kind of making a big thing of it, when it was only meant to be just a hill of beans. The waitress came and asked if everything had been all right, and took away the check and the credit card while Debra had the weird idea of telling her no, everything hadn't been all right, because this wasn't her real mother anymore and this wasn't her real sister.

And there was something else, something that was trying to come at her like some invisible bird or a giant bat, and she wondered if she might have to flail her arms around in the air to keep it away from her, because it was dark and terrible and explained everything, everything she'd never wanted to know.

"You okay?" Madlen was asking her. Her voice sounded like it was coming from a long way off.

"I guess," Debra said, and got out of the booth very fast and darted her eyes around for the rest room sign and made it there just in time, and afterward she looked at her face in the mirror and could hardly recognize it, pinched and white and tearstained and kind of crumpled-looking, like a balloon with the air starting to come out of it.

"Shit," someone was saying as the door burst open and banged shut, and Madlen's arms were around her suddenly, holding her while the shivering went on and on and Debra couldn't think of anything to say. "For Jesus

Christ's sake," Madlen said through her teeth, "was that the only way she could think of telling us?"

"She didn't," Debra said haltingly, "she didn't like having to tell us, you could see that."

"Tough *shit!* She could have rehearsed it a bit, couldn't she, got her lines worked out, instead of telling us she'd got a real busy fucking afternoon and then just throwing it in our faces while she happened to have the time?"

"It's okay," Debra said. It wasn't so much the shock of finding out she was a kind of stranger to these people after all this time, though that wasn't too easy to handle; it was the other thing, the dark and terrible thing.

"Look, Deb," she heard Madlen saying, "what difference does it make? Does it make any difference to you?" Holding her tight, her arms right around her, their heads pressed together, her breath on Debra's neck.

"I guess it doesn't," Debra said at last, and then had to break away and go into a stall for some toilet paper to blow her nose on because she'd left her purse in the booth.

"Then what the hell are we talking about?" Madlen said. She was leaning against the tiled wall with her feet together and her arms folded across the peacock-blue halter top Deb had given her for Christmas, staring at Deb and waiting, her eyes wide and very dark.

"It's okay with you?" Debra asked her when she'd flushed the paper down the john.

"You bet it's okay with me. We're still sisters, aren't we? We share the same room and everything, and do everything together. Isn't that all that counts?"

"I guess," Debra said, and leaned against the wall like Madlen was doing, folding her arms.

"Look, Meg and Laura are sisters, aren't they, and they hate each other's guts, and they don't mind who knows. That makes us *real* sisters, doesn't it, compared with them? I mean, who cares whose goddamned womb

anybody comes out of, so long as they love each other?"
She waited again, and when Debra said nothing she
pushed off the wall and came over and took hold of
Debra's hands and said, "You love me, don't you?"

"Sure."

"I don't want just 'sure,' Deb. I want to *know.*"

Deb found herself wondering, in the next beat of a
second, what love really was, knowing there was a whole
slew of different reasons for loving somebody, but not
being able to think straight enough right now to know
which of all those reasons applied to Madlen. So she took
a short cut and decided that if Madlen ever got killed in
an accident or got sick and died, it would be the end of
the world for her, and she'd want to die too. Wasn't that
love?

"Jesus—" Madlen started to say, but Debra cut in real
quick.

"Of course I love you, of *course* I do." And Madlen
put her arms around her again and they both broke out
crying.

It hadn't been too long ago when that happened.
They'd got over it and Mom hadn't said anything more.
But the dark and terrible thing had never gone away, and
it was this: It hadn't come as any surprise to Madlen that
day in the restaurant.

She'd already known.

She'd known for a long time, for years and years.

One night when they were very young kids, three or
four, Maddie had gotten out of her bed and crept downstairs, thinking she was asleep. Debbie thought maybe
she'd gone down to listen to what Mommy and Daddy
were saying in the sitting room behind the closed door.
Her sister liked listening at keyholes, Debbie knew—she
liked secrets, her own or other people's, it didn't matter
which. Then soon afterward Maddie had come scamper-
ing up the stairs, and then Mommy followed to tuck

them both in. "You're so cold!" Mommy said, but her sister didn't answer, and Mommy fetched an extra blanket for her. Debbie didn't say anything either, because she knew how her sister had gotten cold—she'd been standing down there in the hallway listening at the door. When Mommy had gone downstairs again, Debbie waited for her sister to tell her about the secrets she'd found out, because usually Maddie did that, whispering and rolling her eyes, but on that night she didn't say anything to her at all, even "goodnight and God bless"; she just covered her head with the bedclothes like she wanted to shut everything out, and Debbie had known as she drifted off to sleep that something terrible had happened in their house tonight.

It frightened her for days, because Maddie didn't seem like Maddie anymore, didn't act like her. She was okay when they were downstairs with Mommy and Daddy, having breakfast and getting their coats on for kindergarten and times like that, but when they were alone together she was different, quiet all the time and not looking at Debbie or talking to her.

Then she got over it, and started talking to Debbie again and playing with her in the sandbox behind the house like nothing had happened, and Debbie started letting herself feel happy again, because when her sister had been like that with her it had been horrible, and scary, and made her chest ache.

And then after a while the little things had started. Debbie told her sister she couldn't find her special Barbie doll anywhere, so they hunted under the beds and all over the house without any luck, but the next morning Mommy found the Barbie doll at the back of a closet, and asked Debbie what on earth she'd been thinking of, hiding it there and then forgetting, and Debbie had felt the whiteness coming into her face as she looked at her sister, knowing what must have happened, and Mommy caught her look and turned to Maddie.

"Madlen."

"Yes, Mommy?"

"Did you hide Debbie's Barbie doll in the closet?"

"No." She stared at Mommy without blinking or looking away, her eyes very dark.

"Are you sure?"

"Yeah." Still staring, her mouth tight.

But she'd been given a spanking just the same, because Mommy had figured out what had happened too.

Then there were other things missing, Debbie's sleeping-eye Mickey Mouse and a pair of her brand new sneakers and even her toothbrush, and Debbie wouldn't have said anything, so as not to get her sister in trouble, but of course Mommy soon found out her toothbrush was gone and started hunting again till she found it, and the other things too and all in the same place—on top of a wardrobe this time, and Maddie came in for an awful lot of really hard slaps and once or twice got a stick on her bottom, which made her scream, and Debbie started trying to take the blame for things, so her sister wouldn't catch it anymore. But it didn't do any good because Mommy always seemed to know what was going on. The worst time was when she told Maddie she wasn't going to have a jealous little girl in this house and if she didn't stop getting at poor Debbie then she could just get out and stay out. That really got through, and Maddie curled up on the floor underneath her bed that night, like she wanted shelter, and stayed there till morning even though Debbie tried to coax her out.

Then the little things had stopped.

Debra lay watching the restless flickering of the nightlight outside the cell as a wind got up and found cracks in the window frames and went whistling along the passage.

The little things had stopped, and the big things had begun, and she and her sister were playing in the bathtub, splashing in the water, and suddenly Madlen was leaning over the bathtub pressing on her shoulders, laughing and laughing, and Debbie felt the warm rushing of the water burying her head as her sister kept pressing and pressing her down, laughing and squealing, her face big and funny-looking because of the water, her mouth open and the squealing fainter now as Debbie started choking under the water and couldn't get her breath and began kicking and scrambling with her heels slipping on the bathtub and her elbows hitting it as her chest started to ache bad and she couldn't breathe anymore because she was choking too much and panicking now and trying to scream but couldn't manage it, and then the squealing above the water stopped and Madlen wasn't pressing her down anymore so she kicked out again and again and came up through the water into the air and tried to clamber over the edge of the bathtub away from the terrible water, then Mommy was there and pulling her out of the tub as she went on choking and choking and Mommy put her down on the bathmat with her face against it and slapped her on the back a lot and said it was okay, honey, everything was okay, while the water came spluttering out of her onto the bathmat and she heard Madlen saying she slipped, she slipped under the water and that was why she was squealing for help, and Debbie knew that something terrible had happened, and later when she was in bed and Mommy and her sister were there she could see by Madlen's face that she mustn't tell what had really happened, so she just said they'd been having a game like Madlen said, and she'd gone under the water and couldn't get out because everything was so slippery.

That had been the first of the big things, and after that there was the accident with the car rolling away, and then the broken strap of her left ski when they'd been on the slopes in Vermont, and then the stuff in her cereal that had made her sick for weeks with Dad threatening to sue the cereal company, and then the thing with the horse that had bolted—there'd been so many of them, the big things, and every time one of them happened Debra thought it was going to be the last one, made herself believe it was going to be the last one, but it never was; there was always another one, and tonight she knew who'd set the bed on fire in Sister Patrice's cell—it was Madlen, because she knew somebody might smell smoke coming through the cracks around the secret door in the North Chapel, and go in there and save Debra before she could die. She'd wanted them to think it was from the bed.

They don't die of their burns. . . . They die of smoke inhalation.

Turning her head, she could just make out Madlen's sleeping face, a blur in the darkness. Madlen was turned toward her—she always slept on her right side—and her dark lashes made delicate wings against the paleness; she looked like an angel, asleep on a cloud.

She's a long way from being an angel. You know that.

Be quiet. I want to go to sleep.

You won't ever face the truth, will you?

I told you, be quiet.

The candle in the passage hadn't gone out. It mustn't ever go out. She wouldn't be able to stand the dark, or the truth that was always waiting for her in it.

Then Sister Denise was talking to her as she slipped into a dream, and Father Giovanni was there too, looking wonderful—no, *gorgeous,* as Nicky had said, with his kind eyes and the clefts in his cheeks and a lock of dark hair always across his forehead, like it must have been since he was a boy. *When you're ready, my child, I'm*

*ready to listen. . . . And nobody else would ever know.
. . . Remember that. . . . Nobody. . . .*

But she would never tell him. She was a Keeper of the
Secret.

She woke later, not knowing what time it was but
sensing that something had changed, and in a moment
saw that the nightlight in the passage had gone out—and
even though she tried to stop it the truth came rushing in
with the dark and she couldn't get out of its way.

She's trying to kill you.

In the silence she could hear Madlen's breathing, close
to her in the next bed. She breathed like an angel, softly,
innocently, her eyes closed under the tiny wings of her
lashes.

I know.

You admit the truth at last?

Yes. She's trying to kill me.

The voice in her head didn't say anything more, she
supposed because there wasn't anything more to say.
That was enough, wasn't it? That was quite enough.

Lying on the hard narrow bed with her skin crawling
with nerves, and feeling more alone than she'd ever felt
in her whole life, she knew she should really be feeling
relieved, now she'd faced up to this terrible thing at last.
But she didn't, because she also knew, deep down, that
on the other side of this terrifying truth another one was
waiting for her in the dark, so much more terrifying that
she hoped she would never have to find out what it was.

13

"Our mother," Madlen told Debra as they sat on their beds during evening Recreation, "is a hypocrite." She turned her head to make sure her sister was listening.

"She is?" Debra asked in surprise. They'd just been given their first letters that had arrived with this morning's mail, from Mom, Alice Thompson, and Jeff Soderberg (who had written to Debra personally), and Madlen had just opened the one from Mom.

"Listen to this: *Hi, guys! Dad and I very much hope you're settling down all right in your new world up there.*— 'Up' meaning north, or does she assume we've gone to heaven?—*We think about you every day. Let's have some news about yourselves, and remember, if you'd like me to come visit with you, you have only to let me know. We miss you guys! Love and kisses—Mom.*

"Like I say," Madlen fumed as she lowered the letter and looked across at Debra, "that woman is a hypocrite. You know?"

"Well—" Debra began, trying to think of something nice about Mom.

"I mean, for Christ's sake," Madlen cut in, "they think about us every day? Do you believe that? They wouldn't have time! And they miss us? You believe that too? The only time those people missed us was when we weren't there to man the machine for them. Right?" It had become a family phrase—"Okay, kids, man the machine and beep us while we're away." So they'd be sure to get any phone messages, especially Mom, with her realty business.

The way Debra heard it, as she sat with her knees bunched up under her black woolen bathrobe, was that Madlen was still upset about the way "those people" had treated them all those years, never having time for them or paying attention to their grades and things like that, and it was coming out in anger.

"I guess I feel sorry for them," Debra said, and passed the letter back across the space between their beds.

She prayed for Mom and Dad every night before she went to sleep, a kind of habit she'd picked up from all the other prayers going on in this place, which she found rather selfish, always asking God to have mercy on *us*, save *us* from sin, give *us* our daily bread, and stuff like that. It wasn't often they were told to pray for other people, except when somebody was sick. Sister Denise had told her privately after Vespers one evening that Madlen had prayed for her "with constancy and vehemence" while she was recovering from shock a week ago when they'd found her in the bell tower.

Madlen, praying? Debra couldn't imagine that, but if Sister Denise said so, well, then. . . . She certainly remembered Madlen crossing herself that time when they found the bones in the sacrificial chamber.

Maybe enough of this stuff would finally get through, and she wouldn't try to kill her anymore.

Debra was always getting thoughts like that flashing through her head, now that the candle had gone out and she'd faced the truth at last. You couldn't really say it was all she thought about now, but it was close. Because facing the truth wasn't going to be enough. She would have to do something about it.

"Alice is really cute," she heard Madlen saying. "So shy and formal." She tilted the mauve-colored letter to catch more light from the oil lamp. "Listen—

"Dear Madlen and Debra: I hope you like being nuns. I haven't seen you in your habits yet, and cannot wait. I bet you both look real saintly. I know you went there to be away from everything, but I hope you don't want to be away from me too. So would you mind if I came to visit with you when you can receive people? That will be next Saturday, the 18th, did you know? So please write back real soon and let me know. I'll have to ask Jeff Soderberg to drive me there, would that be okay? Gee, I do miss you both, you have no idea! Write soon, please! Love you. Alice."

Madlen passed the letter to her sister. "Why don't I let you read them for yourself, for God's sake, I'm so selfish! But look how she crossed out 'uniforms' and put 'habits' instead, and crossed out 'cute' and put 'saintly.' I really love Alice."

"Do you love me?" Debra asked.

It had just come out of her mouth without her even thinking, but she was waiting with her breath held like it was the most important question in the world. Which it was.

Madlen was still holding the sheet of mauve paper across, staring at her in the silence.

"Do I love *you?* Is that what you said?"

"Yes."

Madlen was off her bed in a flash, dropping the letter and holding Debra in a bear hug, rocking her thin shoulders back and forth while Debra felt the tears coming and couldn't stop them. In a minute Madlen let go of her but caught her hands, which still hadn't healed completely, hurting them without meaning to or even knowing, staring into her sister's face as the tears kept coming. "What the fuck is this, sweetie?" she asked quietly.

Debra couldn't think of an answer for a while, because the question had surprised her too. She couldn't remember asking it before, ever. But she knew it was awfully important.

"I—I just guess I—needed—" was as far as she got before Madlen was saying it for her.

"Reassurance?"

"Yeah. Reassurance." She wiped her face with the back of her hand.

"Why?"

Because you want to kill me.

Couldn't say that. Couldn't ever tell the truth, the enormous new terrifying truth. She'd already worked something out, and that was that Madlen didn't actually know what she was doing those times, wasn't actually herself. So if Debra said a thing like that, it would be like telling somebody they were crazy. Somebody who couldn't ever keep their hands still or rolled their heads around all the time like those poor kids they'd been to visit with at the Institution "to learn about life," as the principal had told them. You couldn't tell people like that they were crazy; that would be shocking. You had to pretend they were okay, and just like everybody else.

Was Madlen crazy?

"Why do you want reassurance?" her sister asked her again, not looking away even for a second, her eyes very dark and intent with the need to know, the real, true need to know, as Debra could see.

"I—I guess it's just this place," she said, and tried to find the handkerchief in the pocket of her bathrobe. "Sometimes it's kind of scary." It wasn't what she'd meant to say, but it would have to do.

Madlen found a handkerchief in the pocket of her own bathrobe and gave it to her, still looking and listening very intently. "You mean that awful mess I got you into?"

"Yeah," Debra said. "I guess." She wasn't finding it easy to breathe now; she hoped she wasn't going to hyperventilate and need a brown paper bag. Where would she find a brown paper bag around here? Nobody went shopping. The thing was, she was getting very close to the truth here, because when Madlen had gotten her into that "awful mess" she'd done it on purpose. That heavy scuffling sound Debra had heard in the passages that time hadn't been another bat or anything small, as she'd known perfectly well. It had been Madlen, and not far away. That was why Debra had called out to her, two or three times. But Madlen hadn't answered, and the sound—the sound of her feet and her robes—had faded into the distance.

Madlen hadn't answered, hadn't stopped, because she had things to do. She had to go and light the kindling in the big chamber along there, and get the smoke started, so it would kill her.

She wiped her face with Madlen's handkerchief. It was kind of her, she thought, to let her use it.

"I could kill myself," she heard Madlen saying quietly.

She'd said the same thing years ago, when Dad's Buick had run away—*If I thought it was my fault, I'd kill myself.*

"Well you don't need to do that," Debra told her. "I'm okay now. It just left me kind of scared, that's all."

"If I get you into anything like that again," Madlen said, watching her intently, "that's what I'll do."

It wasn't easy for Debra to look so close into her sister's eyes when she was saying things like that. Because, what did she mean? Did she mean she'd feel so bad if she got her into a mess again that she'd kill herself out of guilt, or was this actually the plan she was working on? If she got lucky next time there was an "accident" and Debra actually died, they'd call it a murder-suicide, wouldn't they, if she left a note saying what she'd done? Was that what she was planning?

It couldn't be.

"You just mean," Debra said, "you're sorry it happened. Right?"

"Pissed off with myself, yeah. Real pissed off."

"Well that's okay. We don't need to talk about killing."

In a moment Madlen said, "I guess that's right. I just have to make darn sure it never happens again." She gave Debra's hands a squeeze and saw her wince and let them go like they were suddenly red hot. "Oh *Jesus,* I'm always forgetting. They still sore?"

"Little bit."

"You know something, sweetie? You could do with a better sister than the one you pulled out of the lucky dip."

"I like this one fine. Who's the next letter from?"

Madlen picked it up. "Here. You open it this time."

"No. I like the way you read them."

Madlen picked at the flap of the envelope to get it started and then ripped it open, glancing down at the signature. " 'Aunt Helen,' it says. Do we have an Aunt Helen?"

"I never heard of one."

"Well this is really something new." She tilted the single sheet of paper to catch the light and began reading.

"*Dear Madlen and Debra: You probably never heard of me, but I'm your Mom's sister. We never really got on, for various reasons, and we haven't talked to each other since you were just rolling around in your cribs. So that's why you probably don't know me.*

"*But I've been hearing about you both from time to time, because I live locally, in Weldon, and a friend told me your Mom and Dad weren't getting along too well either, and that you were kind of unhappy about that, as I can imagine. Then somebody else said you'd signed up— though I guess that's not the right way to put it!—as Sisters of the Sacred Light.*

"*I guess that threw me a bit, a couple of girls your age and still not out of high school. But I suppose things got that bad that you decided to drop out and hole up somewhere more peaceful. I can imagine that too.*"

Madlen glanced up from the letter. "Our Aunt Helen has a lot of imagination, right?"

"It can be a real pain," Debra said.

"What?"

"Nothing. Go on reading."

"*It must be a surprise for you to get this letter, and it was a long time before I made up my mind to write it. But I thought you might need a friend around you at a time when your whole world has so drastically changed, and that's really why I'm writing. So if you'd care for me to visit with you some time at the convent, would you drop me a line? I sure hope you will, because from what I*

hear about you, you're a couple of really nice
young people, and I don't have that many friends
myself. Yours sincerely, Aunt Helen."

Madlen passed the letter to Debra. "Whad'ya know?
Nuns one day, nieces the next. Is there no end to what
our karmas have in store for us?"

"Our what?"

"Our fates."

Debra didn't want to think about that. "She sounds
rather neat," she said.

"Yeah?" Madlen was looking at the last envelope to be
opened. "I don't think I'm that crazy about meeting any
sister of Mom's. This one's just addressed to you." She
passed it to Debra.

"You don't want to meet our new aunt?"

"She sounds kind of weird, coming at us out of the
blue like this. And besides, if she's anything like Mom. . . .
You meet her and tell me how you get on." With a quick
grin—"You be the guinea pig." She seemed more interested in the last envelope. "You know who that one's
from?"

Debra thought she recognized the writing. "Jeff Soderberg?"

"Your Prince Charming, who else?"

Debra couldn't tell whether she was being sarcastic;
Madlen always had fun being deadpan.

"I don't need letters from Jeff," Debra said.

"You bet you need letters from Jeff." Madlen got off
her bed and dropped onto her own and picked up the
script of *The Phantom of the Opera* that she'd smuggled
in when they'd arrived. "He's a real neat guy."

Debra was listening carefully. She always listened carefully these days to everything her sister said, in case there
was anything she should catch. But right now it didn't

sound like Madlen was jealous about Jeff Soderberg; he'd never seemed to turn her on at school.

Debra opened the letter and saw the heading, "Weldon Police Department," which gave her a start, and the thought flashed through her mind that Dad had killed Mom at last in one of their fights. Then she remembered Jeff's father was a police officer, and he was proud of him.

Dear Debra: I don't know if you expected me to write to you, or if you would rather I didn't. So you need to tell me. I just want to say I miss you an awful lot. I knew it was going to be pretty bad, but this is something else. You looked so beautiful that time when we said goodbye, holding the flowers and everything, and it didn't seem right that you should go into a place that looked so cold and stony. But you must have had your reasons.

Will you be staying there long? I know this sounds kind of silly, but I started marking off the days on a calendar I bought specially to hang on my wall, and when my Dad asked me what I was marking off I said it was to the end of semester, which worked okay because he knows I think our school is the pits. I can't tell him about you, because he says I'm too young to start dating—I mean he's really out of the Ark.

And anyway I don't mind sort of keeping you a secret. It makes it special.

I try and understand why you wanted to go in that place and be a nun, but I can't. I just hope it won't be for long. I want you to know that however long it is, I'll be waiting to see you again, and

*that I'll never see anyone else, ever. You are a
sweet soul, and I'm lucky I'm even allowed to
write this letter to you. Just thinking about you
makes me feel, gee, I don't know, like I swallowed a whole sunset.*

*Please write to me if you'd like me to come
visit with you. Alice and I have worked it out that
the first chance would be on Saturday, the 18th.
I live only for the hope that I can see you then,
even for a little time. Answer my prayer if you
can. Jeff.*

There was a PS: *Say hi! to Madlen for me.*

"He okay?" Madlen asked from the other bed.

"I guess. He says hi! to you."

"He going to give Alice a ride here?"

"He didn't say." She felt Madlen watching her steadily.

"You want him to come here?"

Debra turned her head now. She mustn't stop eye
contact with Madlen just because she couldn't be sure
now what was going on in her mind. In fact it was better
for her to look into her sister's eyes to see what was there.
"You want Alice to come here?" she asked.

"Sure. She's a lot of fun."

Alice was Madlen's number one fan—except of course
for Debra herself—and always made sure she got a front
row seat when there was a show.

"Okay, so I'll tell Jeff he can come." She watched her
sister, but Madlen had her eyes on her *Phantom of the
Opera* script, so Debra couldn't see them. She still wasn't
sure if Madlen was jealous or not, because more guys had
asked Debra for dates than they had Madlen, and Jeff
was one of them. It was important that she shouldn't be
jealous.

Or there might be another accident.

"Madlen?"

"Huh?"

"Shall I tell Jeff he can come?" She couldn't make out whether Madlen was really dug in to her script or was just pretending, to make it look like she wasn't interested in Jeff Soderberg. Or jealous.

"Sure," Madlen said, and looked up. "Then he can give Alice a ride here, and I can talk to her and you can talk to him. It'd work out fine." She kept her eyes on Debra, and they didn't look anything but frank, and friendly.

"Okay," Debra said, and looked away so that her sister could go back to her reading. "I'll tell him he can come."

"Fine," Madlen said, and Debra listened carefully to her tone. It sounded okay, but then her sister was an actress, and she always had to remember that.

But what was it going to be like, now that she'd decided to face the truth? She was going to have to watch Madlen's eyes all the time, every minute when they were talking, in case they changed suddenly, went cold, showed something that Debra didn't want to see, would never want to see, would be terrified of seeing. And she was going to have to listen carefully to Madlen's voice, in case that too changed suddenly, and went cold, telling her something she didn't want to hear, would be terrified of hearing.

She was going to be walking through the dark, watching and listening for the thing that was waiting there for her. The last accident.

14

"Bless me, Father, for I have sinned."

Giovanni half-turned his head as he listened to the voice coming through the iron latticework, recognizing it at once as Sister Nicola's.

"It has been two days since my last confession. I said my penance and went to Holy Communion."

The priest waited. According to practice, Sister Nicola should now make her new confession.

But the silence went on, and in the silence Giovanni heard the rustle of linen, as if the novice were rearranging her robes. He found it disturbing.

"Tell me how you have sinned, my child," he said in a moment.

"I confess to Almighty God and to you, Father, that last night I had sex again, in my thoughts, and touched myself there."

Once more the priest waited. She'd said this before, three times in the past week, and he didn't know what he could do for her. There were others who came to confessional with the same problem, but he didn't believe them all. He was the only man in this place, and some of the younger novices, having taken their vows of chastity without fully understanding the self-discipline those vows demanded, were finding it tough going, more than a month after leaving a world where maybe they'd been playing around a little. In girls their age, a month was a long time.

Those were the ones he believed, and he never instructed them to do penance. The others were just trying to make mischief, already bored with the life they'd imagined was so dramatic. It happened all the time, in all the sisterhoods; you got dropouts.

"I'm touching myself there now, Father," the voice came through the lattice, and Giovanni leaned his head back against the velvet-padded wall of the box. This woman Nicola was starting to be a problem.

"The confessional," he said quietly, "is hardly the place for the commission of sins."

There was silence again, and this time in the silence he heard the sounds she was making for him, and again he was disturbed. Part of the problem was that if he were to tell these girls the truth he would advise them to just go on doing what they were doing and not worry about it. They had to have relief, and this was the only way they could get it. But the truths in life weren't always his privilege to tell: The vows of chastity were sacrosanct.

"Father," the voice came through the latticework, "I always think of you, when I dream about having sex."

His eyes still closed, Giovanni didn't answer her, but let the silence—and the sounds within the silence—go on, as he brought this woman's face into his mind, the dark Italian eyes and the sensual mouth that no veil in Christendom could render innocent. Through the partition her breathing was faster now, and suddenly he realized what was happening to him—he'd let the silence and these sounds go on because he wanted to share in them, and could feel his own body responding.

He snapped his eyes open, crossing himself. "My child, if you feel you must do this, then you must do it in the privacy of your—"

"Oh God . . ." she was crying softly, "Oh Giovanni . . ." as her breath came tiding out, "this is for you, Giovanni . . ." and she began moaning, and he sat there in the confines of the box with no hope of saying anything that would stop her now, sat there so close that if it weren't for the iron grille he could have reached out and touched her. And then she climaxed, and he closed his eyes again as if he could shut out the sounds that way, and in the darkness behind his lids he was aware that as he called on the Lord for strength and patience he was at the same time sharing in this woman's passion, in the celebration of her body's most primeval force.

When it was over he heard his name again, coming softly on a sigh, "Oh, Giovanni. . . ."

Opening his eyes and lifting his head, his hands clasped in supplication, Father Giovanni whispered a brief prayer, and the very fact of his having to seek strength in the Lord made him aware of the danger he was in. When he was ready he said with his face turned to the lattice, "Sister Nicola, I want you to come and see me in my office at the beginning of Recreation today. We won't be alone, of course."

But they were alone.

"Sit down," he told her, and went behind his desk.

They were alone because when Giovanni had thought about it afterward, he realized it just wouldn't be possible to ask anyone else to be here, least of all Mother Superior or the Mistress of Novices, the most qualified to ensure propriety. Because although this was simply to be the

severe bawling out of a novice by the head of the convent
staff, he knew there was a risk of this young woman's
refusing to play by the rules, and if she did that in front
of Mother Superior the outcome would be certain: Sister
Nicola would be thrown out of the convent.

Giovanni didn't know why she'd come to the convent
anyway—though he meant to know, and pretty darn
soon—but it might be that she'd had good reason, and he
didn't want her to get hurt by having to leave.

There was also something else he wanted to discuss
with her, and it was even more important than the question of her broken vows. This was another reason why he
hadn't called Mother Superior along: She lacked discre-
tion.

"You know what I'm going to say, Nicola, but I might
as well say it, to avoid any misunderstanding. If you can't
control your natural urges I'm going to insist on your
keeping them strictly private."

He noticed she hadn't sat down, as he'd told her; she
was standing at the window, her hands on her hips and
her robes swept back to reveal her lean figure, an attitude
in a nun that was almost a sin in itself. "So you've got a
view of the windmill," she said, "on the hill. That's neat.
The sun sets behind it, right? That's the west?" She
turned to look at him. "I love being here in your room.
I didn't think I'd get the chance." She flashed him her
quick Italian smile. "I'm grateful, Father."

He leaned back in his ancient swivel chair, feeling one
of the springs poking into a buttock until he shifted
around a little. He'd noticed how this girl had called him
"Father," saying it softly and letting it linger, giving it
intimacy. Her whole approach, in the confessional and
now here, could be looked on simply as an attempt at
seduction in the cheapest sense of the word, but he had
the impression there was more than that going on. These
dark eyes had great depth, and there was an intensity in

Nicola's whole body that was vibrating in the very air of the stuffy little room, so that he felt that if he moved his hand toward her he would feel the heat—or get burned.

She wasn't, he thought, just playing games, Sister Nicola.

"I decided," he said in a moment, "that it wasn't necessary, after all, to have someone else here. I've chosen to rely on your intelligence and your good taste not to provoke me to my face, as you've been trying to do in the confessional."

She turned, leaning her head, her shoulders and her arms against the wall beside the window, her pelvis thrust forward a little, opening herself to him. "Good for you, Father. If you'd called in a chaperone it sure would have looked like you couldn't handle me on your own."

Giovanni's little tin clock sounded noisier than ever today, perched on top of the coffee machine. When Mother Superior was in here with him he never even noticed it, but today you could have heard a spider spinning its web. Somewhere in his mind Giovanni was aware that he might not be fighting on this ethereal battleground for his own vows, his own chastity, but for his whole life as a priest. In this vibration of hers there was an undertone of great danger.

He was also aware that his eyes were taking in the whole of her body under her swept-back robes, noting that she wasn't wearing the regulation binder. Aware too that she noticed this. With difficulty he looked away, asking casually, "What decided you to become a nun?"

Her head still touching the wall, she leveled her eyes down to his at an angle, the heavy lids almost closed. "I thought it'd be a real gas to be a bride of Christ. It sounded so sexy."

His fingers began tapping the smudged manila folder on his desk. "We don't have all day, Nicola. I want to know, for your own sake, why you came to this convent.

You must have taken quite a bit of trouble to bring it off—you're not the standard applicant Sister Denise has to interview. And you seem to be someone who doesn't take trouble to reach trivial goals, so it looks as if it's important to you to be here—and stay here. So if I can help it I don't want to send you away."

"You'd miss me, wouldn't you, Giovanni?" She left her lips slightly parted.

He looked at his watch. "I can give you another five minutes."

Nicola pushed her shoulders away from the wall, hugging her arms, taking a step or two across the creaking board floor, kicking by chance against an old plaid slipper because the room was so small and so cluttered. "So you don't go for the bride of Christ bit? Okay." She paused, then said, "Everything I say in here is like saying it in our little love-booth?"

"The same," he said quietly, "as in the confessional."

"Okay." She began pacing again, her robes swinging, reminding him of the way a fashion model moved. "Well, my uncle tried one or two other places for me first but they didn't think I came across as the right kind of material, even though—as you rightly divine—I took a lot of trouble mugging up on the routine from a nun I knew. Then my uncle heard—his name is Luigi—that the Sisters of the Sacred Light were strapped for funds, so he bought me in for a couple of grand as my dowry because it was this place or the slammer—I married into the Capria family in New York about the time they were taking over the numbers racket in Brooklyn, and I made a little mistake at a party and said something I shouldn't have to the wrong guy, and next day Giulio Capria was found floating in the Hudson off Pier 57. He'd managed to get rid of the cement shoes they'd fitted him out with but not before he'd taken in too much water—can you imagine *drinking* that stuff, with all that garbage floating around? So anyway the message I got through the grapevine was that Renato—he's the godfather—was going to set me up and put me away for a few years so I couldn't shoot my mouth off anymore to the wrong people." She stopped pacing, and stood with her head lifted to watch the winter sundown filling the window with its saffron light. "So I guess I'll be better off here till my Uncle Luigi can find me a boat ticket to some banana republic where the Caprias don't operate. At least I'm not in the slammer getting screwed every night with a broom handle by the brawniest gals on the block."

She remained still for a moment, with the pale yellow light pouring softly over her face as she stared through the window.

"Cry," Giovanni said gently, "if you can."

She didn't turn her head. "I never cry."

"Giulio Capria," he said, "who was found in the river. He was your husband?"

In a moment, "Yeah."

"And you loved him."

She turned her head now. "Jesus, you think I'd marry a man I didn't love?"

"Sometimes there are—"

"Sure I loved him."

Giovanni got out of his swivel chair and left it rocking as he came round the desk and took Nicola into his arms and stood there with her in the fading light of the sundown until at last he felt her tears coming, and pretended not to notice, holding her against him and feeling the beat of her heart beneath her robes as the light drew down, and down, and she let out a sigh and turned in his arms and he released her, going to the stained lopsided coffeemaker and plugging it in.

"It won't be fresh," he said, "but it'll be Italian."

"Molto bene." She moved away, looking at a photo-

graph on the wall near the patched-up crucifix. "Is this you?" she asked him.

"Yeah."

"You look so young. Not young, exactly, I mean so unlined, so inexperienced." She looked round. "How did your face get so much experience in it without a woman to give your life any meaning?"

He left it, taking two paper cups from the cupboard over the sink. "I gave absolution once," he said, "to one of the Lagorio family, on his deathbed. His name was Bruno. Did you know him?"

"Not personally. You were in New York?"

"Yeah." The Lagorios and the Caprias didn't hit it off so well when the numbers racket in Brooklyn changed hands after a shootout in Mario's. "How did you get mixed up with people like that?"

"I liked the feel of all that power."

The coffee was starting to bubble and he poured it into the cups. "Want to sit down?"

"We've only got five minutes, right?"

"Take as long as you need." He didn't know if he could hope to do anything for her. To lose your husband, to have him *murdered,* was tough enough, but she'd been the *cause.* He still didn't know how people could handle things like that in their life on their own, even though he'd known so many, had made it his business to know them. Watching her, he said, "And the power of Christ?"

"That stuff," she said, "is too subtle for me."

"It takes work," he acknowledged.

"I'm lazy. I like things instant. Plug yourself in to a family like the Caprias and kerboom—suddenly you get a whole lot of respect from all the people you meet. You know?"

"You didn't have any respect before?"

She sipped her coffee and found it too hot, and blew on it. "All I've ever had is my looks."

"And your courage."

"Courage?"

"Not to cry."

"Crying's a giveaway."

"Give yourself away to God. Then you can't lose anything." That was what she was afraid of—losing by giving. But she couldn't keep this bottled up forever.

"Yeah," she said.

Twilight was in the room, and half her face was in shadow as she sat in the ancient carved chair opposite his desk. What was she—twenty-three, twenty-four? Married and widowed and condemned in just a few years, waiting now for a ticket to a banana republic where the Mafia had no presence. And until then they'd keep looking for her, and if they found her it would mean the slammer, as she knew.

Whatever she did to provoke him, he couldn't send her away.

"Come and talk to me," he said, "whenever you want to. Whenever I'm free. Here or in the garden or the grounds, wherever."

"I'd like that," she said.

Her face was almost lost in the shadows now as the twilight deepened, but he didn't switch on the lamp. "Meanwhile," he said in a moment, "would you like to do something for me?"

"Spell it out for me first."

It didn't surprise him. She was afraid she might commit herself to giving something away. She couldn't let go of her pain, had to cover it, deaden it, under a show of hard-nosed cynicism where it hurt the most—"Can you imagine *drinking* that stuff, with all that garbage floating around?"

"This isn't about you," he said. "You see a little of Debra, the novice, don't you? And her sister Madlen?"

He'd seen them walking together sometimes in the passages, and knew they had adjoining cells.

"Yeah."

"So you know Debra went through a hard time a week back, though we don't know where, and she says she doesn't remember." He watched her steadily. "Do you think she remembers?"

Nicola leaned her head against the high wooden back of the chair, closing her eyes. "Why don't you ask her?"

"I did."

"And?"

"She won't change her story."

"You want me to change it for her?"

Giovanni came round his desk and perched on the edge, facing Nicola in the gloom. "What I want you to do," he said quietly, "is help me protect her from something like that happening to her again. She nearly got killed, did you know that?"

Nicola opened her eyes. "No. I didn't know that."

Giovanni hadn't given up his investigations during the past week. Taking a lamp, he had gone again into the secret passage, and into the next, and the next, and he knew now that Debra could only have got out of there by climbing the broken supports of the steps that had once led to the bell tower, over a sheer drop. How else would she have gone up there? If she'd managed to find her way back to the North Chapel she would have gone straight to her cell. She'd have had no reason to go up to the tower.

"She nearly got killed," he said again, "and even though it would have been by accident, it mustn't happen again. There was some sort of wild escapade, you see."

Nicola moved her head away from the back of the chair, leaning forward and searching Giovanni's eyes. "That doesn't," she said, "sound like Debra."

"Madlen, then?"

"Maybe. She's into theatrics, that gal. But look, they're friends of mine. I can't—"

"Nicola. You don't seem to get the message. I'm not asking you to snoop on your friends. I'm asking you to help me to make sure that nothing like that happens again. They're younger than you. They're just kids."

"Did you talk to Madlen?"

"Yeah. She says she doesn't know what happened to her sister."

"Do you think she knows?"

He took a deep breath. "Yeah. I think she knows."

"Jesus. She was half out of her mind, while Deb was recovering. She—"

"Like she felt she was to blame."

"I guess that could be."

"So all I want you to do, my friend, is to keep an eye on those two. If there are any more wild escapades planned, I want to know. And in time."

He leaned away from the desk and moved to the door, and Nicola's head turned to watch him. "You gonna bounce me now?"

She saw him smile. "I've got others to see."

She got out of the chair and came to him, reaching for his hands. "It's the first time I've told anyone," she whispered, "about Giulio."

"I know."

"I need you," she said, "in so many ways."

"I know that too. And I'm here for you. And so is Christ."

Debra pulled the coarse prickly blankets right up under her chin, but it didn't do much good: She was always cold in bed. It didn't make any difference how many blankets she had on—Madlen had given her one of her own, though she'd protested—or even whether she could sometimes smuggle in a stoneware hot water bottle from the sick room. She was always cold in bed, and it was still only November.

Debra looked across at her sister to see if she was awake too, but Madlen was curled up like a hedgehog under the blankets, fast asleep.

She'd been to see the mannequin again today.

Debra always knew.

She'd known for a long time, for years: They'd still been in their preteens when Madlen had told her one day that she must never go into the attic again.

"There are bats up there," she said.

"Bats?"

"I heard them squeaking." Madlen was looking very intense, her eyes dark as she gave an exaggerated shudder.

"Oh," Debra said. But there was something about the way her sister was telling her this that made her wonder. Why were there bats in the attic—suddenly? But she knew better than to question anything her sister said—it was usually right, or . . . so strange that Debra didn't want to know any more about it. "Okay," she said, and it wasn't mentioned again.

It was maybe a week later, when Madlen was staying late at school rehearsing for a new play, that curiosity got the better of Debra and she climbed the ladder into the attic through the trapdoor in the ceiling and took a look around. There weren't any bats here; she wasn't worried about that; her sister was into one of her secrets again, that was all, and it might be interesting—they usually were.

It was an October evening, already dark before seven, and Debra had brought a flashlight. A low wind was moaning through the gaps between the tiles, and there were drafts here. There was also a lot of dust, drifting in the beam of the flashlight as she moved around, testing each floorboard before she put her weight on it, because if Madlen got home earlier than she'd thought, and found her in the attic, Debra wouldn't know what to say; she'd been warned not to come up here, and it'd look like she didn't trust her sister.

But a board creaked in spite of her taking care and she froze, her heart thumping a little. There was some kind of a wardrobe against the wall, and a stack of flags leaning next to it, with so much dust on them that the stars and stripes were almost smothered. She froze again, thinking she heard Mom calling from downstairs. She wouldn't know what to say to Mom, either, if she found her in the attic; nobody came up here very often.

Then the voice came again, but it wasn't Mom, it was the girl next door, Mary Beckwith, calling out to someone in the yard.

Debra moved again—and stifled a cry as something else moved with her, something close. Her heart hammering now, she slowly brought the flashlight higher until its glare became dazzling, bouncing off the mirror in the door of the wardrobe where the movement had been, the movement of her own reflection.

"Oh, God," she whispered, "Oh, God. . . ." The saliva was thick in her mouth and she swallowed it, taking a deep breath and waiting for her nerves to calm down.

The wind moaned through the gaps in the tiles, and Debra shivered. She shouldn't have come up here: This place was spooky. But she hadn't found anything yet that looked secret, just a whole lot of boxes and junk and stuff, and she was still curious.

Press on. It was a favorite saying of Madlen's: "Press on regardless."

Debra moved again, and dust rose in a golden cloud as she caught her foot on something and it fell across the beam of light—one of Dad's old fishing poles with the line dangling and a hook still on it, encrusted with the black shriveled remnants of a worm.

A board creaked, and she stepped over it, testing out the next and then going forward again, stifling a sneeze because of the dust, her nerves still tingling from seeing herself in the mirror. She still couldn't find anything that Madlen might have hidden, but there was a door leaning across the gap between the wardrobe and the wall alongside it, and she swung it slowly back and shone the flashlight behind it *and gave a scream as she saw a face staring at her with its eyes bright and alive and she jerked back and dropped the flashlight and stood there quivering.*

The flashlight hadn't gone out, and in the backwash she saw a figure below the face, dressed in black, perfectly silent, perfectly still, its hands pink—no, with pink gloves on. Now the shock was over, Debra could see the eyes in the face weren't staring—they were smiling, even, as motes of dust settled across it in the glow from the flashlight.

Debra swallowed. *Had anybody heard her scream?*

If they had—Mom, or Madlen home early—there wasn't anything she could do about it now, and if one of them came up to the attic she'd say yeah, there are bats here, they scared me to death.

In a moment she picked up the flashlight and brought the beam higher, slowly, slowly, swinging it until it reached the face of the mannequin again—because that was what it was. The smiling face of a girl, with the standard freckles and tip-tilted nose and everything, the eyes bright because it—she—hadn't been here long, or—okay—she might have been here a while but the face had been dusted off, maybe regularly, when—yeah—when Madlen came up here to visit her behind the leaning door.

You must never, ever go into the attic. There are bats up there.

Bats?

I heard them squeaking.

But there weren't any bats here; she'd known there wouldn't be. There was some other reason, some secret reason, for Madlen saying that, and here it was . . . here was her secret, a teenager dressed in a black track suit, or ski suit, whatever, with pink gloves and sneakers, a kid with long fair hair and a smiling face, so lifelike that she looked alive, alive enough to think of her as "she," instead of "it."

Was that how Madlen thought of her? As "she," something—someone—alive?

The motes of dust drifted, gray turning to gold as they reached the beam of light and Debra stood looking at—who?

Did she have a name?

Had Madlen given her a name?

What, then? What was her name?

It seemed important. People had names.

They stood looking at each other in the silence for another moment, but no longer than that because Debra was feeling the urge rising in her to say something—like "Hi!" or "I'm Debra," because it felt kind of rude to just stand here staring in silence—and this was when she had to swing the leaning door back across the gap and come away, because that kind of thing could get to you if you were cursed with enough imagination.

That had been years ago, but she remembered every detail. She'd gone down to the landing and pushed the ladder up into the trap and heard Madlen's voice in the kitchen talking to Mom, and then Madlen had come running upstairs to find her and gave her a little hug like always and said, *"God, you're freezing!* Where have you been?"

And Debra had said she'd been out in the yard trying to get Lissa in—Lissa was their Manx cat, the kind without a tail, and Madlen had looked at her with her eyes deep, maybe sensing the lie, but Debra stuck to her story, shaking inside, and that was an end of it.

Now she lay in the hard narrow bed with the prickly blankets pulled right up to her chin but still shivering.

Because Madlen had been to see the mannequin again today.

She'd smuggled it into the convent in an extra bag; maybe its arms and legs swiveled, or came apart. *Are you sure this is all the baggage you brought with you?* Sister Carlissa had asked that day as she'd checked their stuff in their cell. Madlen had said yes, Sister Carlissa must have been thinking of some other novice. The nun had given one of her famous shrugs, which always made you feel you'd been lying even when you hadn't, but she'd had to believe Madlen.

The mannequin was here now, somewhere, and today Madlen had been to see it.

Debra always knew. Sometimes there was grime on her sister's robe, or her veil was a little bit skewed, like she'd been in a small space somewhere, but always there was that strange light in her eyes, like you saw with Patrice when she'd been praying a lot, "communing with the Savior," as she called it, and Madlen wouldn't speak for a while, seemed preoccupied, so Debra didn't say anything to her either, knowing she needed a little time to kind of get back to reality.

Maybe there was going to be another "accident" soon, she thought as she stared at the ceiling, watching the candlelight. Maybe that was what Madlen went up there to talk to the mannequin about, the girl in the black ski suit.

Because there *was* going to be another "accident."

She knew that now. She'd just been kidding herself along, all these years, believing that every time it happened it would be the last time. But that wasn't true anymore, now she'd made up her mind to face this whole thing. But facing it was one thing. She still had to find a way out.

And there wasn't one.

She couldn't talk to Madlen about it. It would be like telling her she was crazy, and that would be a terrible thing to do to anyone, let alone her sister.

She couldn't tell anyone else. They wouldn't believe her. Or worse, if they believed her they'd put Madlen away in some horrible institution and give her shock treatment and stuff like that, and Debra would never forgive herself.

She couldn't run away. There was nowhere she could run. Not back home, for sure. And she couldn't leave Madlen anyhow. She couldn't imagine life without her, and didn't want to. Between the . . . "accidents" . . . Madlen was more fun to be with than anyone Debra had ever known. She'd even turned their life in the convent into a game, totally wired by what she called the "theatricality" of it all. And she was so wonderfully kind and thoughtful, always looking after her and trying to keep her warm and stopping her from worrying about things. Shecouldn'tever—*ever*—go through life without Madlen.

Debra stopped thinking to listen.

A door had made a sound somewhere, and the candle in the corridor had started flickering. Then there were footsteps, soft ones made by slippers, and in a moment the door of their cell came open quietly and someone was standing there, silhouetted against the candlelight.

Debra shivered. "Is that you, Madlen?"

"Yeah." She closed the door as quietly as she could, though it always gave a click you couldn't stop. Everyone said Sister Carlissa had fixed all the catches, so she'd hear when people were moving around. "God," Madlen said as she pulled the blankets back and slipped into bed, "it's *freezing* in those bathrooms! Some crass dummy left one of the windows open."

"Hurry up and get warm, then," Debra said. "Listen, I'm going to give you your blanket back." She started getting out of bed but Madlen stopped her.

"You will do *no* such thing! Thy need is greater than mine, kiddo. Did I wake you up?"

"No. I didn't even know you were out of the room."

"I had to go and wring out my cute little pink kidneys. The storm didn't wake you up either?"

"Yeah, I guess it did." The storm and the infant skeletons, and Madlen's laughter. Don't think about it.

"Well it's over now," Madlen said. "Even the rain's stopped; I could tell when I shut the window. Now we must get some more sleep, before that diabolical bell starts ringing. Sweet dreams."

"Yeah," Debra said. "Sweet dreams."

15

"Hi," Debra said, thinking it didn't sound nearly enough of a greeting, considering she hadn't seen Alice Thompson for such a long time, almost five weeks.

"Hi!" Alice said with an overbright smile, and tugged her strawberry-red sweater down, the one Debra had given her. It still looked a whole lot too tight, Debra thought. "Where's Madlen?" Alice asked her.

"She's in bed."

Alice's smile died. It had been overbright, Debra knew, because it was the first time her friend had seen her in her robes and veil, and behind the round-rimmed glasses her pale eyes were moving all over, trying to find Debra's hair. "Is she sick?" Alice asked her.

"Not really. It's the curse, that's all. But it gets to her. She's really miffed, not being able to see you. But she says hi."

"Oh." Alice remembered the flowers she'd brought, and pushed them into Debra's hands.

"Oh . . . You shouldn't have! They're so pretty!"

"They've got their stalks in a glass bulb," Alice said, "full of water. Better hold them upright!"

Debra looked around her to see if there was somewhere they could sit. They were in the convent parlor, the big high-ceilinged room, bright with polish and smelling of floor wax, where she and Madlen had come for their interview with Sister Denise, and there were quite a few other visitors here, all talking very quietly, while two or three of the professed nuns moved around, not speaking to anyone but just "sharing the occasion" as Sister Denise had told them. They were also listening, as Debra knew, and keeping their eyes open.

"Look," Nicola had told her after Mass this morning, "think of yourself as a lifer in St. Quentin receiving close relatives, okay? Our ever-lovin' sisters won't be looking for packets of crack or hacksaw blades, but don't try hiding any Betty Jane bras or Mars bars under your habit if your friend brings you stuff like that—anything except flowers. This is still Sin City and you don't want to eat supper tonight on your knees. And remember not to talk about yourself or anything that goes on in this place or what you think of it. All you can talk about is—shit, I don't know—the weather, I guess."

"We can sit over there," Debra told Alice, "on the bench."

"Okay." As they edged among the people Alice was thinking, gee, how could Deb still look so pretty when you couldn't see her hair or her ears or her neck or anything? *Did she still have hair?* Jeff had told her on the way here that they got their heads shaved in places like this. That was a *terrible* thought, especially since Alice herself had a mass of bright ginger hair that rubbed against the roof-lining of Jeff Soderberg's beat-up VW, and Mom called it her crowning glory.

They sat at the end of the bench, right in a corner,

which was a bit cramped but a good place to be, because none of the sisters could come up behind them and listen in without being seen.

"Jeff's here," said Alice.

"Jeff Soderberg?" Debra felt a rush of warmth, which surprised her. She'd wondered why he hadn't come, because in his letter he'd said he'd give Alice a ride here in his Volks.

"Jeff Soderberg," Alice said with her smile beaming again, "who else?"

"Doesn't he want to see me?" Debra found her emotions seesawing inside of her—first she'd expected Jeff to come and then it looked like he hadn't and now she knew he had but he wasn't here in the room with Alice. It was a lot to handle.

"Doesn't Jeff Soderberg want to *see* you?" Alice was grinning like an idiot. She put her warm freckled hands on Debra's. "Listen, I want you and him to have some time to yourself alone, see—" she looked around at all the people "—well, I mean everything in life is relative, right? So I'm just commandeering you for five whole minutes of girl talk first. Or do you want me to bring him in right now?" The look on her face said she'd die if the answer was "yes."

"No *way*," Debra said, but felt unkind, because it left Jeff just standing around by himself out there.

"So how've you been doing in this place?" Alice asked.

"Fine. Still kind of settling in, I guess." *The only thing is, my sister tried to kill me again.*

"Sure," Alice said brightly. "Early days." But she didn't think Deb looked all that happy, seemed worried about something. Well, okay, she'd given up pretty well everything she'd ever known and changed it for a life that Alice privately considered totally *weird*, and that wouldn't leave anyone looking too happy. She wished to God she could just grab Debbie and whisk her out of here and take her away in the car—it would be so *great* to have her back in her life again. But then there was the other side of it, too, and she lowered her voice and said, "It's still going on, at the High."

"Going on?"

"Yeah. Dan Cresser got booked for drug dealing. They say he's for the slammer."

"Oh, *no* . . ." Debra crossed herself, and Alice was quite impressed. It looked like she was asking God to protect Dan Cresser, see he didn't go to jail.

"I was there," Alice said, "when the cops came for him and put the handcuffs on." Her eyes were gleaming behind her glasses. "It was terrible. And some other guy shot himself in the foot, in the main hallway, showing off his gun. I laughed like an idiot because I thought it was really funny, those stupid clowns with their guns, and Joe Bicksby saw me laughing and slapped my face because this guy was a buddy of his, and I brought my knee up in Joe Bicksby's crotch like they showed us how to do in the self-defense class, and oh, brother, did it fix that punk! I left him throwing up in agony."

Debra didn't say anything. It was terrible to hear about all this, but it just proved Madlen had been right when she'd got them both out of their old world and into this one. If only there wasn't this thing haunting her all the time now, so she could hardly take an interest in anything else. Watching Alice with her big round glasses and her beaming smile and her freckled skin, Debra thought how wonderful it would be to run out of here with her, hand in hand, and drive away down the hill in Jeff's VW and—and? Yeah, sure, and go and join a circus or get work at a car wash or the Happyburger, and *without Madlen*. But then Madlen would leave here too, so they could be together again, and Debra would want her to, because then it wouldn't be so bad, except . . . it wouldn't make any difference, would it? Wherever they were, there was still going to be an accident, somewhere along the line. The last one.

So there was no point running away with Alice. She could leave this place any time she liked, just walk out of here; it wasn't really St. Quentin.

". . . So I gave it a try," she heard Alice saying. "Don't you think it's made a difference?"

"Yeah," Debra said.

"You do?" Alice sounded delighted.

"Sure thing." Debra went on nodding, and in a moment got the drift—Alice was always trying new stuff for her acne, and this must be what she was talking about. "I noticed the minute I saw you, but I didn't want to—you know."

"Sure. Do you have a sore throat? It sounds kinda raspy."

"It's nearly better."

"You getting enough Vitamin C?"

"It isn't a cold. There was a lot of smoke around the place," Debra said. "We had a fire."

"Gee! Smoke inhalation. Remember that talk by the fire chief? You taking honey?"

"Sure." Alice really cared about you, like a mother. They hadn't had too much of that, she and Madlen. "How are your folks?" she asked Alice.

"What happened to your hands?" Alice was holding them, and felt how rough they were. She turned them over. "Jeeze, look at these scars!"

"That' was the fire too. Passing buckets, and everything." Debra pulled her hands gently away.

Alice put her head on one side, eyeing her friend steadily. "They got like *this* passing *buckets*?" Then she decided not to say any more. "You have some Vaseline?"

"Sure. I use it every night."

"You do that." Then Alice was beaming again. "My folks? Dad got his job back at Compucenter last week,

and Mom's been baking griddle cakes by the zillion for
the transients on Leary Street—there's a Home-from-
Home drive happening again." She talked a bit more
about that, but didn't think Deb was looking too interested. Maybe she had her mind on Jeff Soderberg, so
Alice said, "Well anyway, your enamored swain awaits
without, so—"

"My what?"

"Your boyfriend. I'll go get him." And suddenly
Debra was enfolded in Alice's warm plump arms and
smelling the sandalwood oil she used instead of cologne
and feeling her tears against her face, and then she was
gone—"Say hi to Maddie for me, okay, and make sure
you take your honey!"—and Debra saw a young guy
with a flat-top haircut squeezing his way through the
visitors and felt glad Jeff Soderberg didn't have his hair
cut that way, and Jeff Soderberg was suddenly standing
in front of her with a bunch of red sweetheart roses in his
hand.

"Hi," he said.

"Why, Jeff! I didn't recognize you!"

Standing there in front of her, hopelessly in love, he
saw right away that she thought his trendy flat-top fif-
teen-dollar haircut was a total catastrophe, and wanted
to turn tail and get out of here and wait till his hair grew
normal again, and then come back in the hope she'd still
want to see him. This whole thing was so critical. Get
something wrong at this stage and he could lose her
forever. Lose *Debra*. It didn't bear thinking about.

But he gathered strength, remembering what she'd said
to him the last time he'd seen her, right outside this place.
You're the only guy. . . . He'd been listening to her saying
that for all these weeks, morning and night and all
through the day, and finally it had got to the point when
he'd thought of cashing in his savings and paying one of
those skywriting outfits to fly a plane around and around

the convent of the Sisters of the Sacred Light with the banner behind it reading YOU'RE THE ONLY GIRL, but he'd never gone through with it because she might be inside praying or something and never see it.

"You look so pretty," he said. But his eyes too were glancing upward a little. "Did they cut off all your hair?"

A thunderbolt came right through the roof at that minute and blew him into bits, because it had been such a *stupid* thing to say. It was just that he'd been spending at least half of his homework time studying books he'd searched out at the library, like *So You Want to Be a Sister?* and *When God Calls* and *The Nature of a Religious Vocation,* so he'd get to know as much as he could about the life Debra was living; and somewhere he'd read about novices having their hair cut off as a sign of humility, and it had shaken him up real bad because Debra had always had the most beautiful fair hair and wore it in long natural waves down to her shoulders, taking his breath away as he'd followed her up and down the hallways at the High, watching it flow and ripple in the light as she moved.

"Yes," she said. "But it's growing back again. We have to keep it short, that's all." He was looking quietly anguished, so she said, "But it's not forever."

Jeff was suddenly aware that a rainbow was flooding the room with a torrent of colors as the voices of a heavenly choir filled the air and a flight of a thousand angels soared aloft through the roof, gold and silver in a blaze of celestial light.

"It's not?" he said.

"I mean . . . I guess it'll be a year or two, but that's not forever." She wanted to keep the hope there in his quiet gray eyes, and not destroy it with a clumsy word. She'd never seen things like this going on in the eyes of somebody she didn't really know very well, the light in them when Jeff had edged his way through the people a minute ago and seen her, and stopped dead, just watching, till she'd looked up at his hair and ruined everything. The thought of it made her nibble suddenly at her lip, and he noticed. He didn't miss anything about her, and somehow she didn't mind.

"A year or two," he nodded. "Sure. That isn't forever." His long mouth formed a smile. "But it'll seem like it, to me."

Suddenly, as the people all around went on talking and smiling and the professed sisters moved among them with the light from the windows flashing across their glasses, Debra didn't want to die.

That was a strange thing to come into her mind, but she didn't have time to think about it now because Jeff was watching her, and she realized he'd just said something and was waiting for an answer. But she couldn't remember what he'd said, and only knew it couldn't have been as important as what she wanted to tell him, right out—*Jeff, I don't want to die.*

He'd think she was crazy.

"Are your folks okay?" she asked him.

"Yeah, I guess." He'd never told her he lost his Mom last year, and was living with his Dad alone in the house, just the two of them, with Dad still going around picking things up and putting them down again, looking at his wedding pictures all the time, tilting them against the light, not ever talking much. Jeff hadn't wanted to tell her things like that.

Debra watched his eyes, watched him thinking. She thought it was like watching the reflections on deep water. They would change suddenly if she said it, told him she didn't want to die. But she couldn't tell him, so she asked him about sports and stuff at the High, and his Volks and his guitar, which she knew he was learning, and he asked her if she was okay, kept asking her that,

like Madlen always did when she thought Debra had
something on her mind.

"I'm fine," Debra kept saying, and then the senior nun
began ringing the big pewter bell that always stood on
the table near the door, and everyone hushed and then
started talking faster and louder again, saying their
goodbyes, and Jeff found himself staring into the dark
infinite void of the coming month, four weeks, thirty
days, seeing the endless hallways at the High where her
long fair hair wouldn't be flowing and rippling in the
light as she walked along, a month, four weeks, of seeing
Dad's quiet set face and hearing him sigh and knowing it
wasn't possible, even conceivable, to break the incredible
news that he'd found a girl to love and her name was
Debra and she'd told him he was the only guy, because
the girl his Dad had found to love for all those years had
died. Thirty-two years, Dad kept saying, I was with your
Mother thirty-two wonderful years.

Maybe a month wasn't so long to wait, when Dad was
going to have to wait forever.

"Do I have to go now?" he asked Debra. He didn't
want to believe it—the bell really meant something else,
there was going to be a tour of the place now for the
visitors, or they were going to be offered some coffee and
buns, or—

"Yes," Debra said.

"Okay—" taking it in his stride "—Well, I—"

"Jeff—"

"Yes?"

"I don't—" but she didn't finish.

"You don't what?"

"You have to go now," she said.

"I—I know." He didn't move. "But what were you
going to say?"

One of the nuns was standing near him now, waiting,
her pale bony hands clasped in front of her with one

finger tapping against the others. "Have you said your goodbyes?" she asked. Her voice was thin, cracked, dry.

"What? I'm never going to say—"

"Jeff," he heard Debra saying, "you take care."

He just looked at her for a moment and then stood back and took a deep breath and kind of woke up and gave her a smile and nodded and said, "Yes. Yes. I hope—" and shook his head because there wasn't time.

He was walking away, shepherded by the nun, when Debra called, "Jeff?" He turned. "I like your shoes."

He seemed surprised, and looked down, then nodded, embarrassed, and was lost among the people.

Walking into the cold autumn air of the morning, his hands tucked into the front pockets of his short military-surplus jacket, Jeff was shouting at himself inside— *Moron! Moron-moron-moron!* Because he'd asked her if she'd had her hair cut off and then stood there answering her questions and asking his own, none of them about anything important because of those hawk-eyed nuns with their granny-glasses iced over with disapproval, while all the time Debra had looked quietly worried about something and he should have made her tell him, so he could have helped her with it, whatever it was. He would have galloped back up here on a white charger and thundered at the big wooden doors and found her and carried her off with him, it made him *sick* the way he fantasized when reality had to be faced.

Alice was waiting for him outside the Volks, holding her scarf close to her face in the frosty air.

"Well?" she asked him when she realized he wasn't going to say anything.

"She liked my shoes." He got in behind the wheel.

"Well, g-r-reat!" Alice had told him that if he ever went to see Debbie wearing his special gold-ribbed high-deck inflatable Superking shoes he should be prepared for her to cut him *dead,* so he'd gone out and spent an entire three months' allowance on some Florsheim brogues with tassels on. It was a start.

Jeff got the motor going, and the two halves of the windshield began chirping like a tiny bird to the vibration, where the crack was. It had embarrassed him when Debra had told him she liked his shoes, because it had reminded him of the multicolored Star Trek monstrosities he'd worn before, to impress her—to *impress* her!

"The hair?" Alice asked him as they got up speed.

"What?"

"The *hair?*" The Volks was making a lot of noise.

"I'm going to let it grow out," he told her, and glanced into the mirror and saw the top of his head and shouted inside him, *Freak! Freak-freak-freak!*

"May the Lord be praised," Alice said with relief, and crossed herself the way she'd seen Debbie do, hoping it didn't amount to blasphemy. As they rattled into the roadway at the end of the drive she asked Jeff, "So what do you think?"

"About what?"

"About Debbie."

"Oh." He felt like something was sinking inside of him, down and down and down, and knew it was despair, because he didn't have a white charger and they wouldn't let him through those doors anyway. "She's not okay," he said in a bit, "is she?"

Alice shook her mop of red hair. "No."

Even though he'd expected her to say that, it felt like she'd hit him.

"So what can we do?"

"I guess we can't do anything," Alice said.

"You may offer them to her," the nun told Helen, "but you must take them away when you leave."

The eyes behind the rimless glasses, Helen thought, had the pale shiny look of oysters on the half-shell. She held the box of marrons glacés candies as if they'd suddenly become obscene, like condoms or something.

"You take them, then," she said, and thrust them into the surprised hands of the nun and left her with them as she moved through the small crowd of people toward the corner, where she'd seen Debra the minute she'd come in.

Debra hadn't seen her yet, to notice, and Helen stopped, wanting to look at her for a while, isolate the small child's face from all the others in here, pretend they were alone. It was a long time since she'd seen her, and then it had only been from a distance, and not of course in a nun's habit.

Debra stood waiting for her aunt to come, wishing now she hadn't asked her, because her mind was so full of things she wanted to work out, like not wanting to die. Did that mean she'd been ready to die before? Of course not: Life was exciting, most of the time. It was just that she couldn't leave her sister, because Madlen was almost all of that excitement, and if she was to stay with her she had to risk . . . an accident.

But now there was Jeff.

It sounded strange, though. She hardly knew him. He'd followed her around from the first time they'd sat next to each other in class, asking her only once for a date—screwing up his courage till he could hardly move his lips, she'd noticed—and then just following her around again. It hadn't bothered her, because he seemed a nice enough guy and not at all threatening or aggressive, and Madlen hadn't told him to buzz off, which she certainly would have if she'd thought he was bad for her sister.

But that was it—it was *because* he was almost a stranger that he'd begun making a difference in her life. That, and the way he felt about her. It came out of his eyes like candlelight, or Christmas, the glow of something she'd never seen before. She'd seen softness in people's eyes when they looked at her, Mom's, a long time ago, and Dad's, and of course Madlen's. But they were her family, and you kind of expected it.

Jeff was in another world, outside, and he was letting her into it, asking her to be there with him, and because of that, because of him, she didn't want to die. She didn't want to just go on waiting for another accident. For the last one.

Not now there was Jeff.

"Hello," she heard one of the visitors saying, "I'm Helen."

Debra turned and saw a middle-aged woman with soft loose hair above a pink embroidered scarf, her smile lighting her eyes.

"Oh, hi," Debra said, and vowed never to say "hi" to anyone ever again when she first met them. It just wasn't enough.

"You can call me 'Aunt' Helen if you want to," the woman said, "but you certainly don't have to." She waited, watching Debra with her smile flowing across the space between them, so that Debra couldn't think of anything to say, just wanted to stand there and enjoy it. "I brought you some candies," the woman said in a moment, "but they're obviously off-limits here, which I didn't realize. I gave them to a nun, though she handled them like they were a bunch of dead rats."

"Candies," Debra thought she should explain, quoting correctly, "are considered to encourage self-indulgence, which is a minor sin." She thought she saw a shadow move across the smile, though it kept on shining. "I mean, that's why she was that way. But gee, it was real nice of you to bring anything at all." She looked around to see if there was anywhere for them to sit. There were two spindly camp chairs near the middle of the room, so she led the woman over to them, because she was still quite slim and wouldn't break one if she sat down. There would have been a risk, with Alice.

"Madlen's not here?" Helen asked. She had lovely eyes, Debra thought, a very soft blue, and they could watch you without looking inquisitive. They weren't anything like Mom's.

"She's—you know—it's that time," Debra told her aunt. "She wanted to meet you, but. . . ."

Although that wasn't true: Madlen wouldn't have been here anyway. "I don't think I'm that crazy," she'd said when the letter came, "about meeting any sister of Mom's."

Madlen had looked really wrung out this morning when Debra had left her in bed—and this was another thing she had on her mind. Yesterday, she'd noticed some blood on Madlen's sheets when they'd got up, but hadn't said anything until later. Then, after First Mass, she'd asked Sister Denise where Madlen had gone, and she was told Father Giovanni wanted to talk to her. Sister Denise was looking really worried about something, and when Debra saw her sister again, Madlen didn't tell her what the priest had wanted to talk to her about—which was unusual, because she always shared things. When Debra had finally asked if she'd hurt herself, because of the blood on the sheets, Madlen said right away that she'd "started" again, two whole weeks early. And by this morning she was really into it, pale and cramping and everything, so Debra had gone to tell Sister Denise.

Two weeks early. . . . Was that possible? Well, sure, obviously, but . . . what had brought it on? Had it to do with something Father Giovanni had said to her? No, because the blood had been there on her sheets when they'd first got out of bed yesterday morning, before he'd talked to her.

It took a little figuring, and pretty soon Debra was

going to ask her sister about her talk with the priest, because if she'd gotten herself into some kind of trouble she wanted to help.

"Bad timing," she heard Aunt Helen saying.

"Huh?" Madlen's curse. "Oh, yeah. But I'll give her your—your—"

"My love," Aunt Helen said. She was sitting very straight on the wobbly little chair, almost like she'd been trained by Sister Carlissa; her hands were folded on her pink suede gloves and her legs elegantly crossed. For the first time Debra noticed a kind of shadow on one side of her face, like the remains of a bruise. "And you're wondering why I'm here," Aunt Helen said, "and why I wrote that letter to you."

"Well, I guess Mom must have told you where we'd gone, and—"

"I haven't spoken to your mother since you were born." Aunt Helen looked down at her hands for a moment, then up again into Debra's eyes. "We had a falling out, you see. But I've been around all the time—I've always lived in Weldon—and now and again I've been catching up with the news about your family, from friends and acquaintances and, oh, hairdressers and people like that. It's not always been good news, as you know, and it hurt me a little when I heard it, about the fights and everything at home. Not too much fun for you, was it?" She touched Debra's hand. "I never had any children, you see. So I—I guess I envied your mother, with her two nice kids. You've been the only 'family' I've ever known. Then I heard you'd come to this place, and your parents weren't too happy about it, didn't even come with you to say goodbye—is that right? So I . . . wondered if you might feel kind of abandoned for a while. That's why I'm here."

In a moment Debra said, "I guess we're okay, Aunt Helen." And immediately she knew she'd got it wrong,

because the shadow passed across the smile again as her
aunt nodded quickly.

"Then I'm very glad, and I don't need to come again,
so—"

"I didn't mean it that way." For the first time Debra
began hoping the bell wouldn't start ringing yet, because
it was nice talking to Aunt Helen and watching the smile
in her eyes. "We're okay, I mean, but please come see us
again if you want."

Her aunt looked quickly away, and Debra thought her
eyes were glistening, but couldn't be sure, because of all
the light streaming from the colored windows. She hoped
she hadn't said anything wrong again.

"Then I'd like to," Aunt Helen nodded. "I would really like to do that. And maybe see your sister next time
around. But you don't need to tell your Mom I came to
see you, when you write to her, is that okay?"

"Well, sure," Debra said, "if you—"

"Like I said, we don't ever talk to each other, and she
might even—you know—not want me hanging around
you two."

"They don't hang around much themselves," Debra
said, and felt good suddenly, because it had sounded just
the kind of thing Madlen would say, straight out and no
fooling.

"Well," Aunt Helen said, "they have their problems,
and I understand that. I had my problems too."

"Was that when—" but Debra stopped short. Maybe
that was when the bruise happened, but she didn't want
Aunt Helen to think she'd noticed it.

"Yes," Aunt Helen said, "that was when." Her soft
mouth had tightened a little. "The doctors say it'll go,
eventually. It's only been two years."

"That's awful," Debra said, and swallowed. It was
hard to believe any man could hit a woman like Aunt
Helen. She was so soft, her face and her voice too, and

she must have had really terrific looks when she was younger. "Some of the kids I know—I knew at school had their Moms beat up all the time."

Debra was watching the big pewter bell over there on the table next to the visitors' book, but none of the sisters was going near it yet. "Why didn't you—" and she stopped again. This kind of thing was so personal.

"Because I loved him," Aunt Helen said. She didn't seem to need complete questions: She saw them coming. "And that's a funny thing, isn't it? It's nothing to do with not having the guts, you see. There was a guy in the street once, beating on a dog, and I was carrying a bag of groceries with a big bottle of 7-Up in it, and I brought that whole bag down on that guy's head and nearly killed him. He had to have fifteen stitches." She looked down at her hands. "I didn't love him, you see. He was just a jerk, a stranger. But I loved Harry so much he could do anything he liked, and I forgave him. It's always the same story—you ask the people at any battered wives' home. We go on forgiving the men we love because we think it's our fault, for not understanding them, for getting them mad at us." Her soft blue eyes were on Debra's again. "But finally I had enough. And you know? When I told him I wanted a divorce he cried like a baby and went down on his knees. But it didn't do any good, because I knew by then that he was exactly that—a baby. And I used to think he was a man. So—" she shrugged her shoulders under the pink embroidered scarf "—so maybe it was my fault after all, for making a mistake like that." The smile came slowly back, making everything okay again. "You're a good listener, honey. You invite confidence, and that's nice. But it must give you a lot to handle sometimes."

"I guess people don't tell me things, much," Debra said, and smiled, shaking her head. "I'm so young. I mean I'm even younger than—you know—my age." She felt the smile dying away because of what she needed to ask. "So it's wrong, to go on loving somebody when they're—when they're a danger to you?"

"It's wrong for you, and it's wrong for them. Trouble is, it's like a trap you've set for yourself, and it takes an awful lot of getting out of." Aunt Helen watched her for a moment. "Why did you ask?"

"Oh, it—I guess it sounds so weird, doesn't it, loving someone like that. So how did you get out of the trap?"

"I found someone else to love."

"You *did?*"

"And this time it really is a man."

"Well, gee, that's—"

"Bless you, honey, you look so pleased."

"Of course I'm pleased! It's a—you know—a happy ending!"

Aunt Helen looked away, her lips compressed. "Sort of. Except that he's such a terrific man that I wish I could have offered him even a half-terrific woman, before she got all beat up. He—"

"But you're beautiful, Aunt Helen!"

"Bless you, honey. But it's not just the looks, you see. You get an awful lot of things beat out of you if it goes on too long. Things like trust, and faith, and self-respect. And the capacity to love with a whole heart again." She turned her head and looked back at Debra. "Don't ever let it happen to you."

"I—I guess—" and then she didn't have to finish it because Sister Carlissa was at the table picking up the big pewter bell.

"You sure you want me to come see you again?" Aunt Helen asked her.

"Oh, *yes.*" She reached for the soft hands on the pink suede gloves, feeling how warm they were in a room as cold as this. "I'd love to talk to you again, Aunt Helen, whenever you have the time."

"It's a deal. Are you happy in this place, honey?"

The soft blue eyes were watching Debra very intently, looking for the truth.

"I—it's okay here. Better than where we were."

"And you have Madlen," Aunt Helen said above the clanging of the bell. "She must be fun to be with, and you're close, I know."

"Yes." It didn't sound enough to say, but what more could there be?

But she's trying to kill me.

Aunt Helen was waiting, and when she didn't say anything more she just put her arms round her in silence and gave her a gentle hug, and Debra was surprised to feel her trembling.

Then the middle-aged woman with the pink embroidered scarf was half-lost in the crowd again, talking to Sister Carlissa and taking something from her and turning for a moment to wave it at Debra with a rueful smile, a box of candies, it looked like, and Debra waved back and watched her go out through the archway and vanish, leaving her with a lump in her throat and a piercing sense of loss that quite bewildered her.

16

There was dew on the grass, jeweled by the light of the winter sun and sprinkling the spiders' webs with diamonds. The earth smelled rich from the recent rain, and the last leaves of autumn made gold spirals through the air, spinning their way to the year's end.

"Look," said Sister Rose. "Come over here."

She was sitting on a tree stump, a black shawl round her habit, her round face on fire in the frosty air. The temperature had dropped again last night, Father Giovanni had said, and there was ice on the buckets outside the goat shed.

"Look," Sister Rose said again, her breath clouding out. "See the difference between these two?" She held up the mushrooms as the sisters came over, their boots scattering diamonds in the grass. "This one's good, the real thing, with the veins the right color and not hidden under a membrane, like with *this* one. And it's almost perfectly round, not wavy, see the difference?" Her raw fingers, sticking out of mittens, prodded the mushrooms as she looked up at the others with her eyes sharp behind their glasses. "And don't think I'm giving you moonshine. There's not many of *these* around, but they want watching for. Eat one of *these,* and you'll need a stomach pump and an ambulance, and that's if you're lucky and there's time." She dropped one of the mushrooms and crushed it under her boot.

Sister Nicola stood looking down, hands on her hips, her dark eyes attentive. Sister Madlen was nearby, holding one of the wicker panniers they'd been given; hers was almost full.

"So I want *everybody* to bring me their basket when they're ready," Sister Rose told them firmly. *"Every* mushroom going into that kitchen has to be personally checked out by *me."* Her round head turned an inch or two. "And Sister Nicola, if Mother Superior sees you standing like that with your hands on your hips like a chorus girl out of Las Vegas you'll eat on your knees from here till Christmas Day, so don't say I didn't warn you."

They drifted back into the trees, where the mushrooms grew more thickly. Nicola stayed close to Madlen, who looked white as a mouse and like she was going to keel over any next minute.

"Is it the 'bitch'?" she asked her. They all had their different names for it in this place.

"Yeah," Madlen said. "The thing is, I'm right in the middle of the month, so maybe that's why it's worse than usual." She'd never experienced a period this bad, with her stomach cramped for two days straight and a high fever at night. Sister Denise had given her Advil, double strength.

"In the *middle* of the month . . ." Nicola said. "Has that ever happened before?"

"Uh-uh."

"So it's the lifestyle in Sin City, kid." Nicola straight-

ened up and looked around her to see who was in ear-
shot. "Sex is a natural urge, okay? It makes no difference
how many beads you count or how many times you kiss
the floor or Mother Superior's ass, it doesn't affect the
hormone production, you know? It goes on producing,
and the result is we come out in hives and gumboils and
panty rash—show me a nun with pimples and I'll show
you a nun that hasn't been putting a single finger on her
G-spot since she signed up as a saint, it stands to reason."

"I don't think that's my problem," Madlen said. She'd
never stopped giving herself relief when she felt like it
since she'd discovered the trick. "I think it's something
else."

Nicola tossed another mushroom into the basket and
then snatched it out again. "Oh, Jesus, this one's got a
hymen." She dropped it onto the grass and put her foot
on it like Sister Rose had done. "You think it's something else? Like what?"

"I don't know," Madlen said. She wanted to change
the subject, because it worried her. It wasn't just the
cramps and the fever—this time it had left her feeling
weird. "So how's Gorgeous Giovanni?" Nicola had said
she'd been talking to him.

"Gorgeous Giovanni is a real guy. You know?"

"Real?" Madlen straightened up and wiped her face,
and the bare winter trees took a little time to steady.

Nicola looked around her again. "Tell you a funny
story, okay? For your little ears only." Her eyes had gone
dark, and the gold lights were in them. "The first time I
ever met a priest was in the vestry at the Church of St.
Patrick's in the Bowery. I was seven years old, and he'd
asked me to bring some stuff in there for him—there'd
been a harvest festival. It was also the first time I'd ever
seen a penis, because that was what he kindly showed me,
and if I'd been a bit older I might have been interested, but
the way I saw it was that he must be another Elephant

Man—I'd seen the movie—and that was where he kept his
trunk. It scared the living daylights out of me and I went
running down the street screaming blue murder, and
when I told my Mom what had happened, my Dad and
my two brothers went round to the church and they beat
that poor schmuck into Jell-O, and when he came out of
the hospital we never saw him again, and at that tender
age I kind of thought he'd been seized by the hand of God
and dumped into a heavenly trash bin or something."

Madlen had found a tree to lean on, and closed her
eyes, her face tilted upward against the sky.

"You all right?" Nicola asked her.

"Sure. I'm just listening."

"Well, it really impressed me, how much damage I did
to that guy, indirectly, and me just a kid. I felt *power*, you
know? But I still didn't think he'd paid enough for the
shock he'd given me, and I made up my mind that one
day when I met another priest I'd use my power to get my
own back, and when I was older I knew the right word
for it. The word was 'destroy.' I would destroy him." She
dropped another handful of mushrooms into the basket.
"This thing's full."

Madlen felt the weight of the sky against her closed
lids, and the strength of the young slender tree between
her shoulder blades. She wished she could take Nicola
into her confidence too, but it would hurt too much to
say, to hear herself say it. "That's why you told us you
were going to love Father Giovanni to death?"

"That's why. I was going to work him up to the pitch
where he couldn't resist me anymore—I've done that to
guys, I can do it—and when I'd made him break his holy
vows and desecrate his vocation and spit in the face of his
precious Christ and all that good stuff, I would have
gotten him run out of the convent of the Sisters of the
Sacred Light so fast he wouldn't have had time to pull his
pants up."

Madlen heard Nicola's shoes moving through the wet grass, and in a moment smelled the earthy smell of the mushrooms in the basket. Nicola's voice was low and close when she said, "But I don't want to do that anymore. Because, like I say, he's for real."

"How did you find out?"

"That he's for real?"

"Yeah."

"Oh, we—we talked in his office a while ago. There's something I need to get off of my back, and I know he can help me with it. Of course, he's going to bring Christ in on it, but who knows? Whatever works."

"What kind of thing?" Madlen asked her. "But don't say, if you don't want." She had something she wanted to get off of her back too.

In a moment Nicola said, "I need to grieve. I need to grieve, real bad."

Madlen opened her eyes. "I'm sorry."

"So far, I haven't let myself. I'm scared. I've seen people grieving, screaming and hollering and tearing their hair, goes on for days—you know? And it doesn't look like a whole lot of fun. But maybe the blessed Father can help me through it, and he can bring Christ along for the ride if he has to." She watched Madlen's pale set face for a moment. "You look like shit, baby, you know that? Why don't I take you back inside? Then Deb can look after you."

"No."

Nicola played that one word over again and listened harder, but still couldn't quite get the tone. "You don't want Deb to look after you?"

Madlen wasn't looking at her, just looking at nothing, at space. "I'd be tempted to talk to her," she said, "the way I'm feeling right now. And I don't want her worried, more than she is already."

Nicola was still trying to find the channel. "Tempted to

talk to her about what? Don't want her worried about what? I mean, are we going to have a conversation?" It looked like this kid needed help, *both* of them needed help. She remembered what Giovanni had told her; she thought of it every day: "So what I want you to do, my friend, is to keep an eye on those two. If there are any more wild escapades planned, I want to know. And in time."

But this didn't sound like wild escapades. It sounded more serious than that.

"Look," Nicola said, "any time you want to get *anything* off your back, I'll pick up on the first ring."

"I know."

But it would be so hard to say.

She didn't move away from the tree; she needed to feel its strength against her, its security. She'd heard of a farmer, once, who went out first thing every morning and leaned against a giant oak, letting its vibrations flow into him to give him the strength he needed for the day.

Nicola didn't move either. She just stood there watching Madlen, not saying anything, still trying to tune in to her vibes, because she sensed there was something more that needed to get said.

In a little while Madlen turned her head against the trunk of the tree and looked at her through half-closed lids, her face white in the winter sunshine. "That's just one of the things going on, Nicky."

"Okay."

"The worst of them is—is a problem I have with my sister. With Debra."

Another leaf came floating from a limb above their heads, spinning in silence and leaving a trace of gold in the memory, the air so quiet that they heard it touch the others on the grass when it landed.

Nicola waited.

"She thinks I'm trying to kill her," Madlen said.

17

"Bless us, O Lord, and these Thy gifts, which we are about to receive from Thy bounty, through Christ, our Lord."

"Amen."

Dead branches, gathered over the years from the woodland below the hill, to be chopped and stacked against the north wall of the convent, were burning in the fireplace of the Great Hall again tonight. Before Father Giovanni's time, Mother Superior had decreed that no fire should be lit until New Year's Day, but the priest had pointed out that Sister Denise was having to spend a fortune on chilblain ointment and eucalyptus oil for the indigent among the sisterhood, and the mention of finances had brought Mother Superior to a quick change of mind, which didn't surprise him. Firewood, after all, cost nothing.

Debra was sitting between two other novices—Sister Nadine and Sister Sylvia—at the "low" end of the table furthest from the hearth; it was held that the fires of youth were quite sufficient to keep their circulation going in wintertime. But mittens were permitted even at table, thanks to the intercession of Sister Denise.

Nicola was across from Debra on the other side of the long trestle table. Sister Carlissa, Mistress of Novices, made it her business to note the development of incipient friendships among her charges and to discourage it by separating those in question whenever she could; service to God demanded the eradication of individuality and communion with others, and if any felt the need for friendship then they had only to befriend the Lord. In the case of natural sisters there was more tolerance, and a double cell apportioned them if they so wished.

At the "high" end of the middle table, Mother Superior raised her fork as a signal that the meal could begin. Those whose vision was blocked by their neighbors waited for the sudden rattling of silverware on china. At the extreme "low" end of the novices' table were the penitents, kneeling to their meal.

Madlen wasn't among these, though she'd been heard breaking Profound Silence before breakfast today. Given a choice, she'd elected the chore of serving at table, together with six other penitents, and eating last. But tonight she felt almost herself again, and thought it might be partly because she'd been able to screw up her courage and take Nicola into her confidence this morning when they'd been picking mushrooms.

Nicola had been quiet for a minute, just watching her with her dark eyes very deep. Then she'd said, "She thinks you're trying to *kill* her? Oh, Jesus, this has to be quite a long story."

"Not really. I think she heard about sibling rivalry, that's all, when she was just a little kid, and it kind of got to her."

"She blew it up into some kind of monster?"

"Right. From then on she thought I was jealous of her, and doing things to hurt her." She told Nicola about Dad's car, and that time with the runaway horse. "She's got a lot of imagination, even worse than me. Then, when we were in our mid-teens, Mom broke the news that Debra was adopted, and I think that got to her too— made things worse. She started thinking I was secretly looking on her as a stranger, you know?"

In a moment Nicola asked, "And were you?"

"Of course not. We were so *close* by then."

"Still are," Nicola said. "Aren't you?"

"Of course. You can see that." She was glad now she'd taken the plunge and brought this whole thing out, because it had been locked up inside of her for so long. "But she's still scared of me, and that's so *terrible.*"

"How do you know?" Nicola asked. Her voice was very quiet.

"That she's scared of me?"

"That she thinks you're trying to kill her."

"I just *know.* Just by the way she looks at me, after one of these accidents—like with the horse? I mean, kids get into a whole lot of scrapes, don't they, when they're growing up together? Bloody knees, broken arms, teeth knocked out, you name it. But the difference is, Debra doesn't think they were accidents." Madlen tossed her head suddenly, as if she were trying to shake all the terrible thoughts out of it. "Can you imagine what it's like, Nicky, *living* with that? When all I feel for her is *love?*"

"No fun. So why don't you put it on the line with her?"

"Look," Madlen said, putting a hand on Nicola's folded arms, "there's a funny thing about being real close to someone." She gave a rueful little smile. "You're so close, you can't be open. The relationship's too sensitive. You mean I should tell Debra, 'Hey, you think I'm trying to kill you, but that's a lot of bullshit.' Jesus, I don't know how she'd handle that."

"You have to do it, kid," Nicola said. "You have to do it."

Madlen looked away through the trees, thinking how surrealistic the scene was, with the dark bare trees and the nuns in black, all of them bending over to touch the ground, like it was a new way of praying. Sister Rose was still sitting on her tree trunk, way in the distance.

"We're going to get punished," she said, "for talking instead of getting on with the job. Sister Rose is watching everyone."

"Fuck Sister Rose. You have to do it, Maddie. You have to straighten it all out with Deb."

Madlen looked at her, apprehension in her eyes. "I'm too scared. And you know what? I think she'd just deny it anyway; she'd say everything's fine."

"She's scared too."

"Right."

"Well, shit. Let me do it for you. For both of you."

Madlen shook her head. "If anyone's going to do it, it has to be me. But I don't want to give her that much hurt. It's such a—"

"Jesus Christ," Nicola said, "you're both so intent on not hurting each other you're both ripping each other's heart out."

"Yeah. I guess we are. So—" Madlen's hand brushed the air "—so one day I'll work up the courage."

Nicola turned away, watching the others for a while, seeing Sister Rose and feeling the rebellious itch to wave, turning back, looking at Madlen, seeing her eyes were wet. "Have you talked to anybody else?"

"No."

"Talk to Giovanni, then. This kind of thing is his field."

"I know. I've thought about it. He's real, like you say,

and I like him. But he's an authority figure, and this is so very personal. I could tell you because you're a friend."

"I'd like to help."

"I know. You're helping now. This is Confession, right? That always seems to lighten things up."

Nicola had picked up the basket of mushrooms. "I'm here for you," she said, "when you need me."

Sister Rose had taken the basket from them and checked every mushroom in it before she put them into her big canvas sack. She hadn't handed out fifty Hail Mary's to Madlen and Nicola for talking.

So tonight it was mushroom pie in the Great Hall, and after grace had been said a lot of the sisters silently thanked the Lord for Mother Superior's fondness for the home cooking that had produced, over the years, what were charitably thought of as her ample proportions. For some of them it was the only thing that made the cloistered and celibate life of the convent bearable: They ate well.

As Madlen hurried among the tables helping to serve supper, Nicola watched her sometimes, relieved to see the pallor of the morning had gone from her face, though nobody would say she looked at her ease, which was no big surprise.

Nicola watched Debra too, sitting almost opposite her at the table between Nadine and Sylvia. You couldn't ever tell what Deb was thinking, what she was feeling. Madlen threw things off more, acted them out, but the younger sister kept close to herself, and maybe that was the problem: She turned things over in her mind too much, with that imagination of hers, till they grew into something they weren't.

It must feel pretty bad, Nicola thought, living with someone who believed you were trying to kill them. But what was it like for Debra? Wasn't she living with the fear, day after day, of dying? Of being killed? It made no difference that it wasn't true: It was true for her.

"Nicky?"

Madlen was trying to put her plate down for her, but they were all sitting so close.

Nicola leaned sideways to make room. "Thanks, honey," she whispered. "Feeling okay?"

"Sure." Madlen hurried off again for more plates.

They were halfway through their supper at this particular table when Sister Nadine, sitting next to Debra, crouched over suddenly and clutched at her stomach, her young face squeezed in agony, and a hush fell as her moaning grew louder and she writhed on the bench, until Sister Denise was suddenly there with her arms around her, asking her what the problem was, but the young novice couldn't speak, could only moan, doubled over and locked into herself, rocking from side to side.

Sister Denise called to Madlen for saltwater, saying she must be quick, they needed to induce vomiting, but Nadine was unconscious before the saltwater arrived, and Nicola heard Sister Denise telling someone to call Emergency for an ambulance.

It was just after ten o'clock that night when Father Giovanni got back from the hospital and went straight to Mother Superior with the news that for his own good reasons the Lord had called Sister Nadine to his side.

"Lord, have mercy on us in this hour of our despair."

"Lord, have mercy."

"Give us, O Lord, Thy comfort, and lift up our sorrowful hearts."

"Give us, O Lord, Thy comfort."

They knelt in candlelight in the North Chapel, numbed in the chill of the early morning and by the news that Mother Superior had given them immediately after Mass.

Following the Special Prayer for their beloved Sister Nadine, those who felt the need for counseling were told to meet with Sister Denise in the novices' classroom behind the parlor. For many of the sisters, especially the younger ones, it was their first understanding of the nearness of death in life, and the sometimes mysterious working of God's will.

As the early light of day pooled in the windows of Father Giovanni's crowded little office, Sister Rose sat facing him in the carved oak chair, her black shawl over her habit and her face pale beneath the web of broken veins in her cheeks, her eyes wide with concern behind her glasses as she stared at the priest.

"So," Giovanni said wearily, "tell me your part of it, Rose."

She had asked to talk to him in private, immediately after Mass. He would have sent for her in any case, as she knew.

"The mushrooms were gathered in baskets, Father, as usual. I then put them from the baskets into a big canvas sack—again, as usual—when the harvesting was done. I'd warned everybody, beforehand, what to look for, and what to beware of. But I never just leave it at that. When they brought me their baskets, I checked every mushroom." Her plump body rocked forward in emphasis—"I checked *every single mushroom,* before I put it into the sack. As usual."

Giovanni shifted the little Rock of Ages paperweight on his desk. "This isn't the first mushroom hunt you'd supervised, Rose." He was putting off the dreaded question, and knew it, and excused himself. The night for him had been sleepless.

"I dare say it was the hundredth, Father." She sat watching him, never looking away, seldom blinking.

"So, when your sack arrived in the kitchen, it couldn't

have contained one single poisonous mushroom. Is that right?"

"That is right, Father. Not one."

"Who carried the sack home?"

"I did."

"Where did you put it?"

"Onto the shelf in the larder."

"Who else was there when you did that?"

"Sister Laura and Sister Valerie."

"Nobody else?"

"No."

Giovanni drew in a breath. There were dark patches under his eyes, Sister Rose noted. She felt for him. It had been a bad day, and a bad night.

"Laura and Valerie," he murmured. Two of the professed sisters, both splendid cooks and ardent defenders of their faith—nobody was allowed in their kitchen without good reason. There wouldn't have been anyone unauthorized hanging around the sack of mushrooms, then, after Rose had left. "Did they take charge of the sack right away, or was it just—"

"Sister Laura was opening it when I left. She said how good they looked." Rose's breath caught as she said it; Sister Nadine was—had been a sweet child, no more than nineteen, an orphan, without a bad thought in her head despite the fact that after her mother died her father was acquitted of her murder, and the next day shot himself. This convent had been the child's new home and haven.

"Then that closes any gaps," Giovanni said, and had to force his eyes to meet the sister's, unable to put off the question any longer. "So do you have any thoughts that might help?"

"I greatly fear I do, Father." Rose rocked herself forward again. "I know the poisonous mushrooms weren't in the sack. Sister Laura and Sister Valerie would have checked them again anyway—we none of us underestimate the danger here; in this state mushroom poisoning's not uncommon." She took a breath. "The bad mushrooms must have been put with the rest of them some time later."

In a moment Giovanni said, "You mean deliberately."

"I mean deliberately."

Rose watched him for a little time, and then sat back. In the stillness of the November morning they could hear the rooks calling among the elms below the hill, and a bucket clanging in the distance by the goat shed. In a moment Giovanni lifted himself like an old man from his chair.

"Would you like some coffee, Rose?"

"I would, Father. We've the day to get through, haven't we?"

"Quite a few days, Rose, quite a few." He went across to the stained and dented percolator.

"Let me help," Rose said.

She got out of the chair and found the coffee while Giovanni poured water into the percolator, thinking how outrageous it was that with the child Nadine already lying in the mortuary the smell of coffee could bring a breath of pleasure into their lives. Maybe not pleasure, then, but comfort, and that was permissible, God knew.

While they sat with their steaming mugs he asked Rose for the names of those who had been with her on the mushroom hunt, and she gave him a list, totaling fifteen.

Before she left him he said, "Death was certified at the hospital as having been caused by gross phalloidine toxicity. Nobody questioned, of course, that it was anything other than a tragic accident, though a routine report will go to the coroner's office." Giovanni's dark eyes rested on the sister's for a moment. "But in view of what you've told me, there'll have to be an inquiry, with Mother Superior and myself in charge. We may decide to ask the help of Bishop O'Brien, and possibly, at a later stage, the police."

"The police?" Sister Rose had been here at the convent for more than twenty years, and had come to consider it, as all the older professed sisters did, as their own private world, where judgment was to be rendered in the name of the Lord, there being none higher.

"On the one hand," Giovanni told her, "we have to protect the good name of the Sisters of the Sacred Light; on the other hand we must avoid the temptation of resorting to a cover-up."

Sister Rose looked down. "Whatever you do, Father, will be in accord with God's guidance."

When she had gone, pulling her shawl around her and managing to close the door without a sound, Giovanni sat at his desk doing nothing for a while, doing nothing and seeing nothing, but feeling the weight of the day already trying to bear him down. Looking back at a life that at the time had seemed difficult, harrowing, even dangerous, with knives drawn in the shadows where he'd walked at night, he now saw it had been easy compared with what he was called on to deal with now, in the ostensible seclusion and safety of an order devoted solely to the love of God.

Debra polished the tall silver candlestick on the altar.

So it had happened again.

There'd been another accident.

She could see her reflection in the rounded silver stem, looking terribly young, her cheeks fat like a child's, like an angel's.

What was it like to be an angel?

It had been a mistake, of course. They'd been meant for her, the mushrooms, *those* mushrooms. She should be in the mortuary now, instead of Nadine, lying on her back like a wax figure with her hands folded across her chest and her eyes closed, not smelling the horrible chemical smell she'd heard about in those places, not seeing anything or hearing anything or thinking anything, just a cold wax figure, not feeling the cold.

What was it like to be Nadine?

What was it like to be dead?

It was like that.

It was a cold silent nothingness, made of wax.

18

"I don't like to think about it."

The rake left claw marks through the soft earth, its tines rolling the leaves in a rustling wave toward the pile.

"You don't have to," Debra said.

Smoke curled upward in a blue-gray rope from the bonfire, scenting the air with winter.

Madlen began shaking again, shaking all over, leaning on the rake for support, her face white and her eyes shut and her teeth clenched to stop them chattering. Debra went over, putting an arm around her.

"It's okay," she said. "I'm still here." It hurt to see Madlen like this.

"I know," Madlen said through her teeth, "I know. You're still here, thanks to Christ's mercy." She'd been saying things like that, Debra had noticed, in the past week or two, using Christ's name like she really meant it, not making fun or being "theatrical." "But it was so terribly *close* . . . I could have put that plate down in front of *you,* right next to Nadine. . . ."

The rooks called among the elms, their cries raucous in the steel-gray stillness of the air.

"But you didn't," Debra said, feeling her sister's body shaking so hard she couldn't stop. "I'm like a cat, you know? Nine lives."

Madlen clung onto her, her eyes squeezed shut, tears creeping from their lashes onto her cheeks. Debra had never seen her like this before; she'd been crushed with guilt after Debra had been found in the bell tower that time, but not as bad as this. Maybe it was because somebody had actually died. Poor Nadine.

"I might not have been standing here now," Madlen said, "holding you like this. I would've been on the phone, calling Mom, telling her to come as soon as she could because something . . . oh, Jesus, Jesus Christ. . . ."

"Don't *dramatize,*" Debra said. "It wasn't your fault, anyway, with the mushrooms. They got in there by—by accident."

The smoke curled and twisted from the glowing nest of fire among the leaves.

They didn't. They were meant for you.

Debra caught her breath, hearing the voice. She'd heard it before—it was just her thoughts talking, she knew that, but they were the thoughts she didn't dare think out loud in her mind, because they scared her.

"You think it was by accident?" Madlen was asking her.

"Sure," Debra said, like she was reciting something. "Nobody would do a thing like that on purpose. Would they?" She pressed her sister close, to make it sound true.

"I don't know," Madlen said, and for the first time heard a note of despair in her voice. "I don't know."

Also for the first time, she felt today the onset of what she could only imagine was a migraine.

* * *

Lying in her hard, narrow bed that night, Debra watched the candlelight through the open transom above the door, scratching the palms of her hands where the skin was still healing. She'd slept for a while and then something had wakened her—the squeaky shoes, she believed, of the guardian as she crept past on her rounds, listening for anyone talking in their cells; even whispering was breaking Profound Silence.

It had taken Debra a long time to get to sleep, because it had really hurt her to see Madlen like that today when they'd been raking the leaves, and to feel her body shaking in her arms. She hadn't been acting, Debra knew that. Sure, Madlen was great on the stage, but in real life she was straight up, and never pretended.

So what was really going on?

There was only one answer.

Madlen stirred in her bed, and her sister looked across at her. Maybe she was finding it hard to go to sleep too—was still dramatizing in her mind the thing about the mushrooms, that Debra could have died, instead of Nadine.

There was only one answer, yes. If Madlen had been doing these terrible things, all along—

Trying to kill you—

Okay, trying to kill me—if she'd been doing that, she didn't remember it, afterward, did she? Every time it happened, she must have what Sister Denise called retro—retro-something amnesia. Loss of memory, like Debra herself had pretended to have after they'd found her in the bell tower.

She lay watching the flickering light of the candle, and the way the shadows in the cell moved to and fro, like half-seen people in cloaks coming at her through the walls. It was scary, and she stopped thinking of it that way—it was just a candle, that was all, out there in the passage.

Loss of memory, then, or Madlen wouldn't feel so terribly upset about it afterward, genuinely and terribly upset.

"You okay?"

Debra's scalp tightened at the sound of her sister's voice in the quietness.

"Sure." Madlen must have been awake, watching her, catching the glint of her eyes in the candlelight.

"Can't you sleep?"

"Something woke me," Debra said, "just for a minute."

"The guardian?"

"I guess."

"I heard her too. Sister Janine's on tonight. She has squeaky shoes."

Turning her head, Debra saw that her sister was leaning on one elbow, watching her in the gloom.

"Yeah," Debra said.

"So go to sleep, sweetheart. No thinking."

"No what?"

"Thinking. You know? About Nadine, or anything."

"No."

"It didn't happen." Debra could hear her sister's voice trembling now. "I—I mean it didn't happen to *you.*"

"I know. But poor Nadine. She didn't deserve—"

"I'm sorry for Nadine—" and suddenly there was a rustle of sheets and Madlen was leaning over her, and Debra felt a tear splash onto her face "—but if it had happened to you, sweetheart, I would've died too. I mean that." Debra felt a kiss on her forehead, where the tear had fallen, and then her sister was back in her bed, saying, "So we mustn't think about it, okay?"

"Okay." Debra could hear Madlen rubbing her legs under the bedclothes. "God, it's freezing tonight! Are you warm enough, Debbie?"

"I'm fine. And thank you for coming to see me."

"I'd go a million miles."

19

"You're not, I hope," said Bishop O'Brien, "opening that especially for me."

Father Giovanni had taken the bottle of bourbon from a drawer of his cluttered desk, and was peeling away the lead foil. "I tried everywhere for Irish malt, without any luck. I hope this is acceptable?"

"I accept anything from the grain or the grape. Bourbon is handsome—" he lifted a wide, fleshy hand "—but not just for—"

"I'm going to join you," Giovanni said, and pulled the cork.

Ensconced in the huge carved chair with his feet on the edge of Giovanni's desk—"I hope you don't mind," he'd asked him—O'Brien watched the lean, muscled face of the priest from the Bronx, which today looked strained, hollowed from loss of sleep. The telephone call had been brief and cryptic—Johnny needed to talk to him, and had asked when he could come to the bishop's house on the edge of town. But after two hours of struggling with the fallout from the National Conference of Catholic Bishops at the University of Notre Dame in the summer, O'Brien felt the need of a run out somewhere, and had climbed into his vintage Volvo.

"Cheers," Giovanni said, and lifted his tumbler.

"Amen."

Faintly through the wall they could hear the convent choir rehearsing the *Messiah*.

"You didn't see Mother Superior," Giovanni asked, "on your way in?"

"No." Was this the problem, then?

"But you'll see her before you go?"

"Courtesy demands it."

"She needs to talk to you as urgently as I do," Giovanni said, and took another swig of bourbon. They would have seen the bishop together, in the ordinary way, but Giovanni wouldn't have managed to get a word in.

"As 'urgently,' " the bishop prompted him.

Giovanni put his glass down on a pile of ecclesiastical reports; he didn't often take a drink, and this stuff was already going to his head via an empty stomach. "We lost one of our sisters, Bishop, the night before last. A young novice. From mushroom poisoning."

O'Brien took his feet off the desk and sat up straight. "May God keep her soul."

"Amen." Giovanni found himself leaning with his back to the wall, as if he felt the need of its support. "I didn't call you until I'd got all the facts I could. They are these."

Ten minutes later the bishop was also on his feet, prowling between the stained and battered coffee machine and the lopsided filing-cabinet, avoiding the plaid slippers poking from beneath the desk. He was on his second glass of bourbon, though the priest hadn't touched his own again.

"So how much can we rely," O'Brien asked, "on the testimony of Sister Rose?"

"That's the problem. Without her testimony, it would have been put down as a tragic accident."

The bishop stopped pacing and looked at Giovanni. "*Could* have been put down," he said carefully.

The notes of the *Messiah* rose in faint crescendo through the wall, sounding as if someone had left a stereo switched on in another room.

Giovanni didn't answer. His bishop had jumped ahead of things right away, versed as he was in the politics of the church.

"*Could* have been put down as an accident," he said again. "That's why we need to know for *certain* whether the word of Sister Rose is reliable."

Giovanni felt the stones of the wall cold against his shoulder blades, but didn't move; he also felt their strength. There were times when a man, even a man of God, had to reach out for support more palpable than even the presence of the Almighty. "I would take the word of Sister Rose," he told the bishop, "as I would take yours."

O'Brien turned away, gazing through the window at the mill beyond the elms. "We shouldn't overestimate the worth of my word, Johnny, or anyone else's. He who tells the truth in this world should keep one foot in the stirrup."

"I know this sister well enough," Giovanni said carefully, "to assure you that if we tried to cast doubts on her word, she'd be unshakable."

"Good enough. We need to know where we stand. But of course the testimony of one witness alone could never make a case for the prosecution. I speak metaphorically. You've not finished your inquiries, right?"

"No."

O'Brien rested his heavy arms along the back of the chair, and Giovanni noticed how like a bull the man seemed, short-necked and massive-shouldered, his strong head tilted upward a little as if to face a challenge. "Any suspects?" he asked the priest.

"Not really. Sister Nadine was well liked, a quiet girl with some trauma in her life we were helping her to deal with quite well."

"The last person anyone would want to poison."

"The very last."

"So we have to ask ourselves who *could* have done such a thing, with malice aforethought, whether they were fond of Sister Nadine or not. Who could have, in fact, simply introduced those mushrooms into the meal that night with a view to poisoning *somebody*. Any-body."

"That's been in my thoughts too—that it could have been a random act."

"Of an unbalanced mind."

"Right."

"And?" O'Brien watched him with his head thrust forward.

"There are three or four sisters here," Giovanni said reluctantly, "who could be described as special cases. One has a harelip, and in the middle of a nervous break-down she once screamed that she'd come to the convent when she heard there were no mirrors here."

"Not uncommon," the bishop sighed. "A variation of anorexia. Was Sister Nadine pretty?"

"Not exceptionally. And in these cases the one who thinks of herself as disfigured often seeks out attractive friends. All I'm saying is that this one might be feeling the urge for revenge on society. We've got quite a few women here who've escaped from the rational world because they're . . . irrational."

"That's par for the course too." The bishop turned and faced his priest directly, one arm now hooked over the back of the chair. "And you've talked to them?"

"Not yet. There hasn't been time."

O'Brien locked his thick fingers together and studied them for a moment, the facets of his three jeweled rings catching the light. "So we have two issues to resolve. One concerns Sister Rachel, who—"

"Rachel?"

"The one who supervised the mushroom picking?"

"Rose."

"Rose, then. You're obviously satisfied with her integrity, so I accept that when that sack of mushrooms was put into the kitchen it contained no poisonous ones. But they could have found their way into the cooking process by other means, accidentally. Anyone could have picked them at some other time, taking a trip on their own and bringing them back, not recognizing them for what they were. So the first thing we have to do, quite clearly, is to tell the kitchen staff that mushrooms, henceforth, are strictly off the menu at this convent. Forever."

"I've already done that."

"Well and good. The major issue concerns the police: should we call them in at this stage? I don't think so— and you know why."

Giovanni had to think for a moment, had to think politically, like a bishop. "You mean the repercussions. . . ."

"Let's talk turkey. This convent would have to close."

The music of the *Messiah* came back to fill the silence.

"It'd be as bad as that?" Giovanni asked.

"I rather think so. As it is, its economies are such that you can't afford to lose the bounty coming in from the wealthier relatives—especially parents—of the sisters here, and I can guarantee that more than a few of the younger ones would be hauled out of the place by their parents or guardians once they heard the police had been called in to investigate a case of suspected homicide. We have to remember that some of these younger women were brought here for their peace of mind and safety—or came here of their own accord for the same reason, as refugees, if you will, from the wicked world outside." He shrugged his massive shoulders. "There are plenty of other orders and other convents around who'd be happy to take these people in, together with their dowries. Have you talked to this poor girl's parents yet? Sister Nadine's?"

"Her mother was murdered, and her father killed himself just after he was acquitted. She's from a foster home."

"No problem there, then."

Giovanni turned away, not wanting O'Brien to see the disgust in his eyes. "No, Bishop, there's no problem there. But right now I'm more concerned with the welfare of the sisters here in our care than with the future of the convent."

"As indeed you should be, and you have my blessing." Bishop O'Brien looked at his watch. "I'm glad you called on me for support, Johnny. You may rest assured you will always have it. Now, let me leave you with my opinion to mull over. I think it would be a disservice to the Sisters of the Sacred Light—and to the Mother Superior here and her staff—for us to call in the police on a matter which seems likely to be either completely accidental or the tragic result of some ill-considered prank on the part of someone suffering from mental aberration. In either case a man with your track record should surely be able to get to the bottom of it in short order, and incidentally—despite your understandable lack of interest at the moment—save this convent from extinction." He tugged at his topcoat and buttoned it. "I have every faith in you, as I'm sure you know. You're the soldier in the field, and this is the battleground. So fight the good fight, Johnny, in the name of the Lord."

"I gotta have another hit, Johnny. . . ."

"No."

He'd been telling her that for an hour now. This one he was going to save.

He'd been in the Bronx three weeks already, working the streets and working them at night, and so far he hadn't saved a single goddamned one of these kids.

"Get me another hit, Johnny, for Christ's sake. . . ."

"No."

He pulled his arms tighter around her. They were lying together on the floor of a room high up in a condemned tenement, been lying there on the bare boards for a long time, ever since she'd crashed, writhing and screaming and hitting out as he'd come for her, then collapsing suddenly, going limp, so he'd thought she'd died on him like Sugarplum, the little black kid, had done a couple of nights back, his huge eyes rolling in the acid glow of the street lamp and his body going limp, just like this.

"You okay?" he whispered to Jenny.

"Gimme a fucking hit."

Jenny . . . a name that made you think of wildflowers and chintz curtains and the smell of baking bread. Fourteen years old and shot to hell with the promise of the virus in her after selling herself up and down the street for the price of another hit.

The rank river smell was coming in waves through the holes in the wall where the windows had been, drifting on the stifling heat of the night, strong enough in itself to make him puke without anything else going on—she'd pissed in her pants, Jenny, God knew when or how many times, and she wasn't going to stop; that stuff she'd been hitting was a diuretic apart from more exotic things, and she didn't know she was doing it anyway.

"For Christ's sake—" she was sobbing again now "—get me another fucking hit, you *bastard*."

"No."

But it took an awful lot of saying. All she could think of was getting out of hell, and all he could say was no.

She was like a stick in his arms, a stick with rags on, and stinking of herself, her filthy hair against his face, her knees—they weren't knees, they were just bones—her bones sticking into him, her shoulder blades like a skeleton's under his hands. She could be playing possum, limp like this, trying to get him off his guard and then wrench herself away and go crashing down the stairs and into the street to offer what was left of herself for the price of another ticket for the slab.

Then she began kicking. "They kick a lot," Doc Finklestein had said in the crowded, blood-spattered emergency room at three in the morning a week ago when Giovanni had taken a kid there. "We have to restrain them," the Doc had said, his tone apologetic, his red eyes losing focus from lack of sleep as he buckled the straps and the kid spat in his face.

"Stop that," Giovanni told the girl in his arms. "You a horse, for Christ's sake?"

But she went on kicking until it exhausted her. "Wanna fuck me, Johnny?" she whispered. "Fuck me for a hit?"

"You're under age." A thousand and fourteen years old and still in her teens.

"If you can give them enough of your time," Doc Finklestein had said, "while they're going through the withdrawal stage, it can often help them deal with it. Enough of your time, enough of your attention."

"Enough of my devotion?"

"Even some of that can help," the Doc had said. But Giovanni knew by the faint smile what the man was thinking: Give this eager young saint just a few more months of life on streets like these and he'll start worrying about how to get the shit off his halo.

When the kicking was over, Jennifer slept for a time while the tugs hooted on the river and the smell of the city lay over them in the heat of the empty room and the rats ran riot along the walls, one of them starting to take exploratory nibbles at Giovanni's ankle until he kicked out and heard it thud against the wall, squealing.

He tried to get a little sleep too, but now she went wild again, and this time it lasted for an hour or more while he held on tight and talked to her and sometimes had to slap her face to get her attention, and some time before dawn she became still again, and in the aura of her rag-and-bone body he felt a quiescence that told him they'd made it through the night, and he picked her up and carried her down the stairs and through the street to the hospital while she defecated on him, her small hollowed face turned to the night sky and her mouth open like an angel singing.

"Well, well," said the medic in Emergency, pretending surprise. "What have we here?"

"What we have here," Giovanni said, "is a soul with the remains of a body attached that needs fixing. Are you any good at that?"

"We're even better." The medic took the girl in his arms, looking at Giovanni over his glasses. "Now go get some sleep, padre, or you'll be keeling over right here on the floor and getting in our way."

Giovanni often found himself thinking back on his stint in the Bronx as an eager young savior of souls, wondering if he'd really done any good, had really managed to save any worth saving, or had simply delayed those kids for a while on their chosen way to the trash heap. But sometimes he decided that yeah, he'd put up a fight for them, win or lose, and that had to be what counted.

But it had been a different kind of fight than the one he was engaged in now, because here among the Sisters of the Sacred Light he was confronted with the insubstantial figments of the mind within the mind that conjured shadows of suspicion, heard whispers in the dark along the endless corridors of night as dream followed dream in surrealistic procession, fading with each new dawn.

For a fight like this one, to be waged on the fragile, ultrasensitive terrain of the human mind, he would need to choose his weapons with the most exquisite care.

20

"Hello."

Just a whisper.

The flame of the candle flickered between them in the draft.

"Hello," Cathy whispered back.

Her eyes were smiling.

Madlen knelt on the bare boards, in the position that had become so familiar since she'd entered the Convent of the Sisters of the Sacred Light. Her knees were used to it: They'd developed calluses, but in this position, at this moment, she didn't feel like she was praying.

She was just visiting Cathy.

But then, maybe that was a bit like praying—praying for her to come home again.

Cathy watched her, with mostly her face showing, her face and the pink woolen gloves, the black ski suit lost in the shadows.

"It didn't work," Madlen told her, and felt the migraine begin throbbing as she said it. "The thing with the mushrooms." She was getting used to them, the migraines, but that didn't mean they were any fun. Sometimes they made her sick to her stomach, and Sister Denise had started worrying.

"Oh," Cathy whispered.

In the silence they heard the call of a long-eared owl through the gaps in the roof tiles. Madlen liked that. She liked Cathy to hear what she heard when they were together, didn't want her to feel isolated up here; they were sharing the voice of the owl, and that was nice.

Madlen never went right up close to Cathy. Even years ago when she'd seen her in the street that day and brought her home, she'd always stayed a little distance from her, because this wasn't Cathy herself, her real sister, this was the channel, the medium they could speak through, smiling in the shadows. When the real Cathy came home at last she wouldn't just stand there in her ski suit; she'd wave from the distance and they'd run toward each other like the wind and come together in a huge enormous hug they'd hardly ever get out of again, or want to.

"I'll try again," Madlen said, "of course."

Cathy didn't say anything. That was okay, she didn't always have to say things.

"I'll go on trying," Madlen told her, "till I succeed." She said this with such intensity that her head started throbbing real bad, and she put a hand up, pressing hard and rocking her head like she'd learned to do, because it seemed to help, though not much: It never stopped the throbbing, the hammering, it just let her manage to bear with it.

She'd always told Cathy everything, even about what had happened before she'd seen her in the street and brought her home.

About Debra's face under the water in the bathtub as she

*pushed her down and let her up again, squealing and
squealing, at first with laughter and then not with laughter,
squealing and then just bubbling, her eyes staring up from
the water, staring wider and wider with her mouth open and
her lips peeled back and her neck stretched and her hands
on Madlen's arms trying to tug herself upward out of the
water till Mommy came in to see what was going on.*

*And about getting out of Dad's car and going round to
the back and pushing against the cold shiny chrome, pushing and pushing and not moving it until suddenly the car
started rolling down the slope and she watched it getting
smaller and smaller with Debra inside and then there was
the sudden blaring of the horns from the street and the huge
fiery feeling inside of her bursting out as she saw the other
car crash into Dad's and roll it over with bits of metal
flying off and flashing in the sunshine and she ran around
the house and dragged open the door of the woodshed and
flung herself in there and slammed the door shut and
laughed and laughed till it became crying and she knew
she'd done something so wicked that God would strike her
dead for it even though the stranger had gone now and that
was what she'd wanted.*

The owl called again through the tiles.

But of course the stranger hadn't gone after all. And
still it wasn't working. She was still here, keeping her real
sister away.

I'm not going to have a jealous little girl—

But Mom had never understood.

"She never understood," Madlen said.

In a moment Cathy answered, "Oh," from the shadows, smiling.

Mom was a bitch.

Madlen had hidden the toys and the toothbrush and
things because the stranger didn't have any right to them,
that was all, they were her real sister's, and all she wanted
to do was keep them safe for her till she came back.

"I was keeping them for you," she said, rocking her head in her hands.

"Oh."

She'd have to see Sister Denise again, tell her the migraines were getting worse. Sister Denise had said she'd take her to see Dr. Grant in the town if they weren't better by tomorrow.

"There's something wrong with me," she heard herself saying as she rocked her head backward and forward, tears creeping on her face as she squeezed her eyes against the pain. It was cold in here, but because of the pain she didn't even feel it; she was just a block of ice tilting backward and forward in the candlelight, the migraine drumming and drumming like a hammer trying to break open her head and let something out, whatever it was inside there that was so dreadfully wrong with her. "There's something wrong with me," she moaned softly again in the silence, in the loneliness.

"Oh," she heard Cathy say from the shadows.

The tears came scalding now, from the pain and also from the fierceness of her frustration.

"I want you back," she cried in the silence, *"I want you back, Cathy!"*

Backward and forward, the tears streaming.

The candle began flickering to a draft.

"Oh."

"Cathy . . . Cathy . . ." the pain blinding, *"I want you to come home again . . . I miss you so much!"*

The flame of the candle flickered again, and went out.

"Oh."

Father Giovanni climbed the narrow flight of stairs to the passage that ran north-south along one side of the building, a passage that had served at one time as access to storage rooms, dormers, and garrets, as he'd discovered soon after coming here when he'd thoroughly explored the entire place.

But a few moments ago when he was passing along the corridor below, he thought he heard a cry from somewhere higher, and had taken it for a night bird, but then it had come again, and he changed his mind: There seemed to be words to the sound, however unintelligible.

There should be no one there at this hour, during Vespers—or at any other time. Mother Superior had told him she'd thought of having the abandoned rooms cleaned out regularly when she'd taken charge of the convent—but for what purpose? Let the owls roost there in peace. Giovanni had agreed; ancient buildings had shadowed corners asking to be left alone, affording space for the past to brood.

As he reached the passage under the roof Giovanni saw a figure coming toward him carrying a candle, its shadow thrown behind, and the hairs rose at the back of his neck. His mind was prey these days to thoughts of the unnatural, following Sister Nadine's death.

"Who is that?" he asked softly.

The figure came on, unhearing, and he waited, seeing now by the veil that it was a novice, her eyes so blinded by the candle's flame that she hadn't seen him yet.

Then when she was closer still he recognized her. Softly again, so as not to startle her—"Sister Madlen?"

The candlestick wobbled, then was held away from her as she stared along the passage.

"Yes?"

It sounded almost as if she'd been expecting him—or someone. "Father Giovanni," he said quietly.

She stared at him for a moment, the sheen of dried tears on her cheeks, her face bloodless, and as she swayed suddenly he caught her and held her close, feeling at once how cold she was.

"I—I thought I heard something up here," she said,

her voice strained, "a bird fluttering, maybe trapped . . . I came up to look."

Quietly Giovanni asked, "And did you find it?"

"No. But I looked all over. And then another migraine started." He saw that her eyes were closed, squeezed tight. "It's pretty bad."

Father Giovanni led her down the narrow stairs, not asking her anything more but leaving her in peace. In the sick room he asked the nun on duty to look after her, and sent for Sister Denise.

And then, climbing again to the passage under the roof, needing to know why the child Madlen had really come here, he went from room to room until he found the one where the smell of candle-smoke still lingered, and there he moved around with his flashlight, finding nothing until he pulled aside a rough curtain of sackcloth and looked into the eyes of the mannequin.

"How many Eves are there in the history of mankind?"

Sister Carlissa waited, looking from one to another of her class.

"Two, Sister Carlissa," little Patrice said.

"Right. But since you've been the first to answer the last three questions," the Mistress of Novices told her, "I'd like you to leave the next three to someone else. But that's good, Sister Patrice, very good." She ran her gaze along the two rows of novices. "All right, what is the difference between the two Eves?"

Madlen found her mind was blank as she sat there on the hard wooden bench, though she'd been studying the Novena for weeks. Her head was still aching.

Debra just plain didn't know.

The morning silence smelled of floor wax and the mustiness of the dry rot in the ceiling beams.

"Sister Nicola?" the Mistress of Novices said.

"I pass."

Nicola had slept badly.

"Can't you even take a guess?"

Nicola shook her head, wise to this bitch's tactics:
When you were invited to take a guess you'd invariably
get it completely wrong, and that gave Carlissa the
chance to make you look an idiot.

"The first one was called Eve," somebody said, "by
God himself, when he made his first daughter. The second one was called Ave Maria, when God's messenger
told her how deeply beloved she was by God and his
Son."

Nicola, in the back row, glanced across at Madlen and
Debra sometimes, though she couldn't see much of their
faces because of their veils. She'd slept badly because
some time in the night the guardian's squeaky shoes had
woken her up, and it had been so cold she'd pulled the
thin hessian rug off the floor and draped it across the bed
on top of the comforter, and then lain there thinking for
a time.

There'd been something on her mind, ever since she'd
seen that poor kid Nadine go down like that at the supper
table, three nights ago now. It was something that had
kind of stolen up on Nicola, like a slow replay of the
scene that had seemed to go so fast at the time, with
everything happening at once.

Giovanni had questioned all of them who'd been anywhere near Nadine, and they'd all said the people who'd
been serving that particular table were Joanne, Madlen,
and Louise, because they'd been doing penance for
breaking Profound Silence, but it hadn't thrown any
light on things because the servers had taken the plates
from the same place in the kitchen, right next to the
ovens where they were keeping hot. Nobody, they all
agreed, had slipped an extra plate in the line anywhere.

But, lying sleepless in her cell last night, Nicola had
run through the replay again, and started worrying. The

thing was, when Madlen had brought two of the steaming dishes to the table for the next in line, and was going to put the first one down in front of Debra, she'd changed her mind and put it down in front of Nadine instead, giving the second one to her sister.

Why?

Or maybe she hadn't changed her mind at all—it had just looked like that. Deb had been in front of her on her right, and the first plate was in Madlen's right hand, so it was kind of awkward for her, having to reach over Deb's left shoulder, so she'd put the plate down in front of Nadine, on her left, and given the second one to her sister. Sure, it could have been simply that. Nicola had done a stint as a waitress in her final school year, and had spilled a whole lot of soup before she'd got her act worked out.

"Sister Nicola, uncross your legs."

Shit.

"I shan't tell you again."

"Okay."

Now just shuddup, and let me think.

So that was all it was, right? Madlen hadn't changed her mind at all. She was just imagining things, and that was too damned easy in this place. It was because of what Madlen had told her about Deb that had started her thinking about the scene at the supper table.

She thinks I'm trying to kill her.

That was what had got Nicola's imagination going.

But it was okay, wasn't it?

Or was it more than just her imagination? Was it something so terrible she didn't want to think about it, hadn't let herself think about it clearly until now?

Okay. Face it.

Bite the bullet.

If Madlen had known she had a plate of poisoned mushrooms in her hand, meant for Debra, she might

have got them mixed up in her mind at the last minute
and forgotten which was which. And had to make a
guess. And got it wrong. And put the loaded one down
in front of Nadine.

Oh Jesus Christ Almighty.

Got them mixed up at the last minute because her
nerves were going off like fireworks, she was just about to
kill her sister and things weren't normal, were they, you
could clean forget which plate was which because you
were going to commit a *murder* right at this very minute
and you couldn't—oh Jesus Christ—couldn't think
straight.

Bite the bullet. Bite down hard.

She felt herself rocking on the bench, back and forth,
just a little, just a slight motion, back and forth, her
hands gripping each other on her lap, suddenly cold, ice
cold, her eyes closed so she could watch the plates right
there in front of her, the first one moving to the right,
then swerving, moving to the left, where little Nadine sat,
hungry in her little tum, waiting for the yum-yum mushrooms.

She thinks I'm trying to kill her.

Nicola opened her eyes and turned her head an inch
and looked down at Madlen in the front row, seeing only
a bit of her face because of the veil, just the smooth
rounded cheek of a young girl, rosy in the cold.

Madlen, I have a question for you.

She thinks I'm trying to kill her.

I have a question.

Are you?

21

"Who is it?"

The knocking came again. Maybe he hadn't called out loud enough.

"Who is it?"

The time on the digital bedside clock was midnight plus five.

A soft voice came. "Nicola."

Giovanni got out of bed, shoved his bare feet into his slippers and went to open the door.

"Come on in," he whispered, and stood back.

There was a glow in the room, reflected from the lights of the town by low cloud; he saw that she wasn't wearing her veil, and that her black hair had started growing again in short curls, making her look boyish. It was the first time in two years he'd seen anyone bareheaded in the convent; it looked in a way grotesque, in a way natural and free, breathtaking.

"I wanted to come to you as a woman," she said softly.

Giovanni closed the door, turning the big iron key. "You look beautiful like that," he said. "Did you always wear it short?"

She came close to him, and he took her in his arms, because she was asking him to; he didn't want to leave her just standing there, so close, ignored. "No." She gave a soft little laugh. "I wore it long, right down my back. And sometimes piled high."

"With a Spanish comb and a carnation."

"You got the picture, Johnny. You could have run your fingers through it, like through a warm waterfall. It would've driven you crazy. It drove a lot of guys crazy." She gave a shiver, a big one. She didn't lift her face to his. He was waiting for her to do that.

"I can imagine," he said. He thought how wonderful she smelled.

In a moment she said, "I couldn't sleep."

"It's so cold, these nights."

"I wasn't cold. I was hot as a tin roof, thinking about you."

"That sounds nice. But my feet are freezing." He led her across to the bed. "Are your feet freezing? I mean, have they cooled down?"

"Are you laughing, Johnny?"

"Yeah. Inside."

"I can hear you. What's funny?"

He lay with his back against the carved oak headboard, which wasn't too comfortable, but with a woman like this in his arms he didn't mind. "Kick your shoes off," he told her, "and dig your feet under the blanket with mine. What's funny," he said, "is imagining what Mother Superior would think, if she knew her least favorite priest was halfway into bed with a stunning Italian woman with short black curls."

"My God, what's going to happen if she comes?"

"You're going to hole up in the clothes closet, like in

a French farce. But I assume you didn't come here shouting the place down."

"Getting past the guardian was the tricky bit."

Giovanni thought how wonderful it was to feel the warmth of her body against his. It must have been ten years since he'd held a woman close. Janine. Her name had been Janine, the last one, and she'd had soft blonde hair and never let him see her with her glasses on, though he knew she wore them, because they left a mark on the bridge of her nose.

Nicola turned her face to his. "Johnny?"

"Yeah?"

"Why did you lock the door?"

"In case Mother Superior comes."

"Are we going to fuck up a storm?"

"No."

"Then why lock the door?"

"Because if Mother Superior found us like this she'd never believe, for the rest of her entire life, that we hadn't been fucking up a storm. Or hadn't been going to. You feel tense, my beautiful amiga. Relax."

He felt her body go soft, curving into the curve of his own. "I wish to Christ you weren't a priest," she whispered.

"Sometimes," he said, "*I* wish to Christ I weren't a priest."

"You do?" She put a hand over his, the one that was stroking her arm.

"Like we sometimes wish we'd never been born. But we don't really mean it. The sun comes out again."

In a while Nicola said softly, "Priests do it, Johnny. I mean, Christ, they're practically famous for it."

"We mustn't exaggerate."

She moved against him, her thigh against his. "Who'd ever know?"

"I would." He moved his mouth against her hair, tasting its warmth.

"You mean Christ would, don't you?"

"No. He'd understand, and forgive. I'd understand, but I wouldn't forgive. I made a vow."

"And that's it?"

"That's it."

"It's all so fucking holier-than-thou."

"Few people," he said, "are less holy than I."

"God, he even gets his nominatives and accusatives right."

"A college kid, yet."

"It's so stupid, Johnny. I mean we were a couple of Italian kids on the streets of New York, once, right? We could have met up and fallen in love and got married and had nineteen little bambinos by now, or close." She moved her hand over him. "Is it up?"

"Oh, yes," he said. "Oh, yes."

"Then for God's sake—"

"Nicky—" he said "—is that what your friends call you?"

"Yeah. But you ain't my friend, bimbo."

"Nicky," he said, "why else did you come here tonight?"

She turned her head to look at him. "You think there was some other reason?"

"Yeah."

"This guy thinks I came here for something other than his dick. That's refreshing."

He waited, not saying anything.

A horned owl called, its sound faint against the window, and Nicola shivered. "There's so much going on in this place, Johnny."

His hand became still, against her arm. "Like?"

"Like that poor kid dying."

Giovanni began listening carefully. "Yeah," he said. "And?"

She pulled him harder against her, but now the way a child would, for comfort. Giovanni listened to the silence, and then in the silence the owl called again, and again Nicola shivered. "I wish those guys'd go to sleep nights. They sound so depressed."

"And?" Giovanni persisted gently.

"Uh? Oh. Things between those two cute little kids. Madlen and Deb."

"Ah."

"I never saw two sisters so close." This time it was she who waited, but Giovanni didn't say anything. "You know?"

"So tell me," he said.

"Tell you what?"

"Whatever's on your mind."

Nicola felt herself hitting the brakes, real hard. When she and Madlen had been talking that time, picking the mushrooms, it had been in confidence—she hadn't needed telling. What Madlen had gotten off her mind was something she'd never want anybody else to hear. Period.

She thinks I'm trying to kill her.

Yeah. That.

"You never saw two sisters so close," Giovanni prompted her. "So?"

Nicola had to think. She couldn't reveal what Madlen had told her, but it could be important for Giovanni to know. Could be vital, essential, a must. Then there was the other thing: Had she blown up that scene in her mind—the scene at the table when Madlen was serving the plates—until it was just a great big wacky balloon? Or could that, too, be important for Giovanni to know about? Vital, essential, a must?

"I think I'm getting in deep, Johnny," she said.

"Then let's get you out before you drown."

She stirred in his arms, blowing out a breath. "I love those two kids," she said. "You know? I really love them." When he didn't say anything she went on, "You asked me to look after them, and that's what I'm doing. I mean, I listen to everything they say to each other, and to me, in case there's anything I think you ought to know about. But it's difficult."

Giovanni got it now. "Sure," he said. "When they tell you things in confidence, how can you pass them on to me? Well it's simple. When you tell me anything, you're telling Christ."

She stirred again, restless. "Look, Johnny, I—"

"Sorry, I was forgetting, you don't go for that crap. Okay, I'll put it another way. When you tell me anything, you're placing a truth in the hands of an infinite grace whose power is such that only good can come of it. And if the truth involves possible danger to anybody, you might be able to avert that danger *only* by telling me, by tapping into that power."

She wanted to think about that, too, but he didn't give her time. Did he have a hunch it was important? Maybe as important as all hell? "It's like," Giovanni said, "you can't swim, and you're watching your best friend drowning in the lake, and you just don't even notice the rope lying there on the bank that you could throw to her."

Nicola took a breath and let it out slowly. "Look," she said, "the best I can do is, if I think there's anything either of those two kids ought to be telling you, I'll make sure they understand they damn well better hurry."

Giovanni thought of Sister Debra's torn and bleeding hands and of Sister Nadine in the intensive care unit with her face wax-white in death.

"You got it, Nicky," he said.

22

Alice Thompson didn't stay long, any more than she had last time, because she wanted Debra to see as much as she could of Jeff Soderberg.

The visitors had brought snow in on their boots and shoes, and there were little puddles forming on the floor of the bright polished parlor. The snow had stopped falling two days ago, but it was still deep on the ground and along the box hedges of the maze behind the building.

First off the bat, Alice hadn't thought Jeff Soderberg was all that serious about Debra Felker, was just totally hung up on her looks like a lot of the guys at school. But she and Jeff had been having coffee sometimes in the mall over the past few weeks, and the way Jeff talked about Debbie was beginning to be something else.

"He's here," Alice told her with a sunny smile, "of course." She looked around. "Where's Maddie?"

"She has these migraines."

"Maddie?" Madlen was never sick, except with the Affliction.

"Yeah," Debra nodded. "But she says hi."

Behind her round-rimmed glasses, Alice Thompson's pale blue eyes watched Debra at an angle. She and Jeff had been worried about Deb when they'd come here last time; now it looked like they had to worry about both of them—because Deb still had something pretty bad on her mind, anybody could see that, despite the angelic smile.

"Shit," Alice said low, "I wish you two would quit this Jesus business and come home."

"It's not as easy," Debra smiled, "as that."

That didn't make Alice feel any the less frustrated. She wanted to ask a lot more about Madlen and her migraines, but she knew Debbie wouldn't say much; she always held things in, especially if they worried her. And Jeff was waiting out there. So she just asked how all the prayers and stuff were going, and Debra asked her if her Dad still liked his new job at Compucenter, and Alice thanked her for remembering, and the conversation kind of tailed off because there was so much Alice wanted to say, and listen to, and there just wasn't the time.

She wrapped Debra for a long moment in a big warm hug smelling of sandalwood oil and said, "Hey, I'm going to write to the Superior Mother here and ask her if you can come out and have lunch with us or something one day, so we can *talk*. Is that okay?"

"Sure. But she likes to be called Mother Superior."

"Whoops!"

Then Alice was waving her fingertips discreetly from the doorway as she went out to fetch Jeff, and Debra was left standing there wishing Jeff hadn't come anyway, because she was worried about Madlen's headaches and about Father Giovanni, who also had his problems, with poor Nadine dying like that. She hated to think of Father

Giovanni being worried, because he was such a great guy and he must be blaming himself for not having been able to stop a thing like that happening—after all, he was meant to be directly in touch with Christ and everything. Debra wanted to keep all this to herself, but of course Jeff would ask her how everything was going at the convent.

He didn't.

They were sweetheart roses again, pink and tiny in a mist of baby's breath. She saw the price tag was still on the paper so she held it toward her so he wouldn't notice; she was beginning to know Jeff, and knew he'd want to fall through the floor over a little thing like that.

She was also, suddenly, deeply glad he was here.

"Improvement?" he asked.

She'd glanced up at his hair without thinking, and he'd noticed, and she realized how awfully careful she had to be, not to hurt his feelings. He was waiting for her now with his breath visibly held, and she said quickly—"You mean your hair? It looks great! Did you let it grow out?"

She saw his shoulders relax under the military surplus jacket as he let go his breath. "Let it *grow* out? I practically *pulled* it out!" His light gray eyes were full of excitement because she thought, yeah, it was an improvement; then they darkened as he said, "Debbie, you remember the last thing you said to me when I was here before?"

She tried to think. "I—I'm not sure—"

"You said, 'I don't. . . .' But there wasn't time for you to finish, because of the bell. I thought it sounded important, though, the way you looked."

Debra tried again, and remembered. She'd started saying, without meaning to, "I don't want to die." The feeling in her had been very strong, like he said—she'd suddenly realized she didn't want to die because there was Jeff in the world now, with his love for her. She couldn't say that, so she just had to lie.

"I don't remember."

"No? Well, it really got to me, see, because I thought you might've been going to say, 'I don't want you to come here again.' "

He waited, thinking this was what it must be like when you're standing with your back to the wall with a blindfold on, tensed for the shots. Or like, maybe, when you're waiting for the biopsy results.

Then Debra was saying, *"No,* Jeff!" And people near them were turning their heads. "Of *course* it wasn't that! I'll *always* want you to come here and see me!"

Jeff gulped, swallowing an entire sunset. "Oh," he said. "I thought you knew that."

"No." His shoulders came up again as he took an Olympic-swimmer type breath, then let it out. "I didn't know. But it's—I mean, you just made my whole year. My entire *life."*

Debra didn't know what to say about that, but anyway he was looking around him now, and saying with his voice low, "Debbie, you're not happy in this place, are you?"

She hadn't been ready for that. "I—yeah, I guess."

But he knew she was just saying that. There was the same kind of deep-down worry in her eyes he'd seen the last time he'd come. "Look," he said quickly, "this is what we've got worked out. I want you to call me the *minute* you decide you've had enough. I'm going to give you a list of phone numbers where you can reach me *any* time, day or night, even if I'm with one of my friends or fast asleep at three in the morning, *whatever.* I can be here in the Volks inside of—" but he broke off as he saw a warning in Debra's eyes.

One of the nuns had come up from somewhere behind him, and was just standing there, but not looking at them, pretending she was watching the room. He knew they were here to listen to everything that was being said—you could tell that, a mile away. And that was outrageous.

"Ma'am," he said, and the nun turned, looking at him with her eyes hidden behind the reflection on her steel-rimmed glasses. "Ma'am, could I talk to my cousin in private, please?"

Debra watched, breathless at his courage.

"But you received the form of protocol, young man, surely. Or you wouldn't have been allowed to visit."

"Ma'am, I need to tell my cousin something very personal, concerning my family, my mother and father. I'd really appreciate your indulgence."

Oh, wow, Debra thought, and remembered Jeff had always come top in English.

"You may rest assured," the nun was saying, "that anything divulged here in this room will never leave it. Am I clear on that?"

"Yes, ma'am." As he turned to talk to Debra again she saw the lingering heat of anger in his eyes. He lowered his voice again. "It's my Dad, see. He wants to marry again, and—you know—this lady looks very nice and she's about the same age, but we'd really like your advice." It occurred to him, even as he ad-libbed like this, that it was really a dream he was making up. If only Dad could get married again he'd stop wandering around the house all weekend picking things up and putting them down and staring at the wedding pictures like that with tears in his eyes. It was almost a year since Mom had died, and seeing him still this way was breaking Jeff up.

"Have I met this lady?" Debra was asking, and he admired that: She really knew how to follow a cue.

"I don't think so. Her name's Molly Brewer, and she's a teacher at Weldon High. She—"

"It's okay," Debra said quietly as the sister moved away.

Jeff let out a breath. "So listen, call me just *any* time.

Alice says she'll come with me and bring some real clothes for you, I mean—you know—things you can be kind of incognito in. Might be a bit baggy on you, though." He gave a breathy laugh.

"Well . . ." Debra said, to give herself time. It would totally destroy him if she said she could leave here anytime she wanted, just walk out or get a taxi and nobody would stop her.

"Alice says you can stay with her folks for a while," Jeff said, "if you don't want to go home—which I guess you don't, or you wouldn't have come here, right? She's told them the whole story, but she did *not* mention your name, okay?"

Watching this boy in front of her, this almost-man, Debra found herself feeling things she'd never felt before. The eagerness in him, the seriousness, was getting through to her. This wasn't her sister, who loved her so much it almost hurt. It was someone "outside," offering her a whole new world if she ever wanted it, and she didn't think Jeff Soderberg was going through a romantic fling that would fizzle out if she ever took her first step into that world. He'd never been "one of the guys" at the High and couldn't care less about football—he was into music more, and took his guitar practice seriously; she knew this from Jenny Tarcher, who would have died for him if he'd asked her to, though he never even looked at her—and she was a cheerleader.

And could anything turn a guy off a girl more than her going into a convent and becoming a *nun?* Maybe for *years?* But here he was, with a bunch of sweetheart roses—again. Debra suddenly wanted to feel Jeff put his arms around her, but even if it could happen here with the sisters watching, the roses would get crushed, and that would be terrible, because it might mean— was "symbolic" the word? Madlen would know—might mean that whatever they'd begun sharing, she and Jeff, was going to get crushed too.

"Okay?" she heard him saying.

Okay what? She'd forgotten where he'd left off. "Jeff," she said, "if ever I decide to leave here, sure, I'll call you. And thanks."

It didn't sound nearly enough as an answer to all he'd offered her.

Jeff's eyes were quiet again, and the light had gone out of them. "Fine," he said softly, and swallowed. "Fine."

He looked as if she'd slapped his face, and she felt tears starting. What had she done this time, exactly? Then she knew. "Jeff," she said quickly, "I didn't mean 'if ever.' I meant 'when.' " She watched his eyes, and saw the light slowly coming back into them, and found she'd been holding her breath, and let it go, and felt a tear spilling over one of her eyelids and quickly wiped it away with the back of her hand.

"Are you okay?" Jeff asked. He moved right up close to her.

"I hate hurting you," she said, "that's all."

He swallowed again. "Hey, I'm tough as a—" but he couldn't think of anything. "I'm—I'm very tough, you better believe it." He gave one of his short laughs.

Maybe that was true, Debra thought, with other people, but she could break through it so easily and without even meaning to. She went on watching his eyes, letting the light in them wash over her like the breaking of a soft gray wave as she felt her heart opening, and began wanting very much to leave this place right now, make her way with Jeff through all these people so quietly they wouldn't notice, they'd be like ghosts, the two of them, gliding softly away, hand in hand, until they were out there under the winter sky, free to go wherever they liked with nobody to stop them.

The longing was in her to get away from this dark,

suffocating world within a world and the terrible things that happened in it, get away from the terrible neverending fear she'd been living with day after day, that Madlen wanted to kill her, a fear that she could leave behind and start forgetting, once she was out of here with Jeff to bring her gently back to her senses.

But she couldn't leave Madlen.

She couldn't leave Madlen especially now, when these strange migraines had started. Sister Denise was totally puzzled by them, but Debra had the feeling they weren't just ordinary headaches, but the pain of something her sister was suddenly having to deal with inside of herself, having to fight with, something so bad that Debra didn't want to think about it. All she could do was stay here and help her sister as best she could, until she was ready to leave too.

So she asked Jeff how his guitar lessons were going, and he asked her if she was warm enough in a place like this made entirely of stone, with the winter here already and snow on the ground, and while they were talking he looked around and slipped a piece of paper into Debra's hand, touching her fingers and thinking with delight how small they were, wanting to take his hand away because she'd feel the blisters on it he'd got from fixing the new muffler on the Volks, and not wanting to take his hand away so desperately that he didn't know what to do.

"Those are the phone numbers," he said, his voice unsteady, "where you can always find me."

"Okay," Debra said, and hid them away in her robes, missing the touch of his hand as if she'd known it all her life.

"Any time," he said, "remember. Day or night."

"I'll remember." And when the big brass bell started clanging she said, "But Jeff . . . you're going to start finding it a real drag, coming to a place like this month after month, so I want you to know I'll understand if—"

"When I first saw you," he said, and took both her hands now, "I knew it was going to be forever."

And as he ran through the snow to the Volkswagen and got in and slammed the door he said to Alice, "Oh, Jesus *Christ,* I got it wrong again, I'm such a *klutz!*" He glared at himself in the mirror. *"Klutz-klutz-klutz!"*

"What happened?" Alice hit the radio off in alarm.

"You know the last thing I said to Debbie?"

"No?"

He told her.

"But that sounds . . . oh, *wow* . . ." Alice said, rolling her eyes.

"It sounds *corny,* don't you see? Corny in the *extreme,* like a line out of a bad movie!" He started the motor, revving it up in a bellow of disgust, and Alice had to shout above the noise.

"But Jeff!"

"What?"

"You meant it, didn't you?"

"Of *course!*"

"Then she'd know that!"

He turned in the driveway. "She would?"

"You bet your sweet ass she would! And you're right—you really are a klutz."

Jeff felt a wave of relief hit him in the chest, and Alice grabbed for her seatbelt as he took the Volks down the driveway roaring like a lion.

"Are you sure you wouldn't rather talk inside somewhere, in the warm?" Aunt Helen asked.

"There's nowhere very warm in there," Debra smiled. "Nowhere private. I'm fine like this." She was wearing a black shawl over her robes, which was permitted after November 1st.

The snow lay thick along the box hedges in the maze, blue-white in the sunshine, spangled with iridescence. It had brought silence across the valley, and you could hear the rooks talking as if they were close by instead of way up in the black skeletonic branches of the elms.

"Father Giovanni was very understanding," Aunt Helen said, "when I asked him if we could be more private this time." She watched Debra with her hands tucked inside the pockets of her pink padded coat, wishing she could see more life in the small pinched face, more peace. The child had looked much the same last time, her young mind plagued with something. Was it just convent life? It seemed to be more than that, something more specific. Madlen? Debra had just told her of the puzzling migraines.

"He's a really nice man," Debra nodded, "but you must have—you know—made a pretty solid pitch to get us a privilege like this. It's terribly special, like when there's a problem in the family or something."

Helen looked away toward the windmill. "Yes," she said, "I guess you could say I made a good solid pitch."

Debra heard something in her voice, but couldn't tell exactly what it was. Aunt Helen sounded amused, but more than that too. She'd put on extra heavy makeup today, Debra noticed, maybe because she knew they'd be outside in the snow-light, where the bruise on her face would show up more, but it didn't help a whole lot—you could still see it, and Debra wished it wasn't there, that it hadn't ever happened. He must have been a terrible man, to do that.

"I love your hat," she said. It was one of those Russian ones, but pink.

"Why, thank you!"

Aunt Helen had a really great smile, Debra thought. "How is your—your friend?" she asked her. There was a new man in her life, she'd told her the last time she was here.

"Fancy you remembering. . . . But then, you know

how to listen, don't you, honey? He's *fine*. We're just—going steady for a while, getting to know each other. But I guess that's kind of old-fashioned, isn't it—'going steady'? What would you call it?"

"Maybe . . . I don't know. 'Seeing each other'?" Debra didn't think she ought to say "shacking up together." But she felt awfully glad Aunt Helen had somebody in her life again, and someone who'd treat her right this time, by the sound of it.

"His name's Charlie," Aunt Helen said, watching her. "Maybe you'll meet him one fine day. There are still a lot of fine days left, aren't there, for all of us?"

"Sure," Debra nodded quickly, but thought it was a funny thing for Aunt Helen to say. It sounded like she was wanting to tell her something, but wasn't sure it'd be okay.

"Maybe, who knows, I'll marry him." She stamped her feet a little bit and started walking slowly through the snow, with Debra beside her. "Would that be fun?" She looked down at Debra's small white face with its mystified expression, and put an arm around her suddenly, giving her a squeeze. "You wouldn't know the answer to a thing like that, honey. You don't know what marrying somebody is like. It'd be my third time, you know? Now doesn't that sound like the story of a dissatisfied woman? But it's not really like that. I lost my first husband—he died. Then there was Harry. You know about Harry. So the way I see it, I still have a chance to find a little happiness if I can. Like I say, we all have a lot of fine days left, and we have to use them."

"You're still young," Debra said. "You're the youngest person of your age I know."

Aunt Helen turned to look at her, laughing softly and giving her another hug. "That's a great way of putting it, honey." They walked on again. "Then there's hope for me. Though I guess I'm too old now to raise a family."

"You never had kids?" Debra asked. She suddenly felt she wanted to know a lot more about Aunt Helen—she'd really been through a whole lot of life.

Helen looked up at the windmill again. "Sure. I had a kid." The snow crunched softly under their shoes as they reached the end of the maze and started back. Nobody else had walked here since the snow had fallen; they were in a secret winter world of their own out here, and it seemed to Debra that when they stopped walking, time stopped too, and waited for them. "I had a kid," Aunt Helen said again. "That was when I was with my first husband. His name was Richard, and you know something? Nobody ever called him Dick. He was too . . . dignified. Too much of his own man for nicknames."

"He sounds great," Debra said. But that wasn't the right word, she knew, for a dignified man. "Great" could mean almost anything, and she wished she had Madlen's talent for words.

"You would have liked him, honey," Aunt Helen said. "But then . . . he went and took sick, suddenly, and we fought the good fight together and lost, and it didn't take long." They were walking in their own footprints through the narrow maze, with snow coming away in little clouds from the box hedge as Helen's coat brushed it. "We were young then, and we didn't have all that much money, and by the time I'd gotten through all the hospital bills I was broke. I mean *broke.*" She gave a short laugh.

"You haven't had a very happy life," Debra said, "have you?"

"Hey," Aunt Helen said, stopping to turn and look at her. "This isn't any sob story I'm into, honey. I've had a great life—I mean you win some and you lose some, right? Anyway, you sure don't want to hear any more of that stuff. Tell me about you and Madlen. Are you going to—"

"I'd like to hear more about you," Debra said, "really." She gave a little shrug under her black shawl—"As much as you want me to know." It was the way Aunt Helen told things that made you want to go on listening: She had a low, kind of sandy voice, and sometimes you could hear the laughter in it when she was telling about sad things, like she meant they hadn't really got her down all that much.

"Okay," Aunt Helen said. "You want to hear about my kid?"

"Yes. Was it a boy?" Debra walked in the footprints they'd left when they'd come the other way, so the deeper snow didn't come over the edge of her shoes.

"No, she was a girl. Cute as anything, one of the few kids I've seen at that age who didn't look like Winston Churchill. But like I say, I was broke, living in an apartment just about as big as a cupboard and going out to work as a waitress, then doing bar work nights, moonlighting. Had to. So there was no way I could bring up a kid, right at that time, no way. I wanted her to have a stable family and everything she needed, you know? So I put her up for adoption. And boy, was *that* tough! I—"

"Adoption?" For the first time Debra realized there were other kids like her around in the world, not knowing who their parents were.

"Yeah. A tough as hell thing to do, like I say. In fact the only way I was able to do it was by following her new parents home in the car, the day they came for her—I had to wait a couple of hours in my beat-up old Chevy, watching the adoption office, tears streaming down my face and everything, the whole soap opera. But I knew, then, where my kid had gone, where she'd be living. And knowing that, I managed to get through, and come up smiling." She gave her low sandy laugh—"Or close."

They turned a corner of the maze, and a robin flew up

from the hedge in a small white explosion of snow. "And then—are you still interested, honey?"

"Of course!"

"Okay. And then I managed to keep going, the first few months, by driving past the house sometimes where my kid was living. Then later her parents moved to another town, so I moved too. I was still a waitress, and a waitress can find work almost anyplace she lands up." She began walking more slowly, so Debra slowed too. "Then it became a way of life for me. I felt I hadn't really lost my kid, see, all the time I knew where she was and that she was okay and getting all the things I couldn't give her." She stopped now, and said, "Anyway, I guess you're getting the picture by this time, aren't you, honey?"

"Well, yeah. It must have been awful for you."

Aunt Helen stood watching her in a strange way, just standing and watching, a smile in her eyes but something quite different behind it, almost like she was afraid of something. "Sure," she said, "it was awful in a lot of ways, but that's not the picture I mean." She drew a deep breath, and blew it out in a cloud on the cold air. "So let's get it over with, shall we? After a long time I heard from people in the town—hairdressers and checkout clerks, people like that who were my friends—that my daughter was having a rough time because her parents had started to fight, and it got so bad she just left home with her sister and went into a convent, so I . . . I went and paid her a visit." She stood back a little from Debra, not wanting to crowd her at a time like this. "Remember?"

23

That night, Madlen had a bad dream, and began screaming.

"I don't want to! I don't want it to happen!"

Debra woke with her heart thudding. "Madlen?"

"Don't let it happen! I'll do anything! I'll—"

"Madlen!" Debra called out and threw her bedclothes
back.

"I didn't mean it—any of it—"

"Madlen!" Debra was shaking her sister now, but the
terrible screaming went on and on, and light flared in the
transom over the door as someone in the passage came
hurrying.

"There's something inside me that won't—"

"Madlen, it's all right! *Madlen!"* Debra went on shaking her, sick with fright because it sounded like such a
terrible dream. "I'm right here, Madlen. . . ." Shaking her
and shaking her until Madlen woke at last and the
screams died away to a moaning as the door of the cell

came banging open and the guardian stood there, Sister
Corrine, with Nicola behind her, wanting to know what
was happening.

"It's okay . . ." Debra kept saying, holding Madlen
against her now, "everything's okay, Maddie, it was just
a dream. . . ." She could feel the cold sweat on her sister's
face as she clung to her, still moaning.

"You gobbled your supper too fast," the guardian
said, looking down with the lamp in her hand. "It should
be a warning." There were doors opening along the passage, and voices whispering. "You've woken everyone
up, do you realize that?"

Madlen didn't hear her; she kept her face pressed
against her sister, burying herself in her arms as she went
on moaning, but softly now, like a child.

Nicola had her arm around both of them. "You guys
need me, I'm right here."

"Return to your cell at once!" the guardian told her
sharply.

Nicola whirled on her. "Shut your damn mouth!"

A look of disbelief came over the guardian's pale bony
face as she hastily crossed herself. "But this is outrageous! You will—"

"Get the fuck out of here," Nicola said between her
teeth, "you understand me? And I mean *now.*"

There was something in her voice that Sister Corrine
had never heard before; it had the sound of a drawn
blade and the guardian took a sudden step back, leaving
without another word.

Later, deep into the night, Debra lay watching the flush
of light on the ceiling, sometimes turning her head to
look at the small carved crucifix on the wall, where the
light caught the gold leaf of the cross.

Madlen was asleep again, her breathing regular. She'd
refused to tell them what the nightmare had been

about—she'd seemed afraid to—and all Debra could remember her screaming was something about not wanting to do something. To do what?

Whatever it was, Madlen didn't want to talk about it, so Debra had just sat on the edge of the bed smoothing her hair until she finally dozed off.

Now Debra was thinking about "Aunt" Helen again. When she'd come back here to their cell after saying goodbye, Madlen had been asleep, breathing heavily because of a drug Sister Denise had given her for the migraine, so Debra hadn't disturbed her. And since that time she'd given it some thought, and decided to wait a while before she told Madlen that she had a mother at last, a real one, of her very own. She wanted to keep her secret for a little, to dwell on it with the awe she'd felt since the soft, dizzying shock had washed over her as she and the woman in the pink Russian hat stood there in the snow as if they'd suddenly come face to face with each other in the middle of the maze, to their surprise.

"It's okay, Debbie," the woman had said—her voice was quiet under the winter sky, as if she spoke from a distance—"it's okay if you don't want to see me again, now that you know."

It was so much to handle that Debra needed help, so she threw herself into her mother's arms, and the thought uppermost in her mind was, *Now I can be safe again.* . . .

"I meant to tell you the first time I came," her mother said as they walked again through the maze, "but I guess I just chickened out because I didn't know if you'd like me. And there were all those people. So I just stuck to the 'Aunt Helen' story, though I never really had a sister—the people who adopted you were strangers. And I went home ashamed of myself for lying." She gave a low, sandy laugh.

The last thing she said, when Debra was seeing her off

in her car, was that she was "doing okay" these days after going back to college: She was now working in a law office as an assistant to the top attorney. "So if you're shutting yourself up here, honey, because you've nowhere else to go, you can just come on home. Both of you, if that's what your sister would like. Just come on home with me."

Debra lay watching the light on the ceiling, still trying to take in what had happened to her. There was another reason why she didn't want to tell Madlen about it, at least for a while. The incredible thing that her sister had talked about as a joke had happened: Debra had a home to go to now, with her own real live mother there, and if Madlen wanted to go with her she'd have to be kind of adopted by a strange lady in a pink Russian hat, and she might not be ready for that.

When Debra felt sleep coming she turned on her side, so the crucifix would be the last thing she saw, with the light from the transom playing on the worn gold leaf and the crown of thorns. And perhaps that was why, as she drifted through the twilight zone before sleep, she heard a voice coming to her through the shadows, soft and clear. . . . *Pray, my child, for your beloved sister. . . . Vouchsafe her the grace of your compassion. . . .*

24

Three days later a windstorm brought the last of the leaves whirling across from the elms, to carpet the stone floor of the bell tower. Performing their penance for whispering during Mass this morning, Debra and Madlen took a rake, a broom, and a sack to the tower and worked until twilight.

They talked very little as they raked and swept and held the sack open for each other. Madlen was still plagued with her headaches; the Advil relieved them for a while but they always came back, and Sister Denise had told her she'd be taking her into the town tomorrow to see Dr. Grant.

The sky had been overcast all day, with low clouds moving in fast from the west, borne on the rising wind. The air was freezing, and the sisters had red noses and watery eyes when they finished their work and came down the flight of stone steps from the tower, carrying the sack full of leaves between them.

Debra had told Madlen about her "new" mother, but
her sister hadn't seemed all that interested. She said it
was "great" and "fantastic" and that she was happy for
Debra, but didn't say any more about it. Debra understood: What with her migraines and her nightmares,
Madlen must be finding it tough to take an interest in
anything going on around her. She was shut in with her
suffering, and Debra had been praying for her morning,
noon, and night in the North Chapel, ever since she'd
heard the voice that time, lying in her bed and watching
the crucifix.

It hadn't come to her in a dream: She'd still been
half-awake when she'd heard it. And the words had been
so clear, even though they were spoken softly, for her
ears alone. The voice would have scared her out of her
wits if she hadn't known whose it was, hadn't known
immediately and without any question that it was the
voice of Christ.

She'd said nothing of this to Madlen, feeling instinctively that it was sacrosanct, a secret not to be shared
with any mortal, even her sister. It hadn't been just something her mind had put together in a half-dream, because
she didn't use words like that. She'd asked Madlen the
next day what "vouchsafe" meant, but that was all.

"It means to grant, I guess. To bestow. Why?"

"I saw it in one of the psalms."

Late tonight, her hands still tingling from her work in
the tower, Debra woke to a sound, and saw Madlen
inching open the door of their cell.

"Where are you going?" she whispered.

"Shh. . . . Go to sleep."

Debra pushed the bedclothes back. *"Madlen!* Where
are you going?" She got her dressing gown from its hook
on the wall.

"I left my rosary in the bell tower," Madlen whispered,
"that's all." It had kept getting entangled with the rake,

so she'd taken it off—a minor sin. "Go back to bed," she told Debra.

"I'm coming with you."

"No!" Madlen stood in the doorway, silhouetted against the glow of light from the lamp at the guardian's post in the corridor. "I don't want you to!"

"Is she there?" asked Debra.

"Who?"

"The guardian."

"No."

So it must be gone midnight, the hour when the guardians themselves went to bed, leaving their lamps burning for anyone who needed to use the bathroom.

"I'm coming with you," Debra said again. Her sister tried to push her gently back into the room, but she resisted.

"I don't *want* you to come," Madlen said. "It doesn't take two of us to fetch a rosary!"

Their faces were close in the gloom, their eyes seeking each other's.

"We go everywhere together," Debra said, and took her sister's hand, closing the door behind them quietly.

It wasn't the sound of the storm that woke Nicola, in the next cell.

It was the silence.

Lying in the dark, she found the dream still running through her head, the same one, the nightmare, with the dark riverwater lapping at the harbor wall, and then the splash, but no cry, no sound of a cry, and it wasn't because they'd put a gag on him, those bastards, before they dropped him in, it was because Giulio wasn't like that, wouldn't have let himself cry out, not even a fucking prayer . . . Giulio, a great guy and a good husband and fantastic in bed, and not a man to cry out in the last goddamned minute of his life on earth. . . . So there was just the splash, and then the bubbles, and then their voices fading away as they went back to the car, and a tug hooting somewhere higher on the river, a sad kind of a sound, like a requiem.

Splash . . . and then silence . . . the same thing in every dream, just like the way she knew it must have been, so why couldn't he have cried out, for Christ's sake, before the black filthy riverwater started pouring into his mouth, why couldn't he tell them to go fuck themselves, or say a prayer or something?

Or call out to her—*Hey, Nicky, the next time you go shooting your fucking mouth off, leave my name out of it, okay? Because look what happens.*

It was the silence that woke her, every time she had the dream, the nightmare.

Silence can wake people up?

Yeah.

Sometimes she woke crying.

"Cry," Giovanni had told her when they'd talked in his little room. "Cry if you can."

"Crying's a giveaway," she'd said.

"Give yourself away to God. Then you can't lose anything."

Sure. She'd have to think about it.

Lying in the dark, she wondered what had happened to the guardian's candle out there in the passage; its light wasn't in the transom over the door. She guessed the draft must have blown it out: There'd been a storm, earlier—it was still rumbling somewhere across the valley. In a while she let her lids slowly close, and there was Giovanni's face, with that incredible depth in his eyes, the faith, the gentleness, the strength. "Come and talk to me," he'd told her, "any time."

And she'd have to do that, pretty soon now. Ask him to help her get the guilt off her mind at last, the grief, before it drove her crazy. Ask him to hold her hands while she cried her heart out, screamed the place down, kicked and yelled and even . . . prayed, if it came to that.

Whatever worked.

And soon now. Maybe tomorrow.

Something woke Father Giovanni late that same night, at much the same hour, but at first he didn't know what it was. A half moon, westering across the valley, sent its light aslant through the narrow window of his cell, and he could see that the door was still shut, and that nobody had come in here.

All he could hear in the silence of the night was a soft singing, like a single note on a violin string, distant, trembling, gossamer-fine. He knew better than to dismiss it as tension along the nerves playing on the membranes of his ears. It wouldn't stop, and while it sounded he couldn't hope to sleep.

It was a while—minutes—before Giovanni began to know that he must leave his bed, and follow the faint distant sound. That was what it was for—to lead him. He didn't question how he knew this; he was used to signals reaching out to him from the regions of the unknown, and knew it was probably a sin to heed them—or not to believe they came from Christ. But Christ spoke with a voice, however soft, and Giovanni had often heard it. This was different, this singing thread that had come to lead him through the night, and cold sweat was on him even as he left his bed and got his woolen topcoat from behind the door. For there were levels of communication, subtle as the trembling on a web, that dwelled in the lattice of universal consciousness for those to hear who would listen, and for this seeming heresy he devoutly hoped that Christ forgave him—and with good reason, for Giovanni believed that Christ himself was born into this same universe of consciousness in order to teach its laws, and one above all others—that the primordial force in that consciousness was love.

He pushed his feet into his slippers and went to the door, shrugging himself deeper into his coat.

Though most of them were narrow, the convent was a building of many windows, and Giovanni didn't think to bring along his flashlight: After four years he knew these cavernous rooms and passages, and the light of the moon was enough to guide him. The faint singing of the violin string had not diminished; he followed its thread, faithful as Dionysius.

Embers still smoldered in the hearth of the Great Hall, and Giovanni was tempted to stir them into flame and warm himself, but the thread of sound was changing now, becoming finer still, drawn to the stretching point, and the sweat crept on his skin, his scalp tightening as he took the passage leading past the North Chapel, the moonlight casting his shadow before him as he walked with his back to the west.

He turned a corner, moving now along the passage that led past the West Chapel—and here Giovanni stopped, standing still to listen, thinking he had heard sounds, perhaps footsteps, but very faint. Looking behind him he saw nothing but shadows; looking above him he saw only the gallery where paintings hung, portraying the lives of the saints.

There was nothing here. Yet the sound of footsteps persisted, echoing faintly among the cloistered walls.

He walked on again, a sudden wave of apprehension chilling him as he turned the next corner and was stunned by an explosion of blinding light and the sound of screaming.

As Giovanni came running he saw Debra pitching down the steps from the bell tower enveloped in flames as the oil lamp crashed to the floor and Madlen began scream-

ing, throwing herself on her sister and beating at her
robes, pulling her to the floor and rolling her over and
over to smother the flames, beating at them with her bare
hands, her own robes on fire now until Giovanni reached
her and smothered those too.

"It's okay, sweetheart!" Madlen cried, her voice hoarse
with shock, *"it's all right, you're okay now. . . ."*

Black smoke clouded around them, catching at their
lungs.

"You're okay, sweetheart, it's all right now. . . ." Madlen
was shaking with sobs, the tears streaming on her face as
the shock went flooding through her in wave after wave.

Giovanni searched Debra's face, saw only soot, no
burns that he could make out. But her eyes were frightened, and he put his arms around her and rocked her
gently, seeing her sister standing there alone with her face
in her hands and reaching for her too and bringing her
into his embrace.

The pool of spilled oil from the lamp flickered for a
time with a dull orange light, and then went out.

"What happened?" Giovanni asked in a little while.

It was Debra who answered. "I tripped on my robes,
Father, coming down the steps."

"You were carrying the lamp?"

"Yeah. I guess I—"

"I was right behind her," Madlen said, "but I wasn't
in time to save her. Dear Christ, why couldn't I—"

"But you put out the flames," Giovanni told her.
"That's all that matters now. . . . That's all that matters."

Nicola woke with a hand on her shoulder shaking her,
and the dark waters of the river swirled away and there
was lamplight and she looked up into the face of the
night guardian.

"Father Giovanni wants to talk to you."

"Now?"

"Yes. Hurry."

Nicola's mind cleared fast. "What happened?"

"I'll take you to him."

The guardian was already holding her night robe open for her, and as Nicola shrugged herself into it she was burning to ask, *Is everybody okay?* But she didn't think she'd get an answer.

The priest was standing below the archway at the end of the passage, his face strained and his eyes hollow in the lamplight as he stared at Nicola and asked the guardian to leave them.

Nicola watched him, waiting.

"I'm sorry I had to wake you," he said.

"No problem." She thought she smelled lamp oil on his coat.

"There's just been an accident, Nicky," he said, "involving the two young sisters. I need—"

"They okay? Just tell me."

"Yeah. No one was hurt." He moved close to her, the raw smell of the lamp oil strong now. His voice was low, hard, as he said, "But they could have been. Debra could have been burned alive. So—"

"Oh Jesus Christ—"

"So listen, you've got to give it to me straight now, Nicky. You understand?"

He waited, not letting her eyes go free. Somewhere the guardian was talking to somebody in the shadowed passage near the staircase; the rest was silence, the whole building, the whole night resting on silence as Nicola stared into the dark face of the priest. Then she took a deep breath and spoke, because now she knew she must.

"All right, Johnny. Debra thinks her sister's trying to kill her. And I think she's right."

He closed his eyes, then, just long enough to let a prayer fly upward.

"That's all I need to know."

25

The window of Giovanni's room was still dark. He had come in here two hours ago, more, after talking to Nicola. He had not switched on the light; he needed to think, to imagine, to cast his mind far and talk to people who were not here, listen to them . . . and that was done more easily in the dark.

Madlen had suffered a migraine attack while they'd been standing there at the bottom of the steps to the tower, the three of them—the child still in her teens who had just tried to kill her sister, *to murder her,* the child who had just escaped death at her hands, and the priest, himself. So he had taken Madlen—half-carried her, she could hardly walk—to the sick room and asked the guardian there to wake Sister Denise. She would give the child some codeine: Advil was no longer strong enough these days when a migraine attacked.

He had sent Debra back to bed, and asked Nicola to move in with her to keep her company; the child was still in shock.

Giovanni had been pacing again, knowing his way in the dark across the threadbare carpet with the sureness of a bear who knows its den; now he was sunk into the chair behind his desk, his heavy black coat still on, his bones weary under the weight of all that must be done, this side of daybreak if not long after. . . . In a minute or two he would get up and make some more coffee to keep sleep at bay.

To murder her, yes, the child Madlen had just tried to *murder* her sister. Let us not turn our eyes away from the grinning truth of things, padre.

"Fight the good fight, Johnny."

Yes indeed, Bishop, just as you say, but the deed is less simple, for I shall need, you see, to outbrave the very angels and tread within the sacrosanct confines of a human mind, there to fight the good fight.

But in the last two hours Giovanni had managed to drag out, confront, and deal with a great many of the monsters that had come to prowl these cloisters in the night.

Bring in the police and have Madlen charged with attempted murder—*no.*

No way.

Evidence? None. Witnesses? None. Without either, no such charge could possibly be brought: He'd be made to look a fool. And what would little Debra tell the police, tell anyone? That it wasn't true. She would protect her sister just as she had before, when Giovanni had talked to her in this room, her hands still raw from her deathly adventure in the catacombs. And what would Madlen tell anyone? Again—that it wasn't true.

Because she didn't think it was.

She herself didn't know the truth. She thought these things were accidents, and after they happened she was distraught, heartsick for her sister. And take this further—even at the very moment when these deadly, mur-

derous "accidents" were taking place, Madlen began
striving to save her sister from harm. This had happened
tonight: He'd seen himself that Madlen had saved her
sister's life . . . in the moment when she'd tried to take it.
If it had happened tonight it must happen that way every
time, because this whole psychodrama was set to a prede-
termined pattern, had to be.

The tin clock ticked on the shelf below the crucifix.

Confront Madlen? Grill her, as the cops would call it?
Sure, he could do that. Stand over her and flail her with
questions, arguments, accusations, letting her get away
with *nothing* as she dodged and dived, bringing her to her
knees at last with the truth coming out of her in a torrent
of tears, with her hands clawing the carpet at his feet for
the mercy of peace.

Sure, he could do that. But what truth would come
out? None that would tell him anything, make any sense.
She didn't know the truth. All he'd get would be an
outpouring of her conscious view of things, which was all
she knew—that her sister, whom she loved so deeply that
she'd die for her, was having these terrible accidents,
and she was scared to death that the next one might be
the last, the fatal one. And even if he could bring himself
to tough it out with her—which he doubted—it wouldn't
be necessary. Madlen was the soul of truth, and she'd
give of it freely: the only truth she knew.

The real truth wasn't there: It never was, for anybody.
Giovanni had meant to go into med-school and psychiatry in the beginning, had taken abnormal psychology at
college and gone through a two-year extracurricular
course in psychiatry itself, and though that had done
nothing more than cover the basics, he'd learned that
consciously "reality" was only a picture show projected
by the subconscious to satisfy the demands of the ego for
a "normal" mode of experience.

The real truth for Madlen was below the conscious

level, buried in a miasma of imaginings whose whole
focus, like a ray of darkness through light, was the need
to kill. The need to kill her sister.

The tin clock ticked.

Sibling rivalry? Sibling rivalry taken to extremes?
It had to be considered. Mrs. Felker had told him, when
her daughters had been considered for the Order, that
Debra, the younger child, was an adoptee, that both had
been told of this in their teens, and that it had made
no difference to their relationship. Perhaps. But only
perhaps.

Giovanni shifted in his chair, its creaking timber bringing the silence home. He was aware of faint light touching the wall near the door, on the west side of the room,
as the planet swung ponderously in its orbit and another
day trembled on the brink of creation.

So what do we do, padre? Let it all go on until by the
nature of things a child is murdered in this, the house of
Christ, and another left bereft, maddened with grief and
looking next for her own death by her own hand?

Separate them? How? They were inseparable. Attend
them with guards, every waking minute, every minute of
the night? Inspect the younger sister's food, every morsel,
search clandestinely for weapons—not your bold short-
sword or a dagger but more innocent-seeming, subtle
tools of destruction—a pillow . . . a shard of broken glass
. . . a needle? And, finding none, complacently overlook
Madlen's hands themselves, the subtlest and most innocent-seeming weapons of them all?

The tin clock ticked in the silence.

Or? Or what, then, if that wouldn't suit? What to do,
padre?

Fight the good fight.

I thought you'd say that, Bishop. You won't let it go,
will you?

Chicken, Johnny?

The priest hunched lower still in his chair, shutting his eyes against the faint light on the wall.

Yes, yes, I knew you'd say that too. Chicken, yes. Shit-scared, scared to death.

Of a little child?

No, scared of going into the *mind* of a little child, Bishop, into the labyrinths of nightmare, to seek the ultimate truth.

So that's what you're afraid of.

Yeah. Of finding the truth, the real thing, curled up like a monster in the mind of a child, and having to face it.

Then try telling your fears to Christ, my son, and see if he wants to help.

And so, as the first light of the new day waxed and took on the color of the palest rose in the window, Giovanni moved from his chair and sank to his knees below the crucifix and prayed for courage, the low resonance of his voice bringing into the little room the sound of a cello string, prayed for wisdom, as the eyes of the Christ looked down from the last of the night's shadows, prayed above all that no harm should be visited upon this child as a result of what he hoped to do, which was to bring good and banish evil, and, if the Lord was merciful, lead her to a state of grace.

"I spent a year in Rome when I was a young man," Father Giovanni said, "studying for the priesthood."

He and Madlen were standing in front of a small framed photograph, now discolored, that hung on his wall near the window. His arm was around her shoulder as they looked up at it.

"Is it a chapel, Father?"

"No. It's just something that in Europe they call a winter-garden, a small paved courtyard under a dome of paneled glass—you find them in a lot of the older hotels.

There are these steps leading down through the ferns, and the fountain stands in the center. You can sit on one of the benches with a book, or just wander around, touching the flowers. Most of the winter-gardens over there are pretty dilapidated by now—the glass domes get broken here and there by storms, so the birds find a way in and build their nests, and weeds start in among the ferns and the geraniums. But that's okay—it gives these places an added charm. This particular one became a kind of refuge for me, when I needed a place to think in peace, far from all the chanting and the moaning going on in the church. The hotel concierge used to let me go there when I wanted—his mother was dying and I was doing what I could to give him a bit of comfort." He looked down from the photograph at Madlen. "It's odd, but the thing I most remember about that little winter-garden was the smell of Italian coffee that found its way in there from the kitchens."

"Smells make us remember things," Madlen nodded.

"Especially coffee, yeah, if you're Italian." Her face was still pale, he thought, but her eyes were quiet now. The migraine attack had gotten to her an hour ago when she was at Mass, and he and Sister Denise had brought her quietly away, and while she was lying down with a damp cloth on her forehead Giovanni had asked her if she'd like him to try hypnosis on her, to see if it would help.

"In some cases," he'd told her, "it's about the only thing that does. But I can't promise a miracle."

"Anything that might work, Father, even if only a little bit."

So two of the sisters were now stationed in the passage outside to keep people away, and Sister Denise was within calling distance in case she was needed. The sun was climbing higher toward the south by now, and Giovanni had drawn the faded velvet curtain across the window. He had also unjacked the telephone and filled the coffee percolator, switching it on to simmer.

"How do you feel, Madlen?"

"Kind of bushed, I guess. It always leaves me like that." Her young face, tilted to look up at him in the shaded light, had the innocence of a saint's, and Giovanni felt a rush of pity for her. Whatever demon was inside her, she didn't want it there. It was starting to drive her crazy, through the migraines.

"Yeah," he said, "you should be sitting down. Try the chair, but let's hope you don't get yourself lost in it."

Madlen stroked the carving along the arms. "It's like a throne. It'd look great on a stage, for *MacBeth* or something."

"I guess it would," Giovanni said, and perched a haunch on the edge of his desk, looking down at her with his hands folded loosely in front of him. "Have you ever been hypnotized before?" He felt the fear trying to come back and get in his way, the fear of what he was going to do, of what he might find, but he managed to ignore it. He'd said his prayers, and maybe they'd be answered. If not, he'd just have to go it alone.

"No," Madlen said.

"It's no big deal. The thing to remember is, you don't actually go to sleep, and when you hear me use that word I'll be talking about hypnotic sleep, which is more like a waking state of awareness. So just relax, Madlen, starting with the muscles in your toes and working your way up, clenching the muscles and releasing them, clenching and releasing." He got off the desk and went over to the little stoneware sink in the corner, finding the earthenware bowl he used for his cereal and putting his blue-and-white coffee mug on top of it at an angle. "Clench and relax . . ." he said over his shoulder, "so you feel a wave of relaxation flowing right through your whole body from your toes to your head." He turned on the water tap and left it trickling onto the mug and the bowl. The coffee was starting to percolate and he switched it off, coming back to perch on the desk again. "Clench and relax . . . you've got it going, have you?"

"Yeah." Madlen said it slowly, and he saw her eyes were closed, her hands lying quietly on the arms of the chair. With her vivid imagination she made a perfect subject. Giovanni lowered his voice to just above a whisper. "Okay, so I want you to imagine you're in that peaceful little winter-garden of mine, standing at the top of the worn stone steps and looking down at the fountain below. Just concentrate on that for a while . . . just for a while . . . there's no hurry . . . take your time."

The water trickled and splashed in the sink, and in a little while Giovanni said softly, "And now you're going down the worn stone steps, Madlen, counting them as you go, counting them from ten all the way down to zero. Can you hear the fountain?"

A whisper—"Yeah. . . ."

"Good, so now you're going down the steps, keeping your hand on the rail all the time. All the time your hand's on the rail you can't fall or come to any harm. And as you take the first step down, number nine, you're going deeper . . . deeper asleep . . . deeper asleep. . . . And now you're on number eight . . . going deeper asleep . . . deeper . . . deeper asleep. . . ."

Watching her in the half-light, Giovanni saw that the child's left hand was lying loosely on the arm of the chair, the right hand gripping the other.

"That's right . . . keep your hand always on the rail. . . ." He led her slowly down to the third step from the bottom. "Can you smell the coffee, Madlen?"

"Yeah . . . smells great. . . ."

"Sure. It's coming from the kitchens in the hotel. And now you're on step number two . . . and going deeper . . . deeper asleep. . . ."

He thought he heard voices along the passage outside, but wasn't worried. His orders to Sister Denise and the two others were that *nobody* must get past them—including Mother Superior.

". . . And your left hand is brushing the ferns as you reach the bottom of the steps . . . and you are now in a deep . . . deep . . . hypnotic sleep . . . and I want you to know, Madlen, that from here on you feel fine, absolutely fine as you go about your day and as you sleep peacefully at night . . . your head feels clear and cool . . . clear and cool at every hour of the day and all night long . . . and you have no memory at all of it ever feeling otherwise . . . no memory at all. . . ." Giovanni waited, then gently moved on. "So why don't you go and sit on the little bench over there, by the fountain? You feel like doing that, Madlen?"

"Sure. . . ."

"It's cool by the fountain, and you can see the water flashing as it falls into the bowl, sending you even deeper asleep. Tell me how you're feeling now, Madlen."

In a moment, "It's such a beautiful place. . . ."

"Yeah, it's a very beautiful place. . . ." And on a deep breath Giovanni took the first step. "And you can be all on your own here, or you can have anyone come visit you, if you want. Is there anyone you'd like to share this beautiful place with, Madlen?"

He waited.

"No."

Giovanni's eyes moved upward a little to those of the Christ on the wall, and for a moment he let them linger there, drawing strength.

"That's fine," he said, looking down again at the child in the chair. "That's fine, but if you ever felt like sharing this beautiful place with someone . . . who would it be?"

He waited again.

"My sister."

"Your sister. . . ." Giovanni said, relief coming into him.

"Yeah. Cathy."

The water splashed in the little iron sink.

"Cathy?" he asked quietly.

"Yeah. My *real* sister."

A chill started suddenly down Giovanni's spine.

"That's very nice. So maybe you'll want to ask Cathy here in a few minutes, to share everything with you."

"I'd like that."

"There's nobody else you'd like along?"

The water splashed quietly from the corner of the room.

"No."

In a moment Giovanni said, "You wouldn't like Debra to come and share this with—"

"No!"

It was almost a cry, and he saw both her hands were now gripping the arms of the chair.

"Okay . . . but why wouldn't you like her to come here, Madlen?"

"She's a stranger!"

"Debra, you mean, is a stranger?" He thought of their closeness, the love he'd so often seen between them, and again he felt something close to heartbreak.

"Of course!" Madlen said through her teeth. "She's not my *real* sister!"

In a moment, "Cathy is your real sister?"

"Of course!" Her hands gripping the chair.

Giovanni let a moment go by, knowing he was now in the middle of a psychic minefield. Within the practicality of hypnosis he could only make suggestions—and those casually. He couldn't argue, judge, approve or disap-prove: Nothing would come of it and he might do damage, perhaps great damage. This child's mind was already in a tumult of confusion, and he daren't add fuel to the fire. But there were things he had to know . . . dear God, there were things he had to know.

"I'd like to meet her," he said at last, "your sister Cathy. Is she . . . anywhere close, right now?"

"They killed her."

The tin clock ticked in the silence.

"I see. Who was it did that, Madlen?"

"My mother. My father. *They killed her.*"

"When did they do that?"

"When I was just a little kid."

"How did they do it?"

"I don't know." Madlen's hands were gripping the chair, the knuckles white, and in the soft curtained light Giovanni saw tears gathering on her lashes. "I only know they killed her."

"How do you know?"

"I heard them talking about it. I used to listen at keyholes."

"Can you remember what they said, exactly?"

"Mommy said . . . she said the most horrible, horrible thing. She said, *'What about if she ever finds out she had a sister who was killed?'* "

"You're sure that's exactly what she said, Madlen?" And Giovanni realized immediately that it had been a stupid question. Any memory surfacing from her subconscious would be one hundred percent accurate.

"Of course I'm sure!"

"But you think your sister might come back, one day?"

Madlen's head tilted and she looked up into the eyes of the priest for the first time. "Yeah, she'll come back. I miss her so much. . . . I can't go on much longer without her."

"When will she come back, Madlen?"

"When I've killed the stranger."

The water trickled in the little iron sink, played in the fountain of her mind.

"Do you really want to do that, Madlen?"

"Yes, yes, yes! Then Cathy can come back!"

"Are you sure?"

"Of course!" The tears were bright on her face now, and her breath came in shudders. "I've told her—I've told Cathy. I tell her everything."

"Where—" and Giovanni stopped, because he suddenly knew where Cathy was. He'd seen her himself. "Maybe," he said, "there's some way Cathy can come back without the stranger leaving." When Madlen didn't answer but just went on staring at him in the half-light he took a risk and said, "Without Debra leaving."

"Debra is the stranger!"

The little tin clock brought the silence in.

"I see. But maybe there's room for her and Cathy as well in your life. They could both—"

"If I can have Cathy back, what do I want with a stranger?"

So there we have it, padre. But keep trying, if only so that later you can't look back and see something else you might have done, and flay yourself for not having done it.

"Strangers often turn into friends, Madlen. Every friend you have now was a stranger once."

"I hate her!"

"I'm sure you'd come to like her, if you just let her stay around with you. She—"

"I'm going to kill her!" The fair, pretty, teenager's face upturned to stare at him, the face of a saint, of an angel, staring at him with this unholy fire in its eyes, the face of the angel of death. *"I'm going to kill her and then my real sister can come back!"*

"I see."

Giovanni took a minute off, knowing there was no

more he could do for Madlen under hypnosis: If it were as easy as that to change people's personae there wouldn't be any need for psychiatrists. And when he felt sure there was no way out he told the child gently, "All right, Madlen, relax now, let everything go . . . just let it all go. . . ." He watched the small pale hands go loose on the carved arms of the chair. "Can you hear the fountain?"

"Yeah." The tears had dried on her face, leaving an unnatural sheen. Had she been crying for Cathy, for Debra, or herself? For all three, perhaps, at various levels of her subconscious. "Yeah, I can hear the fountain. I can see it."

"Okay . . ." Giovanni said softly, "then all you need remember now is that your head is always clear and cool, always at ease with life, with no thoughts of anything that can worry you, with no thoughts of bringing harm to anyone . . . anyone at all. . . . You love life, Madlen, and you love everyone who shares that life with you. . . ."

The tin clock ticked, measuring the silence.

"Just remember, Madlen, that the way to keep your head clear and cool and at ease is to love everyone around you . . . and to know that there's nobody who could possibly come into your life to make it any happier than it is now. . . . Your life is complete, Madlen, your life has all the happiness in it that you could ever wish for, and it has all the people in it you need to give you that happiness. . . ."

The light was strong in the curtained window now, and the rooks were calling in the elms; the day was on the march.

"So when you see a stranger, Madlen, remember she's really a friend . . . a friend in need of all the love you can let her have . . . all the love in your heart. . . ."

Giovanni found his eyes on the Christ again, uncon-

sciously looking for guidance if there were any to be had.
You could never tell: It wasn't always your turn next. In
this way, Madlen, he heard the thoughts running on in
his head, the ones he couldn't say aloud for her, in this
way you can be happy again, with no more migraines,
and give up the idea, the terrible and haunting obsession,
of exchanging, through the ghastly alchemy of murder, your perfect, vital, and loving sister Debra for a
plastic mannequin in a ski suit with pink woolen gloves.

But with his eyes still on the Savior, Giovanni heard
another thought coming into his mind, the memory of
something he'd been saying to Madlen a while ago. . . .
*Maybe there's some way Cathy can come back without the
stranger leaving. . . .*

So what did that mean? Was this the guidance he'd
been praying for?

He let his eyes linger on the eyes of Christ, listening
with all his heart, but that was all he could hear, just the
memory of something he himself had said. Maybe if he
thought about it later he might find meaning in it, but
he doubted it would be of any help in what was to come
as the day unfolded to leave the writing on the wall, the
foreshadowing of appalling tragedy.

Giovanni looked down at last upon the face of the
child in the chair, the face of the doomed angel. "So
when I count to three, Madlen, you'll wake up and look
around you, and take a deep, deep breath. . . . Do you
understand?"

"Yeah. I'll wake up."

"That's right. One. . . ."

While he was counting, Giovanni thought of this
child's future, and again felt a lurch of the heart, envi-
sioning the only future that could become possible for
her if Debra were to remain safe, seeing her at a window
of the institution, hugging her plastic doll with the pink

woolen gloves, while over the years her sister, hiding her tears as best she could, came by to visit her.

Oh Lord, is this Thy will for the child Thou hast created? Is there nothing that I, Thy willing servant, can do in Thy name to show her the grace of Thy mercy?

The tin clock ticked in the silence.

So be it.

"Three. . . . Now wake up, my child, and take a deep, deep breath."

26

Father Giovanni's telephone call to Mrs. Felker, ten minutes later, was brief. The answering machine at her home had given the realty office number, and he'd found her there.

The girls were fine, he told her, but for Madlen's migraines, which they were treating under the supervision of a sister here, a state-registered nurse. There was also something he needed to ask her.

"This may be difficult for you, Mrs. Felker, but remember you have the inviolate confidence of a priest. Can you tell me if there was another child in your family who . . . met with an accident?" As the silence ran on, he added as gently as he could, "Who was killed?"

The silence still ran on, but he didn't break it now.

"Yes," the woman said at last. "Yes, there was. How did you know?"

"I didn't. It was just something Madlen said once, in passing, that put the thought in my mind."

"I guess—I guess she must have overheard something. She used to . . . listen at keyholes sometimes, being, well—"

"Being a normal kid, sure. I used to do it myself."

"You did?" He heard a light laugh of relief. "Well, yeah, we had a little girl a year older than Madlen, before she came, who was killed in an auto accident."

What about if she ever finds out she had a sister who was killed?

Giovanni took a breath. "I see. That was pretty tough for you."

"I guess it was. Is this important, Father? Has it left any kind of—you know—bad impression on her?"

"I think it's possible that these migraines could involve what we might term delayed infantile shock, Mrs. Felker, so—"

"You think I should come and talk to her?"

He didn't miss the reluctance in her tone. "I don't think so, at least not yet. I've a friend who's a psychiatrist in the town here, and maybe I'll have him talk to Madlen. If I think for a moment you should be here, I'll contact you immediately."

Sister Denise was sitting in the big oaken chair where Madlen had sat only an hour ago. So far she'd said nothing, but only listened. She couldn't remember having seen Father Giovanni with a face so drawn, with eyes so defeated, since he'd come to the convent four years ago, and her heart went out to him. The heart of Sister Denise had been moved by this man from the moment she had first set eyes on him, but she had managed all this time to define her feelings for him as simply those for a kindred spirit.

"So there is *nothing,*" Giovanni said, "that we can hope to do now for these two children, without outside help." With an edge to his voice—"Without professional help, official help, from those who haven't the slightest idea of what is going on, but simply the authority to take what steps seem necessary in the eyes of the law and the common good—whatever that is."

Sister Denise spoke at last. "Their parents included?"

Giovanni stopped his restless pacing to look down at her. "Their parents included. And of course if it's left for *them* to make decisions—as it should be, in the normal way—they'll have Madlen certified and slammed into an institution the moment they can get a psychiatrist to suggest it. A convent, an asylum for the insane, what's the difference, so long as the parents are left to go on with their lives undisturbed?"

Denise got up from the chair and moved around, touching things as she came across them, the leatherbound Bible on the stool under the crucifix, a pair of magnifying glasses the priest used for reading in poor light, the coffee mug with the picture of Lourdes Cathedral on it—things that Giovanni had touched, leaving them, to her mind, blessed. "When can Dr. Steiner see Madlen?" she asked him. Steiner was the psychiatrist in the town.

"On Monday, and then only because I told him it was urgent." Today was Saturday.

Denise turned her quiet eyes on him. "In a case like this, how much can a psychiatrist do?"

Giovanni shrugged. "Only as much as he can, like anyone else. To my limited knowledge, this is a case of a delusional disorder—the fixation on Madlen's part that if she kills Debra she can bring her 'real' sister back to life—coupled with dissociative phenomena, which allow Madlen to completely forget that her part in these appalling 'accidents' was deliberate and designed to kill. Sure, a good psychiatrist could make a dent in those things over the years, but he's going to have to visit her in an institution. And that's what I hate most in all this, Denise, the idea of a bright, vital young girl like her spending her life behind bars in the atmosphere of a snakepit."

"I know, Giovanni, I know. But if she doesn't? If she's allowed her freedom?"

The priest took a deep breath, tilting his head back. "If she's allowed her freedom, she'll use it to kill her sister, one fine day." He turned, tapping his fingers on the edge of his desk. "And there is the impasse. Meanwhile, just for today and tomorrow, I want them both to get on with their lives as usual, or at least as far as it's possible. But for Debra's safety they must never be left alone with each other, out of sight—will you pull together a discreet observation team, Denise?"

"Of course."

"At night I want Madlen to sleep in the sick room—you can tell her it's a precaution in case she has another migraine attack—and I've asked Nicola to keep Debra company in their cell, as she did last night."

"And on Monday," Denise asked him with a certain hesitation, "will you want me to go with you and Madlen to see Dr. Steiner? I just need to know if I'll have to rearrange my schedule."

"I was hoping you'd agree to going with us, yes." Giovanni took one of her firm, capable hands. "You're a great comfort to me, Denise."

"I could ask for nothing more."

She drew away from him, feeling, as always, his close presence too magnetic. And then, before she left him, she asked what he thought was a strange question. "Before we surrender Madlen's future to the professionals you spoke about, the officials, isn't there anything at all we can do for her?"

Giovanni stood watching her, caught by her tone. "In what way, Denise?"

"I . . . I'm not sure. Find some other way of getting inside her head. Make a quantum leap of some kind."

She looked away, restless. "I just think that with your brilliant mind and your intense humanity, together with Christ's help, something might be done, maybe, while there's this little time left."

Maybe there's some way Cathy can come back, Giovanni heard his own voice saying again in the far distance of his mind, *without the stranger leaving.* But it didn't make any sense to him.

"With Christ's help," he told Denise, *"anything* can be done, of course."

She nodded quickly as she left the room. "Then let us pray, Giovanni."

27

The wind fluted through the gaps in the roof tiles, like somebody whistling under their breath.

"I'm going to try again."

The flame of the candle flickered in the draft.

"Oh."

"When the bell goes."

"Oh," Cathy said again from the shadows.

Madlen was kneeling, feeling herself to be at prayer, as she always did when she visited with Cathy, praying she'd come home.

But today was different. Today it was going to happen.

The stone was ready.

"Everything's ready," she said.

The flame of the candle flickered wildly in the draft, like it was excited.

"Oh."

During the past weeks, Father Giovanni had been working for a little while every day on the parapet below the roof, where over the years the concrete between the heavy stone blocks had crumbled, leaving them like a row of bad teeth, at all angles, and a danger to anyone walking below along the path by the maze. Madlen had watched the priest from the bell tower as he'd climbed the ladder and rolled each loose block away, making a rope cradle for it and lowering it to the ground. She'd admired his strength as he'd worked with his jacket off and his sleeves rolled up, his muscles rippling. Nicola would have liked to watch him at work up there, but of course Madlen couldn't tell her what he was doing.

"Today it's going to happen," she said.

Cathy didn't answer this time. It didn't matter: her eyes were smiling in the candlelight, and Madlen knew she was listening. Cathy always listened.

While there were still eight or nine of the broken stone blocks left along the parapet, Madlen had gone up there from a dormer window in the dusk one evening during Recreation, and dragged one of the stones along the plinth, leaving it hidden behind a coping. It was heavy, about as much as she could manage, but the parapet was wide and she'd never been scared of heights. The next evening, and the one after that, she'd gone up there again, dragging the stone to the far side of the building and leaving it on the parapet above the red brick alcove where the sisters were allowed to sit and study in the fresh air; when the sky was clear it was a suntrap, as Sister Denise called it—"We need our vitamin D in the wintertime!"

It was Debra's favorite place to read.

As she knelt before the candle, Madlen was aware of a throbbing in her head; it had started when she'd come in here a while ago. But she was used to that now, and if there was going to be a migraine attack it'd come too late, because any minute now the bell would sound from the tower, announcing the hour of two, when on week-ends the sisters were allowed free time, provided they studied.

That was when Debra liked to go to the red brick alcove with her books.

"This time it's going to work," Madlen said, "and then you can come home, Cathy, you can come home at last. You don't know how I've missed you all this time!"

The pain hammered softly in her head.

All you need remember now is that your head is always clear and cool . . . with no thoughts that can worry you. . . .

Where did that come from? It had sounded like a voice, from far away.

Madlen shivered, feeling uneasy. She didn't want to start hearing voices . . . the migraines were bad enough.

"You know what they say when you hear voices? They say you're crazy."

The smiling eyes watched her from the shadows.

"Oh."

"I'm not crazy." But she'd had to say it aloud, and it worried her. There was something wrong with her, she'd known that for a long time, but it was only to do with the migraines.

She shivered again, seeing the flame of the candle and beyond it the smiling eyes of her sister, her real one, Cathy, but the scene was kind of changing as she watched, and she was seeing herself now, like from somewhere above and looking down, a girl kneeling on the floor of a dusty, empty room looking so alone, so shut away from everyone and everything, with only a candle to keep her company, a candle and the plastic figure of a kid in a black ski suit with pink woolen gloves, the kind you saw in a clothes store, while the wind fretted and whistled through the tiles and the cold came in waves over her body and the soft hammering went on in her

head till she couldn't stand it anymore and heard herself
crying out in the empty room—

"Am I okay? Or am I crazy?"

The wind moaned through the tiles.

*"Oh Jesus Christ, am I okay or aren't I? What am I
doing here? Somebody tell me, why can't somebody tell
me? Can't anybody help?"*

Then the tears were streaming on her face and she was
rocking backward and forward with the light of the candle bright and dying away, bright and dying away as
she moaned like the wind in the tiles, her small robed
body hunched over her terror, her bewilderment, *because
something was wrong with her, terribly wrong, dreadfully
wrong, and it wasn't just the migraines, it was something
else, something that had been inside of her ever since she
was just a little kid listening at the keyhole . . . listening at
the keyhole . . . and nobody could help her, Christ couldn't
help and Father Giovanni couldn't help her as she rocked
back and forth with the tears streaming and the pain hammering . . . hammering inside of her head like the tolling of
a bell, the tolling of the bell in the tower. . . .*

The bell in the tower.

Sounding the hour, two o'clock.

"Cathy," she said at last, her breath still coming in
shudders, the flame of the candle brilliant now through
her tears, "I'm okay, really, aren't I? If I were crazy,
you'd tell me, I know that. You always tell me the truth."

The smiling eyes watched her from the shadows.

"Oh."

The booming of the bell in the tower died away.

Madlen didn't move, went on kneeling, took a deep,
slow breath and then another, wiping her face with the
back of her hand, tasting the salt of her tears.

She didn't need anyone's help.

She knew what she had to do, and she could do it
alone.

*All you need to remember now is that your head is clear
. . . and cool . . . with no thoughts of bringing harm to
anyone, anyone at all. . . .*

The wind fluted in the tiles, bringing the voice from the
distance, taking it away.

I know what I want to do, and you can't stop me.

*When you see a stranger, Madlen, remember she's really
a friend. . . .*

"You can't stop me, you can't stop me now!"

She got to her feet and swung around with her robes
flying out and the flame of the candle flickered and
whirled as she moved swiftly to the window and pulled it
open.

The dormer was on the side of the building where she'd
left the stone perched on the parapet, and as she looked
down she saw Debra crossing the grass toward the red
brick alcove below, a book in her hand like always.

Madlen waited.

The tears were dry on her face, itching in the wind, and
in her head the hammering went on, giving her no peace.
But she waited patiently, because soon it would be over,
very soon now, and Cathy would come home again after
so long . . . after so long. . . .

*You love life, Madlen . . . and you love all those who
share that life with you. . . .*

"I only love Cathy! Nobody else, only Cathy!"

Then the waiting was over and she stooped and
dragged the heavy stone to the edge of the plinth and
looked down at the figure on the bench a long way below,
the figure of the hated stranger, and the sky whirled
around the blinding sun and the wind howled and she
gave a cry with no words to it, just Cathy's name, Cathy's
name as she pushed the stone across the edge of the
plinth and saw fragments and bits of moss coming away
under its weight in the instant before it tilted, rocked
back and tilted again, and suddenly was gone from sight,

and as she turned and ran for the dormer she heard a
scream rising faintly from below.

Father Giovanni, hearing the scream from his study, ran
from the building and saw Debra lying beside the bench,
an arm flung out and blood on her veil as she lay still,
facing the sky.

28

When night came, Father Giovanni went alone to the West Chapel to pray.

He felt drained, weary and uncertain of himself, even though it was his belief that the things he had done and the things he was doing now were according to the guidance of Christ.

The memory of Madlen's white, staring face still troubled him like an open wound.

She had been cleaning the silver candlesticks on the high altar, soon after her sister had been found in the red brick alcove, still and silent on the grass. The sunlight, pouring across the altar from the colored windows, was so brilliant on the candlesticks that they seemed to send out rays of luminescence, as from the head of Jesus or a saint in a sacred picture.

Sister Denise had been with Giovanni, her eyes already filled with the pain of what was to come.

"Madlen," Giovanni had said gently, "we need to pray together."

"Pray?" She darted a questioning look from one to the other. "What for?"

"For courage," he said. "Courage for all of us at this time. There's been an accident, Madlen."

Her eyes widened and she gripped his arm. "Debra? An accident to Debra? *Tell me!*"

So he had told her, and Denise helped him as the child struggled in their arms, her screams muffled by their robes—*"It's not true! It's not true. . . . It's not true!"*

They hadn't prayed, after all. The child was beside herself, and Denise had taken her to the sick room, staying with her while Giovanni drove alone into the town, his knuckles white on the wheel.

Now it was night, and he was in the West Chapel, his head bowed before the crucifix. He asked for nothing from the Savior, offered no thanks; he simply needed to feel in his soul that he had Christ's blessing, or to feel, if all had been a mistake, if all were to be lost, that he did not. He needed this knowledge as desperately as a sailor needs a compass to guide him across the bellowing heights of the storm.

After an hour the only knowledge that came to Giovanni was that in being here at all he was perhaps lacking in faith, and should at some later time atone for so gross a sin. For if he had believed his actions of this day had been in accordance with the guidance of Christ, and enjoyed his blessing, then he shouldn't question it.

Rising from sore knees, Giovanni pinched the flame of the votive candle between his finger and thumb, and quietly left the chapel.

In the sick room there was a single lamp burning.

Watching Madlen's sleeping face, Sister Denise felt herself suspended between hope and disbelief, reality and the unknown.

She had talked again with Giovanni many times in the past hour.

Before we surrender Madlen's future to the professionals you spoke about, the official authorities, isn't there anything at all we can do for her?

In what way, Denise?

I . . . I'm not sure. Find some other way of getting inside her head. Make a quantum leap of some kind. I just think that with your brilliant mind and your intense humanity, together with Christ's help, something might be done while there's this little time left.

She saw Madlen's head moving on the pillow, turning to one side.

A quantum leap, indeed . . . and Giovanni had made it. But shall we fall, my beloved friend, or shall we, by the will of Almighty God, reach the other side?

The flame of the lamp burned steadily inside the tall glass chimney.

Its light dwelled on Madlen's lids, illumining her dream, and the block of stone tilted, rocked back and tilted again, and was suddenly gone from sight, and from below the scream rose and then was suddenly cut off.

I must tell Cathy.

She always told Cathy everything, but this time there was going to be the most incredible news of all.

I killed the stranger!

The light grew bright, suddenly.

I killed the stranger, Cathy, and you can come home at last!

The light was very bright now.

I must go and tell her. She moved her head again on the pillow.

"Are you awake, sweetheart?"

"What?" Madlen looked up into the gentle face of Sister Denise. "Yeah, I'm awake."

Looking into the child's eyes, Denise felt a shiver pass

through her: There was no grief left in them, not a vestige of the insupportable anguish that had racked her only hours ago. In these eyes now there was only purpose.

"How do you feel, Madlen?"

"Fine." She watched Sister Denise.

"So do you think I could leave you for a while?"

"Sure."

"Then if you need anything, you just have to call."

"I won't need anything."

"I'll leave the lamp burning, just in case."

Madlen watched her going through the arched doorway of the sick room, and after a while threw back the blankets and got out of bed, picking up the lamp.

Father Giovanni moved on the rickety chair again to ease the stiffness in his muscles.

The door of the dormer room was a little ajar, enough to give him a glimpse of the end of the passage outside, but nothing had changed: It was as dark as ever.

Maybe Madlen wouldn't come.

But she had to come, of course. She had to tell Cathy. Everything depended on that. Everything.

Maybe there's some way Cathy can come back, without the stranger leaving.

Maybe, yeah, and this is it, the only way there is.

For a moment Giovanni closed his eyes. *Praise be, my wondrous friend, and blessed be thy name. Grant us the guidance of thy hand in this little hour, we beseech thee, and let thy endless grace attend whatever will come.*

The owl called again, its soft, piping voice floating through the gaps in the roof tiles, and then at last Giovanni saw faint light touching the wall of the passage outside, and heard the creak of footsteps on the narrow stairs from below.

*   *   *

Madlen opened the door of Cathy's room, making as little noise as she could with the wobbly iron handle. The light from her oil lamp played across the walls.

How would she announce this momentous news?

Maybe just, *"I've killed the stranger!"*

No, that was too brutal. Cathy might have forgotten someone had to be killed before she could come home.

Then maybe, *"You can come home now, Cathy! We can be together again!"*

Yeah, that. It was such incredible news and she wanted to get it right, to rehearse it; this was the most important thing she would ever have told Cathy for the rest of their lives, and her heart was racing at the thought.

Then suddenly she couldn't wait any longer, and swung the lamp toward the shadowed niche—*"Cathy! Cathy! You can come—"*

She stopped dead.

Cathy wasn't there.

It had to be a trick of the light and she held the lamp higher and stared into the niche as the shadows vanished and left just the bare wall with its peeling plaster and a spider's web clinging across the corner.

"Cathy . . ." she whispered, terror coming into her, the terror of losing her real sister again after all this time. "Cathy!" she said sharply and then the panic came and she began screaming—*"Cathy-y-y, where are you? Cathy-y-y, you can come home now, where are you, where did you go?"*

"I'm here. . . ."

Madlen swung the lamp, its flame dancing inside the glass chimney, but the room was bare like it had always been.

"Cathy, where are you? Oh God, oh Christ—"

"I'm here. . . ."

The voice wasn't coming from anywhere inside the room and Madlen whirled toward the doorway, running

outside to the passage and holding the lamp high—
"Cathy! Where—"

"It's all right, I'm here. . . ."

Madlen stood frozen, locked into her panic for one last instant before relief flooded her as she saw Cathy standing at the end of the passage in her black ski suit and her pink woolen gloves, her eyes smiling as she waved.

Madlen set the lamp down and ran blindly into her sister's arms.

EPILOGUE

Father Giovanni stopped and put a match to the pile of leaves, and smoke rose in a thick gray tendril against the morning sky. Working with a rake, he tended the fire constantly, and once, for a moment unnerved, glimpsed a pair of smiling eyes among the flames before the face melted and he heaped more leaves there and stirred them until they caught.

He was up earlier than usual today, to arrange the funeral pyre before anybody came by.

In the distance across the frosted grass was the red brick alcove where yesterday he'd found Debra, still conscious but in shock, and with blood still creeping on her cheek where a flying shard had cut into the flesh as the stone had crashed onto the bench beside her.

It was in that instant that Giovanni had heard the voice again in his mind: *Maybe there's some way Cathy can come back . . . without the stranger leaving.*

The worst had been having to tell Madlen there'd been

an accident, and that Debra was dead. But there'd been no other way: That was the key.

He stirred the leaves again, and a shred of black fabric—a sleeve, he thought—glowed red, took fire, and burned out. Cathy's ski suit had been too small for Debra when she'd tried it on with the help of Sister Denise, so Giovanni had driven into town, to the ski outfitter's near the bank. They had a black suit the right size but no pink woolen gloves, so Debra had put the mannequin's on, stretching them a little. She'd been in a state of nerves, of course, partly from the shock of the crashing stone, but Denise had encouraged her with all the love she possessed. Without Denise, Giovanni thought, they couldn't have got through.

The smoke rose, twisting in the frosty air, and he worked with the rake again.

For Madlen it would take a little time. In that one brief climactic moment, as the stone had plunged from the parapet, her subconscious need to kill "the stranger" had been satisfied, and her "real" sister had come home. But there would be questions lingering in her mind, and Giovanni would watch for them to surface and then deal with them, if necessary under hypnosis.

He plied the rake again, turning the embers over and searching for anything that might be left of Cathy, the girl in the ski suit with the smiling eyes, but there were just the leaves now, glowing with a cleansing fire, and Giovanni stood back to watch the smoke as it drifted upward in the first trembling light of the day.